IN THE LAND OF NI
YAYOI WARRIORS
BOOK ONE

C.G. CHACONAS

Copyright © 2024 by C.G. Chaconas

Layout design and Copyright © 2024 by Next Chapter

Published 2024 by Next Chapter

Cover art by Lordan June Pinote

This book is a work of fiction. Names, characters, places, and incidents are the product of the author's imagination or are used fictitiously. Any resemblance to actual events, locales, or persons, living or dead, is purely coincidental.

All rights reserved. No part of this book may be reproduced or transmitted in any form or by any means, electronic or mechanical, including photocopying, recording, or by any information storage and retrieval system, without the author's permission.

A FOREWORD TO THE READER

This fantasy novel is set against a historical canvas, meticulously researched to ensure authenticity across ancient civilizations. It primarily unfolds in Japan's Yayoi period, around 300 B.C., known as "Wa" to Chinese traders of the time.

Despite the Yayoi's lack of written records, the narrative captures their spirit, blending cultural, religious, and daily life details from various eras. Drawing from local Yayoi sites near Niitsu, Japan, the author infuses the story with a rich sense of place and time.

The book takes creative liberties with language and mythical elements, incorporating demons, monsters, and yokai from various cultures' myths, like the Greek Minotaur, to enrich the fantasy world.

A glossary of characters and terms is provided to guide readers through this imaginative journey.

This one is for Mom

Names and Unusual Terms

Aadi: An ally from India with an enigmatic background, skilled in combat, aiding Pausanias on his quest through India, and beyond.

Adofo: A Black man of Egyptian descent born in Pataliputra, India. A magic user and member of the order.

Akiha: The name of a small mountain in the modern-day town of Niitsu, Japan.

Akiho: Female member of the order.

Akin: Librarian and order member, a stern-looking woman around forty-five with a plump figure and glasses, who works and lives by Lake Inawashiro.

Akuma: "Akuma" is a Japanese term that translates to "demon" or "devil" in English. In Japanese folklore, mythology, and popular culture, akuma are often depicted as malevolent supernatural beings associated with evil, darkness, or malevolent forces. In this book, they belong to the third and most powerful tier of demon.

Anahita: Indian lady with green eyes. One of the head magic users in the Indian army that marches with Pausanias toward China.

Aoyin: An appalling Chinese mythical beast, armed with long, deadly claws, who likes to eat human brains. They look somewhat like upright hyenas.

Ardeshir: One of Pausanias's new guides, a Persian man, whom he meets in Miletus.

Ayana: A friend of Saoka, who entered the order at the same time as Saoka.

Brahminical establishment: A varna as well as a caste within Hindu society. In the Vedic- and post-Vedic Indian subcontinent, Brahmins were designated as the priestly class, serving as priests (purohit, pandit, or pujari) and spiritual teachers (guru or acharya).

Bindusara: Real-life second emperor of the Mauryan Empire in Ancient India.

Blessed: These individuals had pledged a lifetime of service to the order, bound to their commitment. They hold considerable freedom in serving the order, answerable only to the mothers.

Chime: A blessed member of the order, stationed in Kazuno town.

Coenus, Demeas, Gyras, and Megadates: Four Spartan soldiers who make an appearance in Chapter 3, fighting alongside Pausanias. Demeas is dead.

Cuju: An ancient Chinese game where players juggle a ball using their feet to keep the ball from touching the ground.

Daolao Gui: Terrible four-legged beasts with short arms on their chests, that looked something akin to a mix of a green and black colored dog-spider hybrid. They were said to have howls akin to storms. They can attack by shooting poisonous projectiles. Real Chinese myth.

NAMES AND UNUSUAL TERMS

Dilios: A Spartan warrior who helps Pausanias get through Persia, India, China, all the way to Japan.

Duoji: A wolf-like creature with red eyes and a white tail. Real Chinese myth.

Eiko: Female sister of the order.

Eneas: Eneas is an Athenian of good standing who traced his lineage back several hundred years. He rose through the Athenian ranks of society. His main job, however, is as a secret member of the order.

Episkyros: An ancient Greek ball game that involved passing, throwing, kicking the ball, tackling, and wrestling.

Eurotasu: The son of Pausanias and Saoka, navigating the complexities of adolescence while being shaped by the harsh realities of their quest.

Furutsu, Gosen, Yahiko, and Ogikawa: All towns in modern Japan, whose names I am using with artistic license. Of course, back then, these places would have had different names; unfortunately, those names are lost to us.

Hellas: "Hellas" is an ancient term used to refer to Greece. It is derived from the Greek word "Ellas" or "Ελλάς," which designates the region inhabited by the Hellenic people. In historical contexts, Hellas is often used to denote the ancient Greek world, including both mainland Greece and its colonies.

Hirona: A friend of Saoka. She lives in Ni and is a magic user; however, she is not a member of the order.

Hōō: A creature, a yokai, with the beak of a rooster, the jaw of a swallow, and the head of a pheasant; the neck, sinuous and serpentine; and the back of a tortoise. Originally a Chinese myth as fenghuang. A very popular symbol in Japan and China. See Yokai.

Iruru: A blessed sister stationed in the city of Nara, Japan. A dear old friend of Mayuki.

Iry-Hor: Now a twisted half-demon, half-human. He was once like an older brother to Kushim, one of the mightiest magic users of Kushim's people. Like Kushim, he survived the cataclysm. Also, like him, he had believed, or it seems used to believe, in the cause of protecting this world and helping humanity to rebuild. He was the first ruler of Egypt, about three thousand years ago. He also has purple eyes. A little mix of truth and fiction.

Izanagi and his sister Izanami: Central gods of the Japan creation myth.

Ju: An ancient Chinese ball, made of leather and stuffed with feathers.

Kami gods: "Kami" is a central term in Shinto, the indigenous spirituality of Japan. It is often translated as "gods," "spirits," or "deities." Kami can be associated with various natural elements, phenomena, ancestors, and certain human attributes. Shinto believes that kami inhabit both the spiritual realm and the natural world. They are revered and honored in rituals, shrines, and daily life.

Kanashibari: A sleep demon from Japanese mythology.

Kazuno: A town located near a modern-day town of the same name, Kazuno, in Akita Prefecture, Japan.

Keftiu: The ancient Egyptian word for the Greek island of Crete.

NAMES AND UNUSUAL TERMS

Kushim: A sage-like figure, a source of ancient knowledge, guiding the protagonists in their quest against the looming threat of the end of the world. Kushim is thousands of years old and full of magic. He has purple eyes, which are a mark of his people.

Kuzuryu: A nine-headed dragon from Japanese mythology who is a good spirit and loves to eat pears. Can shape-shift into a human.

Longyou Caves: In 1992, farmers near the village of Shiyan Beicun in Zhejiang Province, China, decided to drain several ponds on their land. Draining the water revealed five stone caves. This shocking discovery led to unearthing 19 more caverns. With 24 in total, these carved-out spaces range in size and shape. Scholars remain baffled by the caves' origin. Artifacts within were discovered to be from the period 91 to 48 BCE, the reign of Emperor Xuan of Han. This makes the caves over 2,000 years old. The caves were not documented in any writings of the period. Why were they created? *https://mymodernmet.com/longyou-caves/

Magumi: A mystical wolf spirit, guardian of the natural world, drawn into the struggle against malevolent forces, possessing both wisdom and feral might.

Mayuki: A blessed sister of the order of Wa. She has a sharp tongue and sword, strong magic, and is a senior figure to Saoka, who teaches and befriends her.

Miletus: A city which was once Minoan, Mycenaean, and now Persian. Located close to the modern-day village of Balat in Aydin Province, Turkey.

Mokushiroku: The Japanese word for apocalypse.

Mother Mitsuki: Kind yet serious, resided by Lake Inawashiro. One of three "mothers" of the mysterious order.

Mother Yui: To the south, on giant Lake Biwa. One of three "mothers" of the mysterious order.

Mother Yuki: Further south in the deer realm of Nara, Mother Yuki lived and worked alongside Princess Mimiko, the highest ruler in all of Wa and rumored to be one of the region's most potent magic users. One of three "mothers" of the mysterious order.

Myōbu: A white fox whose job is to be a messenger of the gods. Often imparts good luck. See Yokai.

Nara: Nara was established as the first permanent capital of Japan in the year 710 CE during the Nara period (710–794). The capital was known as "Heijō-kyō." However, its origins as a town go much further back.

Nawarupa: A mythical amalgamation of nine different animals from ancient Thai mythology, an abomination of nature, a creature of nightmares.

Ni: A shortened fictitious version of Niitsu, which is a modern-day town in Niigata City, Niigata Prefecture, Japan.

Older sisters: Ladies who had committed to five-year contracts with the order were entrusted with additional responsibilities and enjoyed the freedom to manage their own affairs.

Oni: Demons in Japanese mythology.

NAMES AND UNUSUAL TERMS

Pataliputra: A real ancient Indian city. Part of the Mauryan Empire at the time period of this book (300 B.C.).

Pausanias: A seasoned Spartan warrior with a stoic demeanor, wielding both physical and magical prowess, on a quest to thwart the encroaching darkness.

Persepolis: A real ancient city of the Persian Empire, located in modern-day Iran.

Philon: Philon was a Spartan king of great intellect, forethought, and cunning. His physical stature was rather unimposing.

Pleistarchos: A fallen comrade, remembered for his bravery and sacrifice in the face of demonic adversaries. Named after a real Spartan king.

Pnyx: Behind the Acropolis stood a symbol of democracy that was little more than a stone stage with a couple of stone steps leading up to it. Nestled into the hillside, there was seating available, designed so the speaker's voice would carry up the hill into the stands, allowing people to hear what was being argued.

Poecas: A diligent Spartan soldier who makes an appearance in Chapter 2, fighting alongside Pausanias.

Polydorous: Another fallen ally, whose valor echoes through the annals of their shared history, a symbol of camaraderie in the midst of chaos. Named after a real Spartan king.

Princess Himiko: The most powerful ruler in all of Wa. Possibly a real-life person from before Japan's recorded history.

Pyu: An ancient people who inhabited modern-day Myanmar from 200 B.C.E. to the mid-11th century.

Ramona: A young assistant of Mayuki and member of the order.

Reikai spirit realm: The term "Reikai" refers to the spirit world or spirit realm in Japanese belief systems. It is the realm where spirits, souls, and supernatural entities exist. In Shinto and Buddhist traditions, the concept of Reikai is often associated with the afterlife, where souls may reside after death.

Rin: A child from the village of Ni who offers juice to Eurotasu the day after his first kill.

Rurua: A blessed member of the order.

Sabas: Nearly 50 years old, gray beard, all knotted muscle, commander of Pausanias's Spartan unit.

Saoka: A Japanese woman, Pausanias's wife, a resilient and compassionate companion, adept in her own skills, sharing the burden of their perilous journey.

Shukaku: A good yokai spirit of Japan. A tanuki or raccoon, that can appear as a man, and often wears the robes of a priest. Roams and helps people in what is modern-day Gunma Prefecture. See Yokai.

Shumoku musume: A good Japanese spirit of myth. Has the head of a snail or hammerhead, but the body and kimono of a woman. Resides in what is modern-day Gunma Prefecture. See Yokai.

Sisters: The lowest members of the order.

Sosuke: A male messenger, mail courier, and forest ranger of the order in Wa.

NAMES AND UNUSUAL TERMS

Sota: A young male soldier, serving in the order.
Stolos and Temenos: Two phalanx commanders in the Spartan army.
Tinayu: The ancient Egyptian word for Greece.
Trireme: An ancient Greek war boat.
Vedic: An ancient religion of the Indian subcontinent.
Vettias: A Spartan king.
Wa: The name for the Japanese islands before the word Japan existed. This name was first recorded by Chinese scholars, and perhaps given to the people living in what is now Japan, with whom the Chinese traded. At the time, the "Japanese" people had no recorded language.
Wakaba: A timid newcomer to the order with a room adjacent to Saoka's. Makes her only appearance in Chapter 4.
Yito and Yuda: Brothers aged nine and eleven, two of a handful of boys in Eurotasu's age group who live in the village of Ni.
Yokai: "Yokai" is a term in Japanese folklore that broadly refers to a class of supernatural creatures, spirits, and monsters. These can take various forms, ranging from mischievous and benign beings to malevolent and dangerous entities. They appear in numerous folktales, legends, and artworks throughout Japan's history. The term "yokai" is a combination of "yo" (meaning bewitching or attractive) and "kai" (meaning mystery or wonder), collectively describing their mysterious and supernatural nature.
Yoko: A silver-haired woman of the order who resides in what is modern-day Kusatsu, Japan. Also, my wife's name. No relation to the character or the hair color.
Yuman: The most elderly man living in Ni, a friend of Pausanias.

PROLOGUE

Kushim entered the dimly lit prison room, the heavy door creaking as it closed. The thick air smelled of rotting flesh and burnt hair, and the flickering torches cast dancing shadows on the damp, stone walls. At the center of the room, bound by mystical restraints, sprawled a grotesque creature—a demon.

Its mottled, leathery skin writhed in the dim light, reflecting purples and greens. Sinewy wings, like those of a bat, clung tightly to its malodorous form.

Kushim's gaze lingered on the demon's eyes—piercing orbs that glowed with an unsettling intelligence. The demon's mouth, filled with jagged teeth, twisted into a sneer as it sensed Kushim's presence. Despite his millennia of existence, the stench of sulfur in the air made Kushim's stomach churn, and the sight of a demon never failed to evoke primal revulsion.

He sat opposite the demon on a rickety stool. Silence hung in the air, broken only by the crackle of the torches. His eyes bore into the demon's, searching for vulnerability. The stillness stretched, a calculated pause to heighten the tension.

The demon remained motionless; its eyes fixed on Kushim.

Slowly, Kushim circled the creature, never breaking eye

contact. From the folds of his worn robe, he produced an ancient relic—a small, ornate dagger with symbols etched into its blade. The blade gleamed in the light. The demon's eyes widened.

Kushim paused, savoring the moment. He took a deep breath. He leaned in, the dagger's tip hovering just above the demon's writhing flesh. "You know why you're here," he muttered. The demon's eyes burned with silent defiance, but it made no sound, no plea for mercy.

In his mind, Kushim replayed the horrors he had witnessed, the devastation wrought by such creatures. He saw the faces of innocents, their lives snuffed out by the malevolence before him. Each memory fueled his resolve.

"Do you feel anything? Regret? Remorse?" he asked, knowing no answer would come. The demon's predictable silence was maddening.

He pressed the dagger into its flesh, drawing a thin line of dark, oozing blood.

The demon's body tensed, its eyes narrowing, but still, it made no sound.

Kushim's thoughts drifted to his own existence. He had seen empires rise and fall, had loved and lost more times than he could count. And through it all, the demons had been there, a constant shadow over humanity's progress.

"Thousands of years," he murmured to himself. "I've lived through thousands of years, watched countless lives unfold. And yet, here I am, still fighting the same battle."

He pushed the dagger deeper, the demon's body shuddering. "Do you understand what you've taken from me? From all of us?"

He knew the demon couldn't understand as humans did. Its existence was a mockery of life, driven by base instincts and a hunger for chaos. Yet, he couldn't stop himself from talking, from pouring out the bitterness accumulated over millennia.

The room echoed with the sounds of the demon's muffled

agony, filling the emptiness inside Kushim. But it never sufficed. Torturing the demon offered hollow reprisal.

"Even after all this time, I still seek answers," he whispered. "Why do you exist? What purpose does our suffering serve?"

The demon's eyes bore into his.

Kushim saw the reflection of his own despair, realizing the answers he sought might never come. He exhaled deeply, slumping back on the stool.

"Perhaps it's not you I'm punishing," he mused. "Perhaps it's myself." He wiped the dagger clean on a rag, the blood smearing like ink on a page. "In the end, what have I become? Am I any better than you?"

He resumed his grim task. The demon's body convulsed. And still, Kushim pressed on, driven by a need he couldn't fully understand.

Kushim's heart, hardened by centuries of conflict, beat steadily in the dim light.

He whispered to the demon, his voice a ghostly echo, "I am Kushim, the eternal witness. And until the end of days, I will stand against you and your kind."

The demon's eyes flickered, a faint glimmer of something unspoken passing between them. For a moment, Kushim thought he saw understanding—or was it pity in those depths? He shook his head, dismissing the notion. Demons didn't feel pity.

With a final, decisive stroke through its neck, Kushim ended the demon's life. As he left the room, the door creaked shut.

CHAPTER 1

281 B.C.E. What is present-day Niitsu, Niigata, Japan.

Dawn arrived, painting the sky with shades of peach and fire as it bounced off three parallel rows of clouds over the forested Mt. Akiha. The golden glow cast on the land of Ni brought the peaceful village below to life. Nestled among lush rice paddies and simple wooden huts, the inhabitants of the village began their day.

Magumi, a white wolf as large as a horse, prowled through the beech trees, her senses alert. For over a thousand years, she had protected these lands.

Her ears twitched, sensing a disturbance—a faint, ominous presence on the wind. Time was running out to prepare Eurotasu, the fourteen-year-old boy under her care. Armies of demons and mercenaries gathered in the north, threatening to destroy the earth. Eurotasu's parents, busy fighting to prevent the apocalypse, had left him in Magumi's capable paws.

How long do we have left? she wondered as her paws splashed through a small puddle. *Will our struggles against the demons be enough?*

At a small clearing atop the mountain, Eurotasu slept outside a straw hut built into the ground. Two Dotaku bells hung high on a nearby tree. A fire pit and a rock pathway led down the rise to a natural spring that fed the basin.

His features held the grace of his enchantress mother, Saoka, and his tall frame was a testament to his Spartan father, Pausanias. As Magumi approached, Eurotasu's piercing blue eyes opened. *By the stars, those eyes are like magic every time I see them.*

"Good morning," Eurotasu greeted.

"Good morning. How did you sleep?" Magumi replied.

"Wonderfully. I dreamed of flying on a giant bird and swimming in deep waters."

"That's amazing," she said with a warm smile. "Are you ready to start the day?"

Eurotasu reached out to pet her head. "I guess, but first…"

Magumi playfully snapped at his hand.

"Hey, bad wolf."

"Stinky human," Magumi retorted with a laugh.

He got up, ready for the day. They moved to the two bronze Dotaku bells. Eurotasu struck them seven times, sending a soft azure magic ripple through the air.

Small teal-colored forest spirits gathered, attracted by the sound. Their forms shimmered with an ethereal glow. Some danced while others sat, vibrating like over-energized toddlers, their curious eyes wide with wonder as they watched the magic unfold. They moved with a playful grace, popping in and out of sight, leaving trails of light that sparkled like fireflies in the dim forest air.

Eurotasu smiled at them, then sat down to begin his morning meditation, a practice ingrained in him since he could walk.

His parents—how I wish they were here not only to look after and teach Eurotasu but to answer so many questions.

As the boy meditated, Magumi joined him in reflection, opening her mind to remember what was lost, take stock of what remained, and ponder the future.

"Hey, runt, stand up. We have a village to protect," Magumi called.

Eurotasu grabbed his bow, quiver, and his father's sword. His father had left it for him to safeguard. Pausanias could more than capably defend himself without it.

Magumi allowed Eurotasu to mount her back, and they trotted off together. They traveled in silence for a while, content to feel the warmth of the sun filtering through the red and yellow maple trees and listen to the sounds of the forest. They descended the mountain, passing a small lake. A fun-loving troop of monkeys scurried past, breaking the relative quiet.

"So, Magumi, can you tell me more about the demons the villagers reported seeing?" Eurotasu asked, eyeing a Kiji bird fluttering overhead.

"My experience spans centuries. I'll sense a demon long before you. You've heard plenty about demons from your parents and me already. How about a history lesson instead?"

"Oh no, not another speech about your first taste of cooked rice—soft, almost neutral, with a subtle sweetness and nuttiness."

"It was sublime. Don't tease me. Over a millennium, I've witnessed humanity's evolution from fur-clad hunters to silk-wearers as rice cultivation reshaped Wa. A diverse array of professions have arisen, including artisans and cooks, while traditional roles like hunting wane, giving rise to specialists such as healers and scouts."

Eurotasu's eyes rolled as he pushed a lazy birch tree branch out of his face. "Huh, isn't that a…"

Magumi twisted to the left, surprising Eurotasu, who held on tight. A hundred paces away, a creature hid in the bushes, the cypress trees blocking a clear view.

"Dismount and ready your bow. Don't move until I tell you," Magumi said, her thoughts racing. *Why hadn't I sensed the Oni?* She positioned herself between it and the boy, getting into a defensive stance.

Then Eurotasu laughed.

"Look, it's just a chiko fox wearing a tattered dress and walking on its hind legs," Eurotasu said, waving at the yokai.

The harmless yokai bore no evil energy. *No wonder I didn't sense it.* "Why do you want to scare people?" Magumi yelled.

It shrugged, laughed, dropped down on all fours, and took off.

"You should have seen your face. 'Dismount and ready your bow,'" Eurotasu said, holding his stomach and pointing at Magumi.

Despite her pride, she smiled. The villagers were safe. "Okay, you've had your fun; let's go back to the hut. Then you need to start your training. We can't waste any time. Next time it might not be a prank, and you are yet untested."

They walked back toward the mountaintop, taking their time winding up the far side. They stopped for a cold drink from a trickling stream. Magumi sniffed at a chestnut tree, knowing its spiny package filled with delicious fruit would fall soon.

The forest air grew still. A low, ominous growl rolled in from the distance, and Eurotasu instinctively reached for his weapon. An unnatural chill raised the fur on Magumi's back. She halted, ears pricked, muscles tense.

A sudden rustling in the bushes further up the stream snapped her focus. Out stepped a monstrous figure—a horned Oni with red and black blistered skin, wild hair, and a large mouth full of sharp teeth. A Namahage. Its wet blisters glistened in the dawn light. It hissed, eyes glowing with malice.

"Eurotasu, stay back!" Magumi growled, positioning herself between the boy and the creature.

Eurotasu's eyes widened, but he didn't hesitate. He drew an arrow from his quiver, his movements swift and precise. "What do we do, Magumi?"

The Namahage advanced, its feet squelching in the mud. Magumi knew they couldn't afford to underestimate it.

"Hold your ground," Magumi said calmly. "Aim for its head but be ready to move if it charges."

Eurotasu nodded, his focus unwavering. He took a deep breath, nocking the arrow. The air grew thick with tension.

The Namahage lunged forward with a guttural roar.

Magumi sprang to intercept it. Her powerful jaws snapped at the creature, fangs grazing its scaly arm. The Namahage recoiled, hissing.

"Now, Eurotasu!" Magumi shouted.

The creature swung its massive arm, catching Magumi off guard and sending her sprawling into the underbrush. She shook her head, disoriented.

Eurotasu's hands trembled as the Namahage advanced on her, eyes burning with malice.

Magumi struggled to her feet, blood dripping from a wound on her side. Eurotasu's arrow flew, missing its mark. The creature turned its attention toward the boy, its growl deepening.

Magumi forced herself to lunge at the Namahage again, her body aching from the impact of the demon's blow. Eurotasu's next arrow flew truer, striking the creature in the shoulder. The Namahage howled, momentarily stunned.

Seizing the opportunity, Magumi lunged again, clamping her jaws around its neck. With a powerful shake, she threw it to the ground. But the Namahage remained relentless, its claws raking across her back as it struggled beneath her. Magumi's grip faltered. The creature pushed her off, rising once more.

She bit down harder, feeling the resistance of its tough hide. The Namahage's strength began to wane, its movements growing sluggish. Finally, with a final savage twist, she broke the creature's neck. The Namahage lay still, lifeless.

Eurotasu stood frozen, his hands shook as he fumbled for another arrow. His breath came in ragged gasps, eyes wide. The bow slipped from his grasp, and he stumbled backward, nearly tripping over a root. "I can't do this, Magumi!" he cried, panic rising in his chest. "It's too much!"

Magumi panted, blood seeping from her wounds. Eurotasu rushed to her, concern etched on his face. "Are you okay, Magumi? What if more demons come?" His hands rested on her chest.

"I'll be fine," she replied, her voice strained. "You did well, Eurotasu. But remember, this is just the beginning. This Oni wasn't as large as others, and it had no magic. Others are far more dangerous."

The forest seemed to close in around them, shadows lengthening as if anticipating the next threat. Eurotasu scanned the trees, every rustle of leaves setting his nerves on edge. Magumi sensed his fear, and though she shared it, she knew she had to be strong for him. She limped forward, the pain in her side sharp with each step, but the urgency of their mission pushed her onward.

Eurotasu nodded. "I'm ready. Whatever comes, we'll face it together. Are you sure you're okay?"

Magumi looked at him, pride and a hint of sadness in her eyes. The path ahead would be fraught with peril, but together they stood a chance. "I am already starting to heal," she said, motioning with her head towards her wound. She closed her eyes, taking a deep, steadying breath. A soft glow began to emanate from her body, bathing her in a gentle light. The air around her shimmered with hues of blue and green, swirling together in a mesmerizing dance of colors.

The glow intensified, centering on the gash along her side. Wisps of golden light wove themselves into the wound, knitting the torn flesh together with delicate threads of magic. The bleeding slowed, then stopped altogether as the radiant energy worked its way deeper into the injury. Tiny sparks of silver flickered within the golden light, adding a celestial quality to the healing process. Magumi's fur, previously matted with blood, began to gleam with a pristine white sheen as the magic cleansed and rejuvenated her. The colors—blue, green, gold, and silver—

twined together in a harmonious symphony, their light casting intricate patterns on the forest floor.

As the final threads of magic settled into place, the glow gradually faded, leaving Magumi's wound fully healed without a scar to mar her pristine coat. She opened her eyes, the luminous colors reflected in her gaze, and gave Eurotasu a reassuring nod.

Eurotasu stared in awe, his earlier panic melting away in the face of such an extraordinary display of magic. "Magumi, that was... amazing. I've never seen anything like that before."

Magumi smiled, her strength renewed. "Magic has its wonders, Eurotasu. Now let's not waste any more time. We have a village to protect."

Eurotasu hesitated, lowering his bow. "What if I'm not ready, Magumi? What if I fail?"

His voice wavered; the weight of his fears heavy in the air. Magumi nuzzled his side gently, trying to infuse him with the strength she herself barely felt. The memory of past battles, both won and lost, flashed through her mind. She knew the cost of failure all too well.

"You are stronger than you think, Eurotasu. But doubt is a dangerous enemy. You must trust in your training and in me."

The forest air grew still again, the wildlife silent as if sensing the impending danger. Magumi's thoughts were clouded with concerns about the demons' increasing presence.

Magumi stumbled, and Eurotasu ran to her side.

"I'm okay, the magic use drains me," she said. "Let's rest here a while. You can tell me about what training you think is appropriate for tomorrow?"

"So, no training today then. Thank you. I am exhausted. Although we haven't traveled very far."

"It's battle fatigue. Seems it even hits boys."

"And older sisters. Now move over; that moss you're sitting on looks nice and soft."

As the afternoon shadows stretched across the sky, Magumi and Eurotasu made their way back to their mountain clearing. The sun dipped low, casting a warm golden hue over the landscape. They settled by the fire pit, the crackling flames providing a comforting glow against the encroaching darkness.

Eurotasu sat on a rock, the weight of the day's events heavy on his shoulders. The image of the Namahage's gaping maw and the bloodied struggle still lingered in his mind. He fidgeted with his bow, the tension in his body palpable. Finally, with a hesitant sigh, he turned to Magumi, his voice barely above a whisper.

"Magumi, I… I'm sorry. Back there, when the Namahage attacked, I… I panicked. I was so scared. I couldn't even hold my bow steady. I let you down."

Magumi looked at him, her eyes softening. She moved closer, placing a comforting paw on his shoulder. "Eurotasu, you have nothing to apologize for. Facing a demon for the first time is terrifying, and you did what you could. It's not cowardice to feel fear; it's what you do with that fear that matters."

Eurotasu's eyes shimmered with unshed tears. "But I froze, Magumi. You fought, and I just… I couldn't move. I thought I would never be able to protect anyone."

Magumi nuzzled his side gently, her voice calm but firm. "You are not alone in this, Eurotasu. We all have moments of doubt and fear. What matters is that you faced it. You drew your bow, you fought alongside me, and you didn't back down. That takes courage. And I believe in you. We'll face whatever comes together, and you will grow stronger with each battle. You are not a coward, Eurotasu. You are my brave companion, and together we will protect this village."

Eurotasu's shoulders relaxed, the tension slowly ebbing away as Magumi's words sunk in. He looked at her, a small smile breaking through his anxiety. "Thank you, Magumi. I… I needed to hear that. I promise I'll be better. I won't let you down again."

Magumi returned his smile, her eyes twinkling with reassurance. "I know you won't, Eurotasu. Now let's get some rest. Tomorrow is a new day, and we have much to prepare for. We will face it together."

As the stars began to dot the sky above, Magumi and Eurotasu settled down by the fire and shared a simple dinner of fish and rice, the calm of the meal contrasting sharply with the day's tension. The warmth of their bond comforted Magumi more than the flames around them. The night air was still, the forest at peace once more, and for the first time that day, she felt a flicker of hope amidst the lingering shadows.

"Magumi, can you tell me the story about my father's first battle again?" Eurotasu asked, his eyes glistening as if he could glimpse the past, his hands clasping the sword that belonged to his father.

"Sure, but then you must sleep," Magumi replied, her tone gentle. "I need to reflect on the past and devise a plan to defeat the demons."

"Foxes too."

CHAPTER 2

300 B.C.E. Near the Caves of Diros, Modern day Pyrgos Dirou, Greece.

The hot sun pierced through the clouds and struck Magumi's face, stirring memories of how Pausanias fought in a boiling, ferocious clash. The aftermath of that conflict would set Pausanias on a journey that led him to these lands.

Red and black. The only colors staining the world. From the heavens to the earth. Everything blazed and churned in chaos. Pausanias gazed around, beholding death everywhere.

Blood, detached limbs, and viscera spattered the ground. Humans howled like beasts through frothing lips. Arrows and javelins jutted out from the dead and dying.

A Spartan trained to be a rock, unyielding and steadfast. He knew no fear.

Oil fires burned, obscuring vision and creating chaos. The

gentle wind did little to disperse the thick smoke. The sickly sweet, acrid smell threatened to strangle him.

The metallic clash of swords and shields shook his body. The thud of hissing arrows and the whispers of thrown javelins racked his nerves. The panicked whinnies of horses melded with anguished wails, eating at his confidence. The piercing horns and war drums buckled his knees.

Still, he did not waver. He tore his spear out of a man twice his age and drew his arm back behind the relative safety of the Spartan shield wall.

Pausanias eyed his brethren. *Push. Push. Don't think, don't react. Do.* His arm pounded up and down, holding his shield far enough to the left to shelter the next man.

Poecas, a diligent and laconic soldier, now screamed louder than anyone. A blind scream, bordering on insanity.

Pausanias tsked himself, narrowly avoiding a spear that penetrated the shield wall. Sabas held that hoplon. Nearly fifty years old, gray beard, all knotted muscle, Sabas commanded Pausanias's unit.

He spared not a glance to see if Pausanias was safe. He bled from countless cuts, seeming not to notice. He roared curses at his foes. "Fucking farmers! Filthy merchants! Worthless scholars! You'll all die."

Pausanias took inspiration, gathered himself, and stepped forward. "Let!" he bellowed.

"Fly!" answered his comrades as they collectively took another step. Spears arced out from the two lines behind him, striking with enough force to tear through the enemies' shields and flesh.

Again and again, they roared. The push began in earnest. The Spartans, eight rows deep, pressed in unison, driving their foes back with disciplined force. Sabas, who coined the chant "Let fly," smiled.

"Fuck them!" Sabas bellowed.

Pausanias's grin widened. *Trying something new.* His spear

snapped against a helmet. He saved Poecas with a deft block, earning only a grunt. Ungrateful bastard.

Sweat-drenched, Pausanias heaved with nausea from the stench of battle.

"Swords and Pincer," Sabas commanded through gritted teeth.

Spears flew, and the phalanx morphed, flanking the enemy with precision. The pincer cut deep, routing the foe as many of the enemy turned to run, creating gaps in their lines.

"Horses!" Sabas bellowed. The Spartans stepped four paces to the right of the next man. The cavalry charged through those gaps, trampling the fleeing men and rounding up any who surrendered.

As the dust settled, Pausanias pointed out two more skirmishes to Sabas, around five hundred and eight hundred paces to the right. The furthest line of enemy contact was holding a small hill.

Sabas patted Pausanias's shoulder. "As you are my second in command, I'd like to watch you take charge."

"My pleasure." As they marched, he gave out orders. "Drink deep from your pouches, men. Hurry to wrap and oil your wounds. We need fresh spears."

The extra dories brought up and provided by the helots would be employed soon. As the men got ready, Pausanias had a knot in his stomach.

"Feeling nervous, boy?" Sabas inquired with a twisted smile. "Need daddy to save you?"

"Eat shit, old man. The only thing I'm nervous about is if I only double your kills. I can't have some grandfather getting anywhere close to my count."

"Good to hear."

"Why is that good to hear?"

"Because if you said anything else in answer to my question, I'd kill you myself."

Pausanias smiled.

The Spartans approached the battle's edge; the clamor intensified.

Sabas commanded his archers to counter the enemy's archers supporting the second Spartan phalanx, which was locked in a standoff.

Upon arrival, the Spartans seamlessly transitioned ranks, allowing fresh soldiers to take the front.

Pausanias' phalanx reinforced the second.

Sabas sent a runner to update the King, who waited two miles back with an auxiliary force.

The enemy's retreat was signaled by an unfamiliar horn. The enemy warriors retreated in a disciplined fashion, launching a volley of spears before falling back with synchronized axe swings. This withdrawal under assault punished any Spartan who dared advance too soon.

The second enemy force swiftly retreated up the hill, skillfully maneuvering to link up with the third force.

The axes were a grave threat even against the sturdy Spartan shields. Pausanias watched as a fellow warrior's shield shattered, an axe cleaving into his arm before a final blow sent him to the ground.

Sabas laughed and said, "I guess they're not all farmers after all."

"You scared, my elderly captain?" Pausanias asked.

"Scared?" Sabas scoffed. "Just means those bastards might actually deserve to die by my hand. Watch this." He played a bronze flute, emitting a sound that halted every Spartan.

"Lame trot!" they echoed, each soldier taking a half-step forward with their left leg and dragging their right leg behind, maintaining a deliberate pace. The legend said an old Spartan once boasted he could defeat an Athenian hoplite with such a gait.

Pausanias smiled as he fell into step.

The Spartans harried the retreating enemy, their extended line gaining momentum.

He moved up into the third line as men in front of him had fallen. He was able to get his spear wet, the terror of his first battle all but gone now.

Finally.

After two swift lunges with his spear, a giant of a man with a massive blue-painted belly fell to his knees, while another Spartan's spear found its way to his throat. *Half of these bastards don't have any armor.*

He blew his own flute, signaling a halt. "Full stop, come around left," he commanded.

Sabas, a row behind, shouted, "Boy, what are you doing?"

"Watch this," Pausanias replied. The Spartans stopped short of the hill.

"They'll get away!" Sabas protested.

"No, they won't. Also, we won't be suckered in," Pausanias assured.

The enemy, puzzled by the sudden stop, hurried up the hill.

"Double time," Pausanias ordered, and the Spartans quickened their pace, ascending the hill to strike the enemy now flanked on two sides. The Spartans' superior numbers and strategic positioning turned the tide of the battle.

A flanking maneuver sealed the enemy's fate. Trapped, they couldn't flee; their screams and tears betrayed their despair. Some, resigned to death, plunged down the hill, disrupting the Spartan formation.

The battle ended; the survivors either fled down the back of the field or were executed, save for ten spared for interrogation.

Silence crept over the battlefield as the clash of swords and cries of combat faded into haunting echoes. Spartans, their breaths labored, let their shields slump to the ground, the reality of their survival settling in as they surveyed the aftermath.

Exhaustion claimed the victors as they collapsed in silence, seeking solace in water, tears, or song.

Pausanias, overwhelmed by the carnage, dry-heaved.

His armor drenched in blood; an eyeball stuck to his sandal.

Trembling, he tried to scrape it off, but his dagger slipped from his grasp, landing in the blood-soaked earth.

"First time's a bitch, isn't it?" said an approaching Poecas.

"Poecas, you survived! I am so sorry; I completely forgot about you and everyone else. Are you well? Any injuries?"

"Who are you again?"

"Best one I've heard all day. Did you see any of my friends?"

"Alive," Poecas said, pointing a little further up the hill.

"Demas, oh Demas, how will I tell his mother? I must find his body. I must," said Pausanias as he stood up.

"No," Poecas said matter-of-factly, pushing Pausanias back down with one strong hand. "The helots will tend to him. Rest, we march soon."

Pausanias spoke to his friend, "I feel guilty for being alive while Demas and so many others aren't. We have won the day. I'm happy and relieved that I don't have to look for his friend's corpse. There's also this deep sense of shame."

Before he had too much time to dwell on anything further, Coenus and Megadates made their way toward him.

They embraced Pausanias, laughed, and cried. These young men grew up and endured Spartan training together. Now they had survived combat together. They were more than brothers.

Megadates shared jerky with his comrades. As they finished their meal, Sabas approached, appearing serious for a man who had just won a great battle.

"What's wrong?" Pausanias asked as he stood.

Sabas pointed with his spear down the hill and back the way they came. "Far in the distance, beyond the oil fires, another fire burns. Look. The smoke is a weird blue. Even stranger, it doesn't wisp about as fumes tend to do but bubbles like boiling water," Sabas said.

"Those bubbles are huge. We are over two miles away, and I can clearly see them!" Pausanias shouted.

Shouts arose from others. Panic rose in Pausanias's chest.

"It's coming from our King's position," Sabas yelled.

"What is it?" Pausanias asked.

Pausanias' gaze followed Sabas' widening eyes, which reflected the deep blue hue of the smoke curling into the sky. Sabas' eyes narrowed, and his lips peeled back, revealing clenched teeth.

When a messenger arrived, panic-stricken, Sabas didn't hesitate to order, "Spartans, to our king with haste!"

They formed a larger phalanx and jogged toward the king's position.

Pausanias gripped his spear so hard it caused his hands to cramp. He couldn't catch his breath. King Vettias himself had helped train Pausanias from boyhood. *I have to help. That man never once looked down on me.*

In the distance, a battle raged.

To the right and center, Pausanias could make out the masses of Spartan men, their red cloaks and bronze armor glimmering through the blue-black smoke. He could hear their screaming and see those closest to the center falling in droves, being pushed back.

To the left, he thought he saw giant insects at first. That couldn't be right, he knew. Insects didn't grow to that size. They didn't conduct military-style wars.

Some of the figures he saw were wielding weapons. Except those figures made no sense. They were too big, some perhaps ten feet tall.

The fuck?

Horns, fur, scales, antennae, and claws. Too many arms, or too many legs, a plethora of eyes.

Now, as his phalanx closed the distance, he could make out more particulars.

Wild snorts, bellows, and roars that weren't meant for humans to hear.

Fear swept through him, and if he hadn't already been so dehydrated, he might have pissed himself. From the nearby drifting odors, some already had.

The fear of what they witnessed caused men to stumble, others to try and turn and run. The phalanx kept moving in step, however, so men had the choice to turn quickly back towards the horror or get trampled.

To Pausanias' great shame, he saw a couple of men he knew choose being trampled.

What a waste.

Screams brought his attention back to the front. Now only a couple of hundred paces from the evil things, he truly saw them for what they were: demons.

As Pausanias grappled with the grim reality, Sabas' command cut through the chaos: "Spartans, protect your king. Protect, protect."

A new, intense rage seized Pausanias, white-hot and screaming to be unleashed. He shut out his thoughts.

The Spartan phalanx crashed into the demons like a tidal wave.

In brief moments of clarity, Pausanias watched his body dodge, shove, and thrust, feeling out of control and beyond the shield wall's safety. His spear broke off in the face of a dog-like monstrosity with three jaws.

Pausanias leapt up and kicked the broken spear deeper into its face, landing in balance atop the fallen creature. Before he knew it, his sword and dagger were out, and he plunged into the chest of a six-legged, boar-like beast. Both blades sank deep, but his momentum caused him to crash almost headfirst into the beast, tucking his chin just in time.

His brain rattled in his helmet, eyes blurring. Miraculously, he held onto his blades.

As the beast reared up, it pulled Pausanias off his feet. Gravity made the blades tear downward, opening the monster from chest to hip. Hot guts rained down, enveloping Pausanias in a grotesque downpour.

He scrambled up only to face the boar-demon's looming

hoof. But before it could crush him, spears from his comrades struck true.

Sabas' voice pierced the din, "Fool, back in line, don't try to be a hero."

A snake-goat demon lunged at them only to be felled by a barrage of arrows and spears.

Pausanias and Sabas retreated to the safety of the Spartan formation, which parted and closed seamlessly behind them.

Re-armed by the helots, Pausanias rejoined the fray, sharing a knowing grin with Sabas. "Gods be damned, there's nothing better than being a Spartan."

A loud explosion erupted to his right, sending men, bronze, and demons flying in a fireball.

Another fireball, three men wide, hit further right, instantly killing scores. Massive, gaping, jet-black wounds, blood spurting in fountains, and severed limbs stunned everyone to a sudden halt.

In the new gap in the line, a man's smoking lower torso still moved forward a step before crumbling to the ground.

Screams erupted as new horrors filled the gaps, tearing into the stunned men.

The Spartans regrouped quickly, becoming horrors themselves.

This was not a fight for freedom, conquest, honor, or glory—those things didn't matter. It was a bloodbath of wills, each side wanting to annihilate the other.

Lucky for the Spartans, they outnumbered the demons ten to one. Pausanias thought they were doubly lucky to have hit the demons' side while they were distracted, as he and Sabas fought from the rear.

Soon the field fell silent as the last demon fell, and cheers erupted. Joy turned to grief as Spartans knelt, weeping.

"Vettias, oh Vettias, no!" shouts went up from all around. Pausanias realized the grim truth—their king had fallen.

He and Sabas hastened to Vettias's side.

Vettias, gravely wounded, lay on a cot. Pausanias, choked with emotion, knelt and took the king's hand. Vettias beckoned him closer, and Pausanias leaned in to hear his final words.

"They came for the jewel from the Caves of Diros. Stupi--, stu--, stupid fuckers didn't know I had it on me the whole time," Vettias said through spat blood, continuing, "Take it to Athens, bring my sword pommel, tell them what happened, and tell them to send you and the jewel to Pataliputra. Tell them, Pausanias."

None of what Vettias said made sense. *What jewel? Where the hell is Pataliputra? How did he know the creatures were after it? Why him? Why Athens? The Caves of Diros were holy relics but just caves all the same. What did they matter?* Before Pausanias asked, he remembered his place and answered, "Yes, my king, you honor me."

"Good, now tell those bleating sheep behind you to shut up. I'd like a little, little time to rest before continuing my fight," the king managed, gasping one final time before passing away.

Pausanias, Sabas, and any man within the vicinity cried blistering tears. Spartan kings weren't figureheads. They fight down in the dirt like the common soldier. Everyone knew Vettias would die for them.

When the time for tears was done, Pausanias stood and whispered in Sabas's ear.

They knelt down together and removed the king's breastplate, revealing, hanging by a thin wire, a purple jewel.

Pausanias took it and hid it under his own armor. They finished removing the king's armor and took up his sword.

Then, they called the helots over to begin cleaning the body and preparing it for transport back to the capital.

Pausanias looked at Sabas and said, "I feel sick to my stomach," before retching all over the scorched ground.

He took a seat, and someone brought him wine cut with water. He drank deeply, laid back on the ground, and slept.

CHAPTER 3

Pausanias awoke to Sabas's intense gaze piercing the darkness. The night still clung to the battlefield, a silent witness to the day's carnage. As his eyes adjusted, Pausanias realized the demon corpses had vanished without a trace.

"What?" he exclaimed, his voice cutting through the silence.

"They up and dissipated like smoke," Sabas replied matter-of-factly. "Magic has a way of returning to its source."

Pausanias's confusion turned to suspicion. "So, what else are you hiding?" he demanded, only to receive a sharp slap across the face. His ears rang with the impact.

"You don't know anything," Sabas retorted sternly. "I'm a Spartan. I don't hide; I confront challenges head-on."

Pausanias's anger flared, but he held it in check. "Try that again, old man, and you'll be the one confronted. But you're right. I apologize. My emotions are raw, and I'm seeking answers." He rubbed his stinging cheek, his gaze fixed on Sabas.

Sabas's expression softened. "Losing a king is never easy, son. I've endured it three times, and it doesn't get easier. There are secrets I've carried, oaths I've sworn to the dead. Now that he's gone and you're entrusted with this mission, I'll share them.

But not here, not now. Soon, I promise." He extended his arm in a gesture of solidarity.

Pausanias clasped Sabas's arm, sealing their unspoken pact.

As dawn broke, Pausanias and Sabas led a contingent of fifty men on horseback towards Athens, leaving the rest of the Spartans to honor the fallen.

Pausanias pulled his cloak tighter against the morning chill. "Sabas, remind me, why did we ride to that forsaken battlefield?"

"Commanded by the Ephors," Sabas answered, slowing his horse. "A strategic move to outmaneuver our enemies."

Pausanias glanced back at the men trailing them. "And those we fought—strangers with unclear allegiances—who were they?"

"Mercenaries, it seemed. Their loyalty as murky as their origins," Sabas replied, his brow furrowed with concern.

Pausanias narrowed his eyes, pondering. "Could they have been in league with the monsters, a ploy to divert us?"

"Possibly. Deception is a timeless tactic in war," Sabas conceded.

A sigh escaped Pausanias. "I answered the call to war with pride. Why then does this victory feel so hollow?"

Sabas remained silent; his gaze fixed on the distant city. "The luster of war fades quickly, Pausanias. What endures is the truth behind our deeds. Let's stop here for the night."

The men gathered around a campfire. Pausanias stared into the crackling flames casting dancing shadows across his face. The flickering light tugged at memories buried deep within him, memories of another fire from a time long past.

The sun hung low over the Spartan countryside, casting a golden hue over the fields. Young Pausanias sprinted through the open space, his laughter echoing as his parents watched with fond smiles.

His father, a towering figure of muscle and discipline, nodded approvingly.

"Keep your stance firm," his father instructed during their training sessions. "Strength and honor, Pausanias."

The peaceful rhythm of their life shattered one night. The helot rebellion came like a storm, fierce and unexpected. Screams pierced the air. Flames erupted from homes set ablaze. Chaos reigned.

Pausanias' father, armed with his spear, barked orders, rallying the few Spartans present. His mother, equally fierce, fought alongside him. Pausanias, barely twelve, stood frozen, clutching a small dagger.

An explosion rocked the ground. Helots, desperate and enraged, surged forward. His father battled valiantly, each thrust precise, each movement a dance of death. His mother's sword flashed in the firelight, cutting down attackers with grim determination.

A helot broke through the line. His father turned, too late. The enemy's blade found its mark. Pausanias' mother screamed, a primal, heartbreaking sound. She rushed to his side, only to be cut down moments later. Blood soaked the earth, mingling with the dirt.

Pausanias wanted to run to them, to help, but a strong hand pulled him back. His uncle, grim and determined, dragged him away, shielding him from the horror. "Live, Pausanias. For them, live."

The campfire flickered, snapping Pausanias back to the present. He clenched his fists, nails digging into his palms. The memory of that night burned as brightly as the flames before him.

In the days that followed the rebellion, young Pausanias trained relentlessly. The loss of his parents fueled a fire within him, a drive to become stronger, to never be helpless again. Every strike of his practice sword, every defensive stance, was executed with a single purpose: to honor his parents' memory.

"Strength and honor. I will protect what remains."

One evening, after a particularly grueling training session, Pausanias stood alone on a hill overlooking the village. Sweat dripped from his brow, his muscles ached, but his resolve was unwavering. "I am their legacy. I will not fall as they did. I will become the shield that protects Sparta."

The flames in the campfire crackled louder, a log collapsing in on itself. Pausanias' eyes, hardened by years of training and loss, reflected the firelight. He rose, the weight of his past giving him strength. He would face the demons, just as he had faced the rebels. With resolve. With honor. For his parents, and for Sparta.

Back at the campsite, his comrades noticed the change in his demeanor. Sabas, his trusted friend and mentor, gave him a knowing look. No words were needed. They had all faced their own battles, their own losses. Pausanias' resolve was clear. He would fight with a ferocity born from tragedy, a determination that would not falter.

As he settled down for the night, Pausanias whispered a silent vow to the stars. "I will protect them. I will honor their sacrifice. Strength and honor, always."

The following morning, the city's silhouette grew larger on the horizon. The great Piraean gate welcomed them into the bustling heart of Athens.

Pausanias observed the throngs of people—housewives, slaves, artisans—all seeking the day's necessities. Soldiers moved in disciplined patrols, while courtesans beckoned from street corners.

Athens was a melting pot, drawing seekers of trade, adventure, and wisdom from across the known world. Pausanias recognized the diverse faces of Persians, Egyptians, Macedonians, and more.

It took another day before the Spartans were granted an audience with the Athenian leaders.

The next morning, Sabas and Pausanias went alone to the Pnyx. "It's little more than a stone stage with a couple of marble steps," Pausanias said, pointing. "Nestled into the hillside, there's seating available, designed so a speaker's voice would carry up the hill."

"The Spartans may be warriors," Sabas mused, "but the Athenians wield words like weapons. Here, even the lowliest citizen is versed in the art of debate."

Pausanias whispered impatiently, "We've been standing for over an hour."

"Patience," Sabas counseled. "They will arrive soon enough."

And indeed, the assembly began to trickle in, exchanging greetings and refreshments.

A thin Athenian approached them. "Welcome, Spartan friends."

Sabas, his patience worn thin, raised the sword pommel and jewel high. "Vettias is dead. We bring his possessions and his request for your counsel."

The Athenians paused; their expressions somber. "Our condolences," a young Athenian offered.

Another pressed, "How did Vettias meet his end?"

"He died as Spartans do," Sabas replied, his voice carrying.

The assembly exchanged uncertain looks, unsure of their role in this unfolding drama.

"What action do you seek from us, Sabas?" the thin man inquired, his gesture dismissive.

Yet one man's reaction was different—a wince at the sight of the jewel and pommel. Pausanias caught the fleeting expression and signaled Sabas. They excused themselves and followed the stranger outside.

A shroud-looking potbellied man with short, thinning hair, brown eyes, and a bulbous red nose introduced himself. "I am Eneas, and I hold the answers you seek. But for the gods' sake, keep those artifacts hidden. Now follow me." With urgency, he led them through a labyrinth of streets to a modest stone house.

Inside, they were greeted with cool wine and an invitation to sit. Eneas drank deeply before beginning his tale.

"I am an Athenian of influence, a shadowy figure in the council. My life has been marked by secrets and encounters with powerful men. And there is one thing that sets me apart, granting me access to the greatest confidences of our world."

Sabas, still skeptical, demanded, "What do you know of this jewel and pommel?"

Eneas rolled up his sleeves, closed his eyes, and conjured a small olive-sized fireball. The Spartans gasped.

Pausanias made for his sword.

Eneas was quick to reassure. "I mean no harm. If I had wanted you dead, it would have been done. I control this city, but I seek to aid you." The fireball vanished, and Eneas produced parchment and pen, ready to reveal his secrets.

"So how did my friend Vettias meet his end?" Eneas inquired, his curiosity piercing the air like a sharpened spear.

The room fell into a hush as Sabas recounted the tale, his voice a low rumble against the backdrop of a setting sun. Eneas listened intently, his face a mask of solemnity. When the mention of demons arose, he offered a silent prayer for Vettias, his composure unshaken by the revelation of otherworldly foes.

Pausanias, his interest piqued, leaned forward. "And this Pataliputra—where does it lie?"

Eneas's eyes gleamed with the reflection of distant lands. "A grand city, the heart of the Mauryan Empire in India," he declared. Questions swirled like leaves in the wind, but Eneas, bound by oaths of secrecy, revealed only fragments of the vast tapestry of knowledge he possessed.

"I will aid you on your journey," Eneas promised, his voice firm. "Remain in Athens for two more days. I shall prepare diplomatic papers, gather supplies, and secure a vessel. Your path first leads to the Persian Empire, where my contact awaits. From there, you will venture to India."

Pausanias furrowed his brow. "Why entrust us with such a task? Surely there are others…"

"Vettias chose you," Eneas interrupted, a hint of finality in his tone. "And you, Pausanias, have yet to grasp the full extent of your actions during the battle."

Sabas nodded, an understanding glint in his eye, while Pausanias's confusion deepened. "I fought as any man would," he protested.

Sabas chuckled. "Not quite, boy. Remember your charge? You leapt through the air, a force of nature, felling a demon and aiding in the demise of another. Such feats are beyond the ken of mere mortals."

Pausanias's denial was swift. "Magic? That's absurd—I…"

Eneas interjected, his voice calm yet insistent. "Magic is indeed rare in these parts, manifesting typically in youth. Yet mine awoke when I was forty-five. Your exhaustion suggests a depletion of magical energy. Am I correct?"

A moment of silence hung between them before Pausanias conceded, a sheepish grin spreading across his face. "I suppose I must have magic then."

The room erupted in laughter, and Eneas called for more wine.

Pausanias, now curious, held up the sword pommel. "What of this artifact?"

Sabas, slightly inebriated, began the tale. "A relic from Egypt, a millennium old, depicting Khnum—god of creation and the evening sun. A simple bronze casting, yet enigmatic, its magic a riddle lost to the sands of time."

Eneas nodded, his knowledge complementing Sabas's account. "A gift from an Egyptian member of our order, its powers unknown, its purpose shrouded in mystery."

As the afternoon waned, Eneas suggested rest. "Stay here for the day. I'll inform your men of their lodgings and set our plans in motion." Pausanias, wearied by the day's revelations, succumbed to sleep, the comfort of Athenian pillows a balm to his spirit.

The following day, reunited with their company, Pausanias and Sabas awaited Eneas's instructions. Sabas shared all he knew of the Order, his voice tinged with a haunted timbre that Pausanias dared not probe.

"Vettias trusted you with his life's secrets," Sabas said, his tone sour with the taste of uncertainty. "I shall do the same."

That night, Eneas arrived with writs of passage. "You'll sail on my ship, provisioned with all necessities, including coin."

Sabas expressed his gratitude. "Upon our return, I shall bring you spirits from foreign lands."

Pausanias added his thanks. "The road ahead is long. Now, if you'll excuse me, I'll retire for the evening."

CHAPTER 4

300 B.C.E. Lake Iwanashiro, Modern-Day Fukushima Prefecture, Japan

---

The sudden appearance of a solitary owl summoned Magumi's recollections of nights spent deciphering cryptic spiritual messages under the guardian gaze of the moon. It, in turn, reminded her of the beginning of Saoka's journey, which started under such a moon.

In Wa, houses unlike any other graced Inawashiro's shores, contrasting with the modest huts around them yet blending into the natural tapestry. The evening sky, a canvas of purples and blues, held the summer sun's lingering colors. Sunsets on the lake were a marvel, with purples and magentas reflecting on the water, prolonging the day. As night took over, the moon and stars shone, fireflies danced, and spirits glowed, illuminating the darkness.

The village at Lake Iwanashiro bustled with activity as the sun began its descent. The houses, constructed from wood and thatched roofs, reflected the people's architectural ingenuity. Women were busy creating intricate pottery adorned with distinctive cord-marked designs, while children played nearby, their laughter mingling with the gentle lapping of the lake's waters. The air was filled with the earthy aroma of freshly harvested rice, a staple that had revolutionized their society.

Among these traditional thatched roof houses stood a series of Zhou Dynasty-inspired wooden houses with red staircases and tile roofs, their three stories towering over the simpler structures. These houses, adorned with statues and encircling gardens, stood as a testament to a different architectural influence, creating a striking contrast against the surrounding modest huts.

On one balcony, Saoka, a sixteen-year-old magic wielder, contemplated her luck in living among such powerful women as those found in the Order. A glowing wind chime caught her eye as she admired her unique features in its reflection. Her black hair, shorter than most, framed her face, highlighting her jade-black eyes. A wreath of maple leaves crowned her head, symbolizing her connection to the land.

Ayana entered Saoka's room.

"Sister Saoka, your divine presence is requested by the mother in an hour's time if it so pleases your majesty," she teased, seizing a white fur pen from Saoka's desk and pretending to await dictation. The two friends enjoyed imagining themselves as important.

Ayana's presence contrasted with Saoka's. Shorter and fuller, with dimpled cheeks and short, boyish black hair, she had a small mole above her lip.

"Your grace, it does please me, and I officially answer in the affirmative. I hope it wouldn't be a bother to relay a message to the mother for me. I wouldn't want to place any burden on such a fair creature as yourself," Saoka responded. *Oh gods, am I ready?*

Saoka glanced around her room. "Ayana, can you believe it's

been centuries since the Order was established? And yet here we are, adhering to the same old rules against unsanctioned magic."

"It's the tradition that keeps us safe, Saoka. Besides, I think there's something special about being part of something so ancient and respected."

"True. But this summons from the mother is unusual. It's well past sunset, and I'm still being called upon. What do you think it means?"

"I'm not sure. But remember, the older sisters manage their own affairs after dark. Perhaps you're being considered for greater responsibility?"

Saoka nodded. "Maybe. I've heard whispers about Princess Himiko's past with the Order. Do you think the Mothers might share some of that history with us?"

"If they do, it would be an honor. Mother Mitsuki, Mother Yui by Lake Biwa, and Mother Yuki of Nara rarely speak of such things. But to serve under their direct orders, like the Blessed... it's every sister's dream," Ayana said, twirling in a circle.

Saoka adjusted her robes. "I just hope I'm ready. My room's a mess, my desk is covered in study materials, my hair... I want to make a good impression."

Ayana placed a hand on Saoka's shoulder. "You will. Your dedication is evident in everything you do. Go face this meeting with confidence. We'll talk together afterwards."

Ayana smiled again, turned, and left.

Saoka's determination swelled. She wanted to be worthy of the traditions she cherished, and her goal to one day become a mother within the Order fueled her every effort.

Saoka gave her clothes one more look over. Then she reached for her notebook but stopped—Ayana had taken her favorite pen, adorned with white fox fur, a memento from a spiritual encounter in the forest. The memory made her smile.

Walking the mossy path, Saoka's attention snapped to a rustling sound. A white fox, glowing like moonlight, stepped out. Its fur shone like fresh snow, and it had wise eyes.

Drawn to the fox, Saoka felt a deep connection. The myōbu, a spirit fox, looked at her. The forest quieted.

The fox danced around her in a celestial ritual.

Saoka offered rice in respect, and the fox accepted.

Planning to confront Ayana about her missing pen later, Saoka grabbed another and dashed out, apologizing to Wakaba, a shy newcomer, as she hurried by. She made her way to the lake, seeking a moment of calm before her meeting with the mother.

Kneeling by the serene lake, the cool water reflecting the pale moonlight, she allowed her memories to surface, stirring a storm within her.

The village lay in the shadow of the mountains, humble huts scattered among the rice paddies. Young Saoka, no more than eight, played near her home, unaware of the storm brewing within her. Her hair, cut short and tousled, framed her face, her eyes wide with wonder.

One evening, a strange feeling coursed through her, a tingling sensation that started at her fingertips and spread like wildfire. Unbeknownst to her, the latent magic within her had awakened. As she reached out to touch a simple flower, it burst into flames, the petals consumed by an unnatural fire.

Her parents, poor and burdened, saw this display. Fear clouded their eyes. Whispers of "demon" and "curse" spread through the village. Saoka's parents, unable to understand or control her burgeoning powers, made a heart-wrenching decision.

That night, under the cover of darkness, they led Saoka into the forest. Her mother's grip on her hand was firm, but Saoka sensed the tremor in it. Her father carried a small bundle, their only parting gift.

"We have to, Saoka," her father said, voice breaking. "You are special, but we cannot help you. This is for your own good."

Saoka's heart pounded. Abandoned? The word echoed in her mind, a stark betrayal from the people she loved most.

Her mother placed a small amulet around her neck, a simple charm for protection. "Stay strong, my daughter. Use your gift wisely," she whispered, tears streaming down her face. With that, they left her, disappearing into the darkness.

Surviving alone in the forest, Saoka learned to harness her powers. She trained herself, controlling the fire within, transforming fear into strength. Her nights were filled with silent cries and whispered promises.

"I will not be afraid. I will show them I am strong," she thought, her resolve hardening with each passing day.

One evening, as she practiced her magic by a stream, a group from the Order found her. Their leader, a stern yet kind woman, saw the potential within Saoka. They offered her a place among them, a chance to learn and grow.

In the present, Saoka stood by the lake, her reflection showing a woman of strength and determination. She had come far from the frightened girl in the forest. The Order had become her family, her refuge.

Saoka blinked, tears mingling with the lake's reflection. She touched the amulet, the only tangible memory of her parents. The pain of their abandonment still fresh, she vowed to prove that her magic was a gift, not a curse.

She whispered to the still water, "I will protect those who fear

IN THE LAND OF NI

what they do not understand. I will be their shield and their guide."

Returning to the Order's compound, Saoka felt a renewed sense of purpose. Her resolve, forged in the fires of her past, would guide her in the battles to come. She was no longer the abandoned child but a powerful sorceress ready to face any challenge.

As she approached the Mother's building, Saoka composed herself to a calm walk, mindful of the older sisters' and the Blessed's watchful eyes.

The Mother's residence, also a place for learning and the Order's library, hummed with magical protection. The corridors were lit by magical paper lanterns.

In the library, Saoka's curiosity led to a stern look from Akin, the librarian. A group of older sisters and a Blessed were in deep conversation, their ranks denoted by shoulder bracelets and a necklace with an ancient clay figurine.

Before facing Akin's scolding, Saoka preemptively addressed her. "I am very sorry for the intrusion, elder sister. I have been summoned to speak with the Mother soon, so I didn't want to wait by her door too early with the possibility of disturbing the dear Mother. I thought I might sit here and gather my thoughts before proceeding further," Saoka explained.

Akin, embodying the quintessential librarian with strict and distrustful traits, responded with a slight tilt of her head. "Well, you thought wrong, young lady. You have not yet reached the rank of older sister. You know the rules, I assume," she stated.

"Yes, sister. I was just thinking maybe it would be alright, seeing as I have permission to come into the Mother's house at this hour, which is highly unusual in itself. But perhaps the Mother wants—" Saoka attempted to explain before being interrupted by Akin.

"I'm sure I don't care; rules are rules and..." However, Akin's words were cut short by another interruption.

"It's OK, sister Akin," a voice intervened. Saoka turned

towards the source and found the Blessed addressing the librarian. Saoka gulped; she hadn't seen this woman before and didn't know her name, leaving her unsure of how to express gratitude.

The Blessed, undoubtedly a wonder of beauty, captured Saoka's attention. Enthralled, she thought, *What a beauty. Oh, how jealous Ayana will be when I tell her I saw such a creature.*

The Blessed had a slender frame and a perfectly proportioned face adorned with medium-full lips painted in a pale red color, showcasing a mischievous yet genuine smile. Her eyes, though on the smaller side, fit her face, complemented by thick and luscious eyebrows, small and dainty eyelashes, and a small slender slightly pointy nose. Her flawless skin and jet-black hair reflected light in the blue spectrum.

After a moment of gaping, Saoka finally bowed. "Excuse me, Blessed. I didn't mean to bother you. Thank you for your kind words; I will take my leave." She turned to go.

"Oh no, you won't get off that easily. Come now, I was growing bored talking with these old hens. Won't you stay and spin me a story? It's not often I meet a young woman who loves to get into trouble as much as I do," the Blessed invited.

Saoka turned back towards the table, mortified. Though she wanted to laugh at the Blessed's joke, she thought better of it. The older sisters around the table did not seem amused. Despite being older than Saoka, none of them were old hens. In fact, to a lady, they were all very pretty. Nevertheless, compared to the Blessed, they might as well be charcoal.

"If... it pleases your Blessedness, your wish is my command," she said with another bow.

"Well, what if I commanded you to jump off the roof, girl, or slit the throat of one of the sisters? Would you?" the Blessed inquired with a curious smile and a wink.

This was a test of sorts, but the nature of the test remained elusive.

"The holy book of Haru says a command can and should be disobeyed if it is illegal or immoral," Saoka replied.

"Yes, disobedient as well. Truly a young lady," the Blessed said with a sarcastic expression. She patted an empty seat next to her and waited patiently for Saoka to obey.

Saoka made her way to the chair. Bowing again, this time to the other ladies, she took her seat, feeling their eyes on her. "It is a pleasure to meet you, Blessed. My name is Saoka. I'm a fourth-year student, and I want to take my Oath as soon as possible. I apologize again for interrupting a meeting of my elders."

"Well, well, aren't you suddenly serious. What a strange combination we have here. Disobedient, a rule breaker who quotes two-hundred-year-old tomes from corners of the library forgotten by even our lovely librarian, and solemn enough to want to take her oath so young," the Blessed finished.

Saoka blushed.

"Reckless, maybe, Blessed, but I do try my best. I want to be a Mother one day, if gods willing, I am able," she said in defense of herself.

One of the charcoal briquettes to the right scoffed and spoke up, "Why would someone like you ever get the idea that she could be a Mother?"

Saoka realized that she didn't know any of the older sisters.

"Well, to start, I can tell you that I have memorized all the names of every sister currently stationed here, and none of you are on my list. I study twice as hard as the other girls, my magic is strong, and so is my will. Also, due to your accent, you're from the south, probably Nara, because of how you wear your hair in a bun with two eating utensils sticking out of them. The people there are doing great things, I have heard, but greatness often leads to arrogance, dear elder sister. The question is, who are you?" Saoka spoke from somewhere deep in her heart. She would not be pushed around.

"You little shit, I'll have your hide for such an insolent tongue. Have you country girls no manners? Do you understand the position you're in here?" said the charcoal briquette.

"And there it is again, the big city arrogance. Decorum is one thing, but insults are another. Manners are only afforded to those who have earned respect by showing manners themselves. I apologized and bowed several times and meant it, but you were the one who cut off the conversation between me and a Blessed. Maybe they forgot to teach you how to greet a sister, big city fast-paced and all. Leaves one to ponder what else you're lacking lessons in," Saoka said.

"Well, she's got some guts, I'll give her that," another briquette with reddish-brown hair chimed in. Murmurs of agreement from another briquette or two and a laugh from the last charcoal sister, a heavy-set but pretty girl with rosy cheeks, short brown hair, and a scar down her neck. Rosy briquette leaned back with her chair, leaving the two front legs dangling in the air, while cupping her hands behind her head to relax. Her sword scraped the floor. Wait a minute, a sword?

She glanced over the table once again, noticing one more weapon propped up against a chair. For some reason, every woman was wearing a dagger at their belt line. While sisters carried weapons and were encouraged to learn at least one, most did not in the houses of the Order.

"Who the hell are you all? Before my courage runs out, I was wondering if you girls were expecting a fight? Most of us don't need armaments in these houses. Or was it out of necessity on the road? Unusual if you were coming from the south, as all the roads there are said to be peaceful. What's more, a group of elder sisters and a Blessed would be accompanied in times of travel with an escort of armed guards. Unless, of course, you didn't come from the south. Oh, fuck, you have been to the north. Forgive my rudeness, but I must know what's going on up there?" Saoka finished with a girly squeal.

The Blessed interrupted before things could get ugly. "Because Saoka is like me, Akina. Now sit quietly, Akina, before I get tired of your ugly mug and turn you into an earthworm," the Blessed said.

Akina's face turned beet red. She remained silent. The other older sisters looked down and shuffled in their seats. Some of them wanted to defend Akina, but all of them were deathly afraid of the Blessed, and none had any desire to get involved.

"Tell me, Saoka, what do you want more than anything?" the Blessed asked, eyes widening with curiosity.

"I... I want to make our Order proud and to protect the people," she replied, a vision of future heroism forming in her mind.

The Blessed gave Saoka a sharp look. "No, what do you really want?" she said with a raised eyebrow.

Saoka's mouth gaped, but no sound came out.

The Blessed continued, "It's OK to say you don't know, young one. But whatever it is you desire, you should follow that passion to the ends of the earth. Do you understand?"

Saoka only nodded.

The Blessed stood up lightning-quick, yanking Saoka to her feet. "Enough. I am happy enough to see the ladies of these lands have some spine, but there are protocols, girl. Those protocols aren't the types of things to break; it's what gets people dead," the Blessed finished.

"Yes, of course, Blessed, I forgot myself in the excitement. My friend Ayana always says I am a whore for knowledge, and it's accurate. How can I make amends?" Saoka asked.

"It's already forgotten. These hens should have been more careful with how they acted, what they said, what they gave away. To think a student figured out all that with so little information. Come on now, Saoka, we have a meeting to attend to, and we don't want to be late. Mother absolutely hates that."

All the other ladies stood up and started for the door. *We?* Saoka thought, more confounded than ever. She held her tongue and took some deep breaths. As they exited the library, she waved goodbye to the librarian, who waved back with a grin.

CHAPTER 5

Saoka's lungs filled with the musty air of the third floor, her heartbeat slowing as she steadied herself. The corridor outside the Mother's room teemed with a sea of robes—twenty Blessed and forty elder sisters—a sight that sent a jolt through her. Twenty Blessed? The thought echoed in her mind, a silent drumbeat of disbelief.

"Can you believe it, Blessed?" Saoka said. "These three compounds shelter half our thousand sisters at any given time."

The Blessed, a serene statue among the murmurs, nodded. "Indeed. And it's the missions that scatter our elder sisters and the Blessed across the Land of Wa."

Saoka cut in, her voice a mix of wonder and curiosity, "But only sixteen Blessed ones in normal times. Seeing more than six together is a rarity."

"The Mother always keeps three Blessed close," the Blessed confided, her voice a hushed thread. "Their magic—it's a shield, a heartbeat for the house."

Saoka's eyes grew wide, her voice a feather's touch, "And yet, here we stand, while I'm rooted to the spot, my mind a tempest of thoughts."

"The Order's men serve in shadows. Rumors speak of secret magic-wielding guards among them."

Saoka's head shook, a small smile playing on her lips. "Just rumors, surely. Magic belongs to the realm of women."

"In Iwanashiro town, a thousand women of the Order thrive with the support of four thousand townspeople. Together, we're a force of five thousand."

"And in summer," Saoka mused, her voice tinged with solemnity, "that number swells with the influx of merchants and travelers."

The Blessed began counting on her fingers, "Among ten thousand souls, only sixteen are Blessed. That's a mere zero-point-one-six percent."

"Yet, before us sit twenty-one Blessed," Saoka observed, her brow furrowed. "The Mother's discussion must bear great weight. And here I am, the sole student among them."

"That marks your presence as extraordinary. You're here for a reason, Saoka. I never gave you my name. I'm Mayuki. Please, take a seat," she guided Saoka to a cushioned bench.

Mayuki leaned in, her voice carrying a note of gravity, "To address your earlier questions—yes, we were expecting a fight, and yes, we ventured north. The turmoil there… it's a harbinger of ill fortune for us."

Saoka's thoughts tangled. Not safe in the houses, danger approaching? What could possibly breach our sanctuary? Then, clarity struck her like lightning. "Demons," she breathed out.

"Damned demons."

The Mother's room doors flew open, a signal that pulled every woman to her feet. A man strode out, his presence a challenge to every rule they held sacred. Saoka's pulse quickened.

Men, forbidden within the Mother's sanctum, were a doctrine etched into their very being. Yet, this man stood defiant, a living contradiction.

The Land of Wa, a realm cradled by the sea, seldom

welcomed outsiders. Tales of people with diverse complexions were confined to the pages of books, making the sight of this man a living legend to the assembled.

He towered over them, his stature magnified by a crown of fur-like black hair. His face, a sculpture of strength, was softened by the warmth in his golden-brown eyes.

Some sisters, their initial shock fading, cast flirtatious glances his way. The whores, Saoka's thought came unbidden.

Clad in Egyptian armor, a leather tunic reinforced with bronze plates, the man was a figure ripped from the pages of Saoka's studies, armed with a spear and a curved sword.

"Most respected ladies, the Mother awaits you," he announced, his deep voice laced with a foreign cadence. "Please forgive my intrusion; my name is Adofo. All will be clarified," he said with a bow and a swipe of his hand.

"At least the towering stranger is polite," Mayuki whispered to Saoka as they passed him.

Inside the Mother's grand room, Saoka lingered at the edge, her eyes drinking in the opulence—from the vivid tapestries to the luminous lamps and the grand desk at the back of the room.

As the doors sealed shut, Saoka's gaze found the Mother. Her timeless grace, with eyes like verdant pools and hair streaked with moonlight, struck awe into Saoka's heart. She bore the youthfulness of one touched by late-blooming magic.

Saoka's mind wandered to the enigma of magic and mortality, recalling the Mother's teachings: "Death is the way of life, but decay is an aberration, and magic is its bane."

The Mother stood, commanding the room's attention. "Ladies, sisters, Blessed—thank you for gathering. The secrets I divulge today must remain ensconced within these walls. Do we understand?" Her voice brooked no dissent.

A chorus of "Yes, Mother," reverberated through the chamber.

"Very well. Where shall we begin?"

"In the middle," Mayuki interjected, her audacity drawing gasps.

The Mother's laughter, a rare melody, filled the room. "Thank you, Mayuki, for the levity," she said, her smile a beacon in the tense air.

"I had prepared a lengthy discourse, but brevity is called for. Demons, in league with humans, advance from the north. Their numbers are unprecedented, their alliance troubling."

A collective intake of breath punctuated the Mother's pause. Saoka's heart raced; such a coalition was beyond imagination.

The Mother's fist clenched. "I bear graver tidings. Our order's roots extend beyond Wa, part of a vast, clandestine network. Our secrecy was a bulwark against demons. This isn't their first pact with humanity, but it is a first for Wa. Until now, only the Mothers knew. Today, that changes."

Whispers swirled like leaves in a storm. A knot of fear and wonder tightened within Saoka.

"You'll need proof," the Mother concluded, nodding to the man. He disarmed himself and sat, a gesture of peace. His blue aura, a whirlwind of energy, captivated the room. Saoka's initial shock melted into admiration as she recognized the truth: men, too, could harness magic.

"Why, Mother, why?" an elder sister cried out.

"Are there others like him?" a Blessed inquired, pointing at the man.

"What of the Order? The implications?" another voiced her concern.

"Enough!" Saoka's voice cut through the tumult. Silence fell, all eyes on her. Who was this young student to command their attention?

Saoka held their gaze. "Our mission remains unchanged. We have new allies. The Order's secrets were kept from love, to protect. If demons approach, we trust the Mother's wisdom," she declared, bowing to the Mother.

The Mother returned the gesture, her presence a calming force. "Forgive us, my sisters. We never wished for secrets. Tonight, we embrace transparency. Some truths must remain veiled, but know this: our actions are always for humanity."

"No time for tears, you cows," Mayuki's voice cut through the somber mood, her tone a mix of frustration and resolve. "Enough with the sobbing and scheming. Let's return to the simple task at hand—exterminating those demons."

A bellow of laughter erupted from the crowd as someone retorted, "Takes one to know one!" The room filled with the sound of mock moos, the tension breaking like thin ice underfoot.

The Mother, a picture of composure, rose to her full height, her back straightening like a reed in the wind. "Sisters, before we part tonight, I have more to share. Take a seat. I'll have rice wine and sweets brought in."

She paused, her gaze sweeping over the gathered women. "Men's magic is a rare and hidden treasure, often mistaken for the work of spirits or enchantments."

Rurua, the formidable instructor of forestry and horseback riding, raised her voice. "Mother, if I may, what becomes of these men?"

As the rice wine made its rounds, tradition dictating each pour for their neighbor, the Mother spoke again. "Those who wield magic are either trained within our ranks or exiled. Those who stay swear an oath of secrecy and find a new purpose among us."

Saoka's head swirled, the rice wine's potency amplifying her dizziness. "Mother, what's the grand scheme? Why the secrecy about men and magic? You mentioned it's to protect us from demons, but it seems like common knowledge elsewhere."

The Mother's eyes met Saoka's, a glint of pride flickering within. "Saoka, you surprise me again. That's precisely why you're here. Listen closely, everyone—the magic that breathes life into demons and spirits is waning. Ages ago, a celestial rock struck our world, ravaging half of its magic. The impact site suffered most, but here, on the opposite side of the globe, the magic endures. What followed was a millennium of ice and endless winter."

Mayuki scoffed, disbelief etched on her face. "A rock from the heavens, you say? Millennia past?"

The Mother's expression softened. "I'll overlook your skepticism, Mayuki. This knowledge comes from the Order, and we Mothers have witnessed the proof. Our duty extends beyond humanity; we are guardians of Earth itself."

A hush fell over the room as the weight of her words settled. "If magic fades, how do we carry on? Can life persist without it?"

"Magic, though scarce in humans and nature, isn't the sole source of life's vibrancy and joy," the Mother reassured.

Sana, a lecturer from the halls of learning, pondered aloud. "The decline of magic is akin to a dwindling species."

"Exactly," the Mother affirmed. "We must allow magic to diminish, lest demons grow too powerful, threatening all existence."

The Mother raised her glass, the rice wine's clarity mirroring the solemnity in her eyes, and took a measured sip. The room fell silent, the air thick with contemplation. Faces, once marked by skepticism, now reflected the weight of her words. A flicker of determination sparked in each woman's eyes, an unspoken pact forming among them. In the quiet that followed, a haunting melody began to rise, weaving through the room like a whispered promise, echoing their deepest fears and steadfast hopes:

> Darkness slaps at my feet
> as water on a lake
> thunder claps fill my head
> broken bones I can take
> empty tombs, goodbye my friends
> demons roam the hills

death of home
blood fire kills

The song spread like wildfire, each woman joining in until the chorus resonated with unity and strength:

Sadness shown across the sky
shone a star that thrills
endless love and that my friends
is why I fight still

The Mother's words, a poignant echo of the Order's founding anthem, stirred the hearts of all present. Its simplicity and depth moved many to tears, reaffirming their purpose.

With renewed spirit, the Mother continued. "Thank you. Now, let's address the reason for tonight's gathering. Blessed Mayuki and her valiant sisters have been surveying the northern reaches of Wa for nearly a year. Demons are advancing on our lands, and while they haven't yet besieged a major city, intelligence suggests an imminent strike on Kazuno. Your mission is to fortify the city, coordinate with local forces, and gather intelligence on the enemy. Mayuki will brief you further. Prepare to lead four hundred men to reinforce Kazuno's defenses. We depart at dawn."

The women responded in unison, "Yes, Mother." Trained for this moment, they stood ready, all except Saoka, the lone novice among them.

"Dismissed. Prepare yourselves, bid farewell—demons roam the hills, and that is why we fight."

As the room buzzed with activity, a gentle hand rested on Saoka's shoulder. She turned to find the Mother's compassionate gaze. "Stay a moment, child," she urged.

The chamber emptied, leaving Saoka alone with the Mother and the towering figure of Adofo. The giant, sensing her unease, seized the moment. "Young one, what do you know of Pataliputra?"

"The Indian city?" Saoka's voice was a mix of curiosity and apprehension.

"Yes, precisely."

Saoka recited from memory, "Pataliputra, the sacred city, stretches in a parallelogram, flanked by sixty-four gates and wooden defenses. It's a nexus of stone pillars and diverse faiths —Buddhism, Hinduism, Jainism."

Adofo's eyes twinkled with approval. "And Jainism? What do you know?"

"Only that it's a path of nonviolence, leading many to forsake meat," Saoka admitted.

Adofo chuckled. "Partly true. I hail from Pataliputra, raised in the Jain tradition. It's more than nonviolence; it's about truth, not stealing, non-possessiveness, chastity, and, for us, battling demons. We Jains are warriors in our own right, aligned with your Order in purpose."

Saoka's eyes widened. "That's admirable. But how does this relate to me?"

The Mother interjected, "Your talents are needed for our northern endeavor. You'll serve as a scribe, documenting the demons, offering insights."

Saoka, her heart racing with a mix of fear and honor, accepted the unexpected elevation to sisterhood. "I swear to uphold our Order and be its exemplar," she vowed.

"You're now a sister, with all rights, and perhaps, in time, blessed," the Mother hinted, a knowing smile on her lips.

"Or a mother," Saoka ventured.

The Mother laughed, "Perhaps a mini Mayuki."

Adofo leaned in, his voice a low rumble. "I anticipate the day, little one."

Saoka bristled. "I am Sister Saoka now."

The Mother's laughter filled the room. "To Adofo, we're all 'little.' And at his age, he's more akin to a grandfather."

Adofo flashed a hand signal—five fingers extended, then two, then three—revealing his true age: five hundred and twenty-three.

"Any questions?" the Mother inquired, noting Saoka's pensive look.

"Where do the demons originate? I mean, the official stories and most of the myths and legends. But haven't we learned more?"

Saoka's pulse quickened, each beat a drum heralding war, as the Mother delineated the ranks of their adversaries.

"The yokai, first-level demons, are spawned from the abyss of death and despair. Their very essence a testament to their vile birthright."

"And the oni," the Mother continued, her voice a somber melody, "are the second tier—cunning, social creatures birthed from humanity's darkest sins. They brandish magic with a skill rivaling our finest sorcerers.

But it is the hybrids that should truly alarm us. These third-level demons, born of both human and demon, wield powers that defy the laws of nature—mind control, shape-shifting… they are the epitome of demonic evolution."

The Mother's eyes shone with an unyielding resolve. "Yet, let us not forget, for all their terror and might, these demons—no matter their power—tremble at the mere whisper of goodness."

Saoka gulped down her fear and found her voice. "Thank you, Mother. Your words have painted a clear picture of the darkness we face. May I be excused? I need a moment to steady my spirit before we step into the morrow's light."

The Mother gave a nod, her gaze affirming Saoka's request. "Go, child. Gather your strength. We will need it for the trials ahead."

As Saoka stepped away, the mood shifted, a collective breath held in anticipation of the battles to come. She slipped into the quietude of the corridor; the wooden walls a cold comfort against the brewing storm within her.

In the solitude of her private sanctuary, Saoka allowed herself a moment of vulnerability. The knowledge pressed upon her, a burden to carry into the dawn. Yet, as she closed her eyes, a resolve kindled within her—a resolve to stand as a beacon of hope amidst the encroaching shadows.

For in the end, it is not just the demons we fight against, but the very essence of fear and despair. And I, newly anointed sister of the Order, will not let that prevail.

CHAPTER 6

300 B.C.E. Miletus City, close to the modern-day village of Balat in Aydin Province, Turkey. Fathers trek through Persia.

Magumi sat in a meditative state, feeling the presence of a lone butterfly. Its delicate flight conjured visions of a once-bustling marketplace, vibrant wings mirroring life's intricate tapestry. She thought of Pausanias, landing in such a market after leaving his homeland for the first time.

Leaning against the side of the trireme's galley, Pausanias sighed. Sabas grunted beside him; the heat of his anger was palpable. Despite their high status, neither man was exempt from oar duty. A Spartan warship had a reputation to uphold. With the winds up and the sails unfurled, the oars were momentarily idle, offering a respite to the weary Spartan.

"Not going to say anything, then? Just stew in it?" Sabas's soft inquiry floated between them.

"No," Pausanias whispered. *If this is a competition to be the softest speaker, I'm damn sure going to win.*

"I miss them, my friends, my king," Sabas said.

"Yeah, so shut up about it already."

"Boy, I have half a mind to end you. When veterans speak, you listen. You've been given an enormous task. I know; I was there. But I'm sitting here behind you all the way. Don't want to be here any more than you do. Goddamn Persians, worse than the Egyptians if you ask me. Almost as bad as the Athenians. You lost plenty, but I lost everything. I've no wife, no children. All my peers are dead! So, if you want to talk, you better do it now."

"I'm sorry. I didn't mean that. I'm bitter, is all. I thought after my first battle, I'd return a hero. Maybe meet a nice girl, the type who wouldn't even look in your ugly direction. Now I'm stuck with an old man, an impossible duty, and half my friends are also dead," Pausanias said, each syllable a stone he spat.

"Good. Rage and bitterness are good. You are going to need it. And since when has a Spartan's duty not been impossible? You stand apart, my friend. The sea's vastness troubles you more than any demon we've faced."

"To leave Hellas, our motherland… it is a burden heavier than my shield, Sabas. The demons we slew, the battles we won —none weigh on me like this departure."

Sabas looked down at his hands. "A week at sea, yet your heart remains in Hellas. Is it the mission's weight that anchors your spirit?"

Pausanias sighed. "The mission is vital, yes, but it's more than that. I've known our lands, our people, our ways. To step beyond… it's a venture into the unknown."

"You are Spartan-born, educated by the finest, and tempered in battle. This journey is but another path to glory."

"Your words are a beacon, Sabas. I can't help wondering if I am ready for the world outside Hellas."

"That is true, but this is a little over the top, wouldn't you say?" Pausanias asked, all anger fleeing his body.

"Chance to be a legend is all." Sabas raised a hand, "One more thing."

"What's that?"

"Your mom never called this dick ugly!"

Pausanias struggled to maintain composure, then burst out laughing, a deep belly laugh. Sabas joined in, as did some of the surrounding men listening in.

"Why does this feel fantastic and fleeting?" Pausanias said.

"That's what your mother said," Sabas replied, ducking a playful punch from Pausanias.

Just then, the wind came to an abrupt stop. The captain signaled oars down, and the hard work began. Three days of sailing and rowing later, they made landfall at the port city of Miletus.

Once Minoan, then Mycenaean, now Persian, it was a melting pot of commerce. With a recorded history of at least a thousand years, Persians, Hellenes, Egyptians, Indians from beyond the Indus River, and countless others came by trade road or by ship.

They would not stay long. With two thousand miles to cover on land to reach Persepolis, they needed supplies, horses, maps, and guides. A lot could go wrong on this journey, so they had to be as prepared as possible. They had travel rites of passage from two kings and an emperor, but these vast distances promised troubles ahead.

During their short stay in Miletus, Sabas hired a guide named Ardeshir, a Persian who had spent his life traveling between Persia and Hellas. Ardeshir offered to show Pausanias around the city, and Pausanias agreed.

"This city is foreign to me. While we Spartans color our towns very little, preferring white marble and red, Miletus is a mishmash of every color imaginable," Pausanias observed as they strolled.

"Even the Athenians stick to blue or purple tones. Here, every house is painted a different color, every window curtain, every flower pot. I quite like it," Ardeshir said, stopping to smell a flower.

"It's almost as jarring as the scents and the smells. These markets have a vast quantity of foods I've never seen. Exotic fruits, piles of pigmented spices, perfume the air. Meats from who knows what animals."

"Cooked over coals, there's nothing better. Here, try one of these," Ardeshir said, paying a local for two kebabs. "The pastries baking in street ovens over there are my favorite," he said, pointing. They continued walking.

"It's outlandish how ignorant I am of the world around me. I thought myself well-cultured, but realize how little I actually know. Damn, it's hot," Pausanias said, stopping to purchase some apricot juice from a beautiful brown-skinned woman at the edge of the market.

"Blessedly, the market's streets are small and tucked between buildings, providing some shade. Those rope lines that crisscross the streets, with their giant multicolored sails, block any midday sunlight that might beam down on us. Quite ingenious, don't you think, Spartan?"

Pausanias grunted, "I do have some extensive drinking to do tonight with my companions. Please join us. For now, though, I think I'll retire to my quarters and take a nap."

The two days in Miletus passed uneventfully, but Pausanias took full advantage of all the delights the city had to offer. He drank a variety of new liquors, some sweet, others sour, and woke each morning with a dry mouth.

On the third morning, Sabas informed him, "All preparations for our journey have been made. As I have traveled to this part of the world before, I made all the arrangements, leaving you with nothing to do save drink and wander."

"Appreciated," Pausanias said through a burp, gesturing for Sabas to pass him a pitcher of water.

Later that morning, as they set out for the city's eastern gates, Pausanias, atop his mount, told Sabas, "How poetic that the sun is rising in the direction of our adventure. Why do the sun's rays transfix a man? Why are those morning hues so inspirational? What is it about dawn and the crisp air that brings about such a sense of wonder, a rebirth, a chance to be anyone, do anything?"

"You might still be drunk, so listen up. Fifty Spartans, twenty more Hellenes, five guides, three tradesmen, and a dozen or so assistants have been paired with twenty Persian soldiers. Not a huge group, but not small enough to be trifled with either. This small command of ours is joining a departing trade caravan. We will travel around two hundred miles together to the next large city. Take a moment to take stock of your surroundings."

Pausanias was still surveying the troop when Ardeshir pulled up his horse next to Pausanias's.

"It's a beautiful sight, eh?" Ardeshir said.

"Not too bad," admitted a stoic Pausanias. "Come, Ardeshir, we have a journey to start." The Persian man broke out in raucous laughter.

"What's so funny?" asked Pausanias.

"I thought I was the guide, and here you are leading me. Do you even know the name of the next settlement we'll reach?" quizzed Ardeshir.

Pausanias started laughing. *I like this man, this Persian. Despite all the history between Hellas and Persia, there were bonds to be forged.*

CHAPTER 7

300 B.C.E. on the road to Kazuno, in modern-day Kazuno City, Akita Prefecture, Japan.

The sight of a solitary hawk soaring high evoked the spirit of a mentor, whose wisdom soared beyond earthly confines. Magumi shifted her weight into a more comfortable position, thinking of Saoka earning the chance to have such a noble, albeit foul-mouthed, mentor.

Saoka weaved through the bustling camp, belongings slung over one shoulder as she dodged soldiers and servants alike. Two stable boys helped her mount a black horse named Coal. The boys' goodbyes trailed behind her, a fleeting sound lost in the morning air. *Focus on the mission.*

Riding to an open field, Coal's hooves dug into the soft earth, stopping amidst a sea of armored figures. A horse and rider approached. Saoka's eyes narrowed, locking onto a familiar face from the night before.

"Name's Akiho. You're to ride with us. Try and keep up."

As Saoka adjusted her gear, another rider approached—a young girl. "I'm Ramona, apprenticed to Mayuki. We can ride together if you wish. I'm sure you have questions."

Saoka smiled. "It would be my pleasure. Nice to meet you. My name is Saoka." They took their place near the end of the long procession of horses and caravans.

Dust rose in clouds as the caravan lurched into motion, the ground vibrating with life. The journey to Kazuno, about 236 miles, would take a week if they pushed hard, ten days otherwise.

Saoka leaned closer, curiosity flickering in her eyes. "How long have you been in Mayuki's service? Is she good to you? What types of things are you learning? What about the others?"

"I joined the Order a year ago. My magical abilities are weak, rendering me nearly useless for certain tasks. But I found other ways to contribute."

"How so?" She adjusted her grip on the reins, guiding her horse to keep pace with the others. The rhythmic clinking of armor and the occasional neigh of horses filled the air. She couldn't help but marvel at the serene beauty of the paddies.

The young woman hesitated, then responded, "I've accompanied Mayuki and the sisters on their journeys, learning about forestry, riding, map-making, and the Order's bureaucratic affairs."

Saoka nodded, appreciating the girl's honesty. She watched a flock of birds take flight from the paddies, their wings beating a steady rhythm against the sky. "And the Order's affairs? Those can be quite complex." *I don't even know how I fit in yet.*

"My physique isn't well-suited for combat yet, but I hope to become a competent fighter."

Saoka smiled softly, encouraged by the girl's resolve. She remembered her own doubts when she first joined the Order, unsure if she could measure up to the expectations placed upon her. "The sisters have embraced you as one of their own."

Ramona beamed. "They take turns teaching me during mornings or evenings when we aren't on horseback."

"Perhaps those sisters are not as bad as I thought," Saoka said, touching her chin.

Ramona giggled. "Oh, if you cross them, they are the worst."

The next three days passed seamlessly. Groups of men arrived at waypoints ahead of time, set up camp, and guided the sisters to the ladies' tents. Campfire meals and laughter filled the air. Saoka found solace in her morning rituals of archery and meditation.

On the fifth day, rain pelted down, plastering cloaks to bodies. By the eighth day, with the deluge continuing, water streamed down Saoka's face as she approached Mayuki, shoulders hunched against the storm.

"So, what exactly should I be doing on this trip? I'm new to being a sister, and I want to be as helpful as possible," Saoka asked through the sheets of rain.

Mayuki didn't answer or even shrug her shoulders.

"Seriously, nothing? Not even a piece of advice? I thought you ladies were going to teach me some things," Saoka said.

Mayuki's face reddened, her words slicing through the air. "Well, excuse me! I didn't receive the news that you had been elected queen of the world. Why, yes, the whole world now revolves around you."

"Hopefully, you wouldn't use that filthy tongue to clean it," Saoka retorted. Her satisfaction was short-lived.

In a flash of lightning, the rain intensified. A sudden force jolted Saoka forward, her hands flailing for balance. She tumbled over her horse and landed in the slick mud. She looked back while rubbing her aching tailbone. Eiko. Not much of a talker, but fiercely loyal to Mayuki.

As she pushed herself to her feet, Mayuki leaned down from the horse to offer a hand and some advice.

"Mother gave you a job to be a scribe, right? Well, do that. Also, try not to get killed," Mayuki said.

"By one of your dogs, or the demons?" Saoka asked.

Mayuki looked out from under her hood and shrugged. "Doesn't matter. Dead is dead." Mayuki galloped off.

Saoka shot a look of disgust at Eiko, who only laughed and followed Mayuki. Saoka remounted, her silhouette a lone figure against the gray sky, her silence as heavy as the clouds above.

The tenth day dawned with clear skies. The sound of mirth pierced the quiet dawn, drawing Saoka from her tent. She joined the ladies at the fire pit for breakfast. Conversations dwindled, eyes flicking in her direction. Mayuki, cup in hand, gestured towards Saoka.

"So, our little empress chooses to connect with the common folk. To what do we owe the pleasure?"

"Just came to see how my moody little princess was doing this morning. Hopefully, there's milk in that cup. Can't have you cranky all day again," Saoka shot back, circling around a swipe at her head from Eiko. Eiko looked shocked and started forward, but Mayuki and her blessed friend laughed loudly. Saoka stepped right up into Eiko's face.

"Eiko, I apologize for antagonizing your master, but that's twice now you've gone after my backside. Do it again, and I'll start thinking you like me."

More laughter.

"You little shit, why..." Eiko tried to get out more, but she was met with a punch to her jaw. Saoka might be the youngest and least experienced of the sisters, but she wouldn't stand for being their punching bag. Everyone fell silent, and Eiko looked down at the sword on her hip.

"Go for it if you think you can," Saoka boasted.

Mayuki growled and stood up. "Listen up, hags, let's not ruin a perfectly good morning. I say you, Eiko, and you, Saoka, are even. If you want to continue, you'll make me angry. Not one of you wants to mess with me when I'm indignant. Shake on it, and let's all relax. Plus, we have a guest, an old friend of mine. She brings news and, more importantly, rice wine."

Everyone laughed nervously. Eiko didn't seem so mad now and offered her hand, which Saoka took straight away.

"Nice punch, bitch," Eiko said.

"You're pretty when you smile," Saoka replied. They all sat down to eat and listened as the unnamed blessed rose to her feet and cleared her throat.

"Good morning, sisters. My name is Chimei, and I come from Kazuno. I trained at the lodges of Nara and have lived here in Kazuno for quite some time. I bring dire news but am relieved to see such a sizeable group of soldiers and sisters here."

Saoka's gaze lingered on Chimei. Of average height and build, Chimei wore a dark red robe that enveloped her entirely. Her sole adornment was a blessed pin. No makeup or hairclips in her wavy hair, which cascaded down to her chin on both sides.

"Our scouts report that the main force of our enemy is only four days away from our gates. We need to make haste to town and help ready the defenses. Steel yourselves; we will likely require all of you in the fight," Chimei continued.

"Now, now, don't go scaring these ladies. Most of them have seen a demon or two in their time. There ain't nothing we can't handle," Mayuki said, taking a big swig of her rice wine. "So how many demons are we talking about?"

"A hundred," answered Chimei.

Wine sprayed from Mayuki's lips; her eyes wide with disbelief.

"And how many men do they have?"

"Perhaps a thousand, but there's something else I have to tell you."

"Out with it then," Mayuki said, taking a guarded stance.

Chimei's shoulders drooped; her gaze heavy with dread. "We believe five of those demons are of the second type, Oni, meaning they can think for themselves, plan, and use magic of their own. Worse yet, we think they have an Akuma with them."

"Shit, holy fuck, shit," Mayuki said, throwing her cup. "An Akuma? A third class? We're fucked."

"Is there no hope?" a sister asked.

"Gods, no," Eiko said.

A collective gasp rippled through the crowd. Saoka nodded slowly, lips pressed into a thin line. She still hadn't seen a regular demon; a second class was rare, and there had never been a sighting of a third class in Wa.

Preempting the hysteria, Mayuki bellowed, "Still, we fight. This changes nothing. We have more magic users than they do by a factor of ten. We hold the walls and the surrounding hills. We have a two-to-one advantage in manpower. We will win!"

"Still, we fight!" all the sisters roared back, racing to get ready to make for Kazuno.

The pace quickened. All the sisters, blessed, and men with horses rode at full speed to Kazuno. By nightfall, they arrived at the edge of Kazuno, dismounting stiffly, gazes flickering with unease.

"I can hardly see anything," Saoka said.

A nearby guardsman pointed. "That thick wall of wood stands around it, the watchtowers spread evenly along the perimeter. A moat encircles the township, which sits up on a large hill. If you squint, you can see fires burning from the towers."

"Your eyes are better than mine. With this fog rolling in, it's like the nearby moat is jealous of me gazing upon the settlement."

They queued at the only entrance still open. It took another hour for the sisters to make it through, and once inside, Saoka stood to the side, taking in the municipality. Kazuno was much like any village around Wa, except bigger. Most homes were triangular straw huts, with a few grander structures. Wooden houses were placed high up on stilts, with staircases leading up, and wooden floors instead of hay. Cleaner and far more comfortable. These buildings were new to Wa.

Saoka's concentration on the buildings was interrupted by loud banging. The metalworks areas worked right through the nights.

Mayuki walked up behind Saoka.

As if reading Saoka's thoughts, Mayuki said, "Approaching army of deadly demons, remember?"

The ladies were led to a clearing inside the village where tents and cooking fires were already set up. They met with the village elders and a couple of other Order members. Mayuki took charge, so Saoka, having nothing to do, wandered over to one of the fires, where Eiko and the others sat down to eat dinner.

"The aromas from those heavy iron pots smell amazing. Much better than the porridge served by the men on our journey."

"Soldiery was of the utmost importance, which meant food preparation took a back seat. This town has competent cooks. They're serving rice with boar, burdock root, and scallion. Take a clean wooden bowl and spoon from that nearby bench and help yourself," Eiko replied.

Saoka sat down on a log around the fire and dug into her food, her stomach growling.

"I guess all the riding and added stress of demons will do that to a person," Ramona joked and pointed towards Saoka's stomach.

After eating her fill, Saoka looked up and wiped her mouth with a handkerchief. Ramona had been watching her but looked away when Saoka noticed. "Dear Ramona, do I still have food on my face?"

"No sister, it's just that, well, I was wondering if you would be okay in the days to come. You have your magic and bow, but have you ever seen a demon?"

"I haven't had the pleasure, but you talk as if you have. What was it like?" Saoka asked. "I've heard stories and real accounts, but all from accomplished sisters and blessed women who bent the world at their whims. I want to know about the demons from someone like myself."

Ramona's face twisted briefly, a shadow of the past darkening her features. She put her arms around herself, shook her head, and cleared a tear from her eye.

"Mayuki and the others rescued me and my brother from a demon. Our parents weren't so fortunate. The Order happened to be passing through my hometown when it attacked.

My family and I had been sleeping in our hut. Without warning, the wall to my left blew open. What came through the hole was horrible.

Eight feet tall with a thick black and brown armored body. It moved like a man on two legs, but it had four arms and a face like an insect, with giant antennae. Two enormous beady eyes and bloody pincers on either side of its mouth.

It jumped on my mother and father and began ripping them to shreds."

Tears brimmed in Saoka's eyes, her head shaking in silent denial.

"Its appendages had spikes protruding out at angles, for climbing and tearing. I watched my parents' body parts fly off while it buried its maw into my father's stomach and started eating. So, when you say you haven't had the pleasure of meeting one, you should be thankful."

The other sisters stopped eating to listen.

"Gods, Ramona, I'm so sorry. I can't imagine what you went through," Saoka said, sobbing. She jumped forward and hugged the little girl. "I'm such a moron. Please forgive me, I didn't want you to relive that."

"It's okay, Saoka. I was saved. I was only five at the time and barely remember my parents now. The demon was scary, but before it turned on my brother and me, a giant white light entered the hut and pushed the Oni back. It was Mayuki and the others. They used magic, a complex combination of wind and fire.

Sooner than I blinked, three women rushed in to scoop my brother and me up, while four more women and six or seven men flanked the beast and began attacking it. That's all I remember." Ramona's smile was tight, her eyes betraying the effort.

Demons had always seemed so far away, a threat meant to be tackled by other people in other places. She perceived them as terrible, but hearing this girl's story shook her.

She realized that all the other sisters were staring at her.

Saoka straightened, jaw set, ready to face the unknown. "Everyone, thank you for taking me on. I have no right to be here. I'm an outsider and a novice. Please forgive my arrogance. I just wanted to fit in and to be of use."

"You ain't the only one, darling," Eiko piped up.

"Shit, we'd all like to fit in. The only place we do is with Mayuki and her band of misfits," said Akiho, revealing a scar—a stark testament to her survival. "I too was attacked by a demon and saved by Mayuki. The difference was I had already become a sister, but I thought I knew everything. Got caught with a back swipe from a giant monkey-looking Oni when I thought I had single-handedly beaten it. Mayuki saw me fall, jumped on top of the demon, and buried her sword through its skull."

One by one, the sisters stood, battle marks glinting in the firelight. Mayuki and her band saved each one of these brave, ferocious women. Every one of them saw demons, fought them, and lived to tell the tale. *Who am I then?*

"I guess you shouldn't judge a book by its cover. I thought you all were just rude and mean," Saoka half-joked.

"And now? What do you think?" asked Akiho.

"Oh, that you're all just a bunch of lunatics."

Everyone laughed. Through her social stumbling, Saoka found a way to bond herself closer to these women.

Saoka saw them in a new light. They were survivors of unimaginable horrors, united by their shared ordeals and the formidable Mayuki. Her eyes softened, respect dawning as she took in each warrior's tale.

"Now I see warriors who've faced demons and lived to tell the tale. Strength, resilience, and camaraderie. I'm honored to be among you," Saoka said with newfound sincerity.

Eiko grinned, and Akiho nodded. Saoka's gaze swept the circle, a silent salute to their shared strength. She listened, absorbing the tales of survival and triumph over the demonic threats that lurked in the shadows.

As the night unfolded, Saoka began to include herself in the sisterhood as someone with potential and a willingness to learn. The scars and stories became badges of honor, connecting them in a shared history of facing the darkness that threatened their world.

In the midst of the storytelling, Mayuki approached, a knowing smile on her face. "Looks like you've found your place, Saoka. Welcome to the misfits," she said, raising her cup in a toast.

Saoka smiled back, grateful. A chorus of chuckles rose into the night, weaving Saoka into the tapestry of sisterhood, shared experiences, and the forging of bonds that would be crucial in the battles that lay ahead.

As she crawled into her bedroll, it dawned on her that in a couple of days, some or all of them might not be around. In the dark, a single tear traced Saoka's cheek, the day's weight sinking in. *Just when I start making friends, we might all die.*

CHAPTER 8

Quill in hand, Saoka greeted the day, words flowing before the camp stirred. She finished her journal entry, dressed, and walked out of the tent, seeking an early view of Kazuno before the town awoke.

Surprised to find people already up, she noted the sense of purpose instilled by impending doom. The town basked in dawn's glow, shadows and light painting a fresh canvas. Saoka traced the wood and iron reinforcements, her touch reading the wall's history. Near the tops of the walls were palisades for archers and magic users. She made her way to a watchtower and climbed up its ladder.

Two watchmen saluted, acknowledging her sister's pin. She walked to the edge and peered out at the surrounding area. Jagged stakes the size of trees lined the base of the wall. Bronze studs added protection to the exterior. Beyond lay a wide moat.

She whistled low, the moat's breadth drawing a line between safety and peril. Perhaps 30 feet wide, a demon would have trouble jumping that distance. On the far side of the water lay more stakes and rolling hills. The town's location, with tree lines pushed back for better visibility, was strategic.

"Tskk." Mayuki appeared, climbing the ladder.

"Good morning, blessed." Saoka bowed.

"Yeah, yeah, boils my blood this," Mayuki gestured towards the hills, frowning.

"What exactly? I thought the fortifications looked decent."

"If we wanted to fight men, they would be. I will have to wake up the General and get him to work. Why are you up here anyway, little one? What do you know of bulwarks?" Mayuki crossed her arms.

"Well, not as much as experienced people such as yourself, but I have read seven books on the subject."

"Tell me then, what else would you have done in the next two or three days to improve things?"

"We need more ways to slow the demons down as they are very fast. Perhaps some funneling channels made of wood and iron works, even any old junk. Every second would be vital. I'm not sure how you intend to direct our magic, but we'll have to deal with magic coming back at us. I can't predict how strong the demons' magic will be, but as you told us, we do have the numbers."

A gruff hum of approval escaped Mayuki. "Not bad. Here's what I want to do as well. One, I want holes dug with spikes at the bottom, covered with leaves and brush at random intervals. Two, I will ask the general to take two hundred men on horseback out of the town and wait in reserve for my signal to flank and hit the enemy in the rear."

"Wait, slow down, I need to write this down," Saoka said as she took out her notebook.

"Three, we need magic users left behind the walls, ready for any surprises they might throw back at us. Fucking Akuma are half human, so who knows what it might have planned."

"And fourth?"

"Yes, well, some surprises are best left unsaid." Mayuki winked and headed back down the ladder.

Watching Mayuki depart, Saoka took stock of the town.

Kazuno's population had swelled with refugees from neighboring towns and villages. "How many people are staying in town?" she asked a watchman.

"About twenty-five thousand."

"How many people of fighting age?"

"Our garrison was about five hundred men. With the addition of yours, that equals a thousand. Maybe twice that number of guardsmen and hunters have trickled in from other towns. So, competent soldiers, I would say two thousand. There is probably another two or three thousand who can fire a bow or stand and fight. The rest would be the elderly and children, I'm afraid."

"Should be more than enough if the men are all as brave as you two. Thanks, guardsmen. I will leave you to it. I too must prepare."

Saoka made her way back down the ladder towards her tent. She grabbed a cookie and a cup of water from the outdoor mess hall. Inside her tent, she got to work on her journal, jotting down details and sketching a couple of drawings.

After about an hour, she attacked her cookie. Excellent—a mix of chestnut, acorn, and walnuts. The people of Kazuno were exceptional bakers. After downing her water, she grabbed her bow and set out to practice.

Saoka's body moved with purpose. Her leg muscles had been improving with all the riding, but her upper body strained with the effort of holding the bow. *Calm like a pond. Release with a breath.*

After an hour or so, she found the other sisters training, some with swords, others with magic.

Realizing she hadn't meditated in days, she decided to sharpen her magic skills. She rolled her shoulders, took deep breaths, and centered herself. As she sat cross-legged in the tranquil garden, the cool breeze caressed her skin, and the rhythmic chirping of crickets enveloped her, a serene wave washed over her mind, peeling away layers of tension and grounding Saoka in an ocean of stillness and clarity.

She practiced hard for the rest of the day.

At night, by the campfire, she sought tutoring about the demons from the other sisters.

Eiko explained, "While strong, fast, and agile, the demons have weak points the same as any other creature. Blows to the head, neck, and heart are the easiest ways to bring them down. Of course, some of them have hardened bodies, horns, or multiple appendages that make reaching those spots difficult. Lost limbs and eyes would slow them down, and, like any animal, enough blood loss will kill them. Still, many demons can fight on with a lost appendage for minutes, and the damage they wreak in that time could be considerable."

Mayuki arrived, catching her breath, hands on hips. She had spent the entire day helping the villagers dig trap holes and set up the funneling sections.

"Sisters, eyes on me, please."

"They usually are," Ramona said, tracing a woman's body in the air with her hands.

Mayuki ignored the comment. "During the battle, the sisters capable of offensive magic will man the walls and rain down their spells on the enemy. Healers should also man the walls as archers but be ready to move behind the walls after the enemy gets close. Those adept at the blessed sight need to use their talents to keep tabs on the enemy."

A blessed walked over to Mayuki, whispering in her ear. Mayuki bowed to her and turned back to the sisters. "Latest scouting report puts the demons about twenty miles away. They'll either be here tomorrow evening or the following morning, so any final preparations you need to see to, do so quickly. It would do you all well to get a good night's sleep; it won't be long now until it will be hard to come by."

As Mayuki's words hung in the air, their weight settling upon the gathered maidens, Saoka felt the gravity of their impending battle. She slipped away from the hushed crowd, her mind racing with both anticipation and fear.

The moon cast long shadows across the tent grounds. As she lay down on her thin mat, she knew that a good night's sleep would elude her—her dreams already troubled by visions of the approaching demon horde.

She awoke to the sound of screaming.

CHAPTER 9

299 B.C.E. Modern-day Bihar, India, and mountains near Bactra, modern-day Afghanistan

> *With each rustle of leaves carried by the wind, the soft murmur of ancient conversations in breezy tunnels echoed in the recesses of her mind. Magumi's memory raced back to when Pausanias first learned the truth of the history of the world, and the enormous scope of his ignorance. All thinking creatures were ignorant, and the battle to become ever less ignorant made life worthwhile, she repeated to herself as a mantra as she slipped into a trance.*

Pausanias's journey culminated in reaching Persepolis, only to be directed by cloaked men to a mysterious mountain town, home to Achaemenids, Greeks, Kashans, and Seleucids.

Massive stone walls, unlike any Pausanias had seen, fortified the town, which builders had constructed into the mountain using stones far larger than those of Egypt's pyramids.

The purpose of such colossal walls puzzled Pausanias, especially since the stone type didn't match the local geology. Inside, the town appeared small but revealed a larger community with workshops, play areas, and training grounds.

A cave entrance led to a vast, torch-lit cavern with eighty tunnels on five descending concentric levels. Pausanias's mouth gaped open.

Who built this place? Before he could ask any questions, a strange little old man walked up to him. Well, not so old; upon inspection, perhaps fifty. Yet, his eyes spoke of age. Stranger still, his eyes were purple. Pausanias himself had unusual blue eyes and had met people with green, gray, and even gold eyes, but never purple.

"Good to meet you, young man, or is it, I wonder? You look like a Greek but stink of demon. What are you? Why are you here? And what do you have in that sack of yours that screams magic?" the purple-eyed man asked.

"I'm not a demon; I'm Pausanias, a Spartan on a mission, and I don't need to explain anything in my possession to you, old man. And who might you be?" Pausanias snarled.

"Kushim of Sumer," he said as he bowed. Pausanias saw much in that bow; the man did not move like an old man. While only five feet in stature, he had perfect balance, hands resting palms down by his hips.

The man wore a simple red cloth around his waist that fell to his calves. His black and graying hair was drawn back in a bun, and he had a long black beard shaped almost into a triangle. His chest was bare, with many scars.

Not a man unaccustomed to danger. Two simple gold bracelets were the only adornments the man had. He carried no weapons. The hairs on Pausanias's back stood up.

Pausanias's mind grasped something, and he took a step forward. "Is this some kind of joke? Who are you really? The city of Sumer disappeared two thousand years ago. Why approach me in such a manner?"

As Pausanias stepped forward, a sword from his escort neared his throat. Pausanias countered with a dagger placed to the assailant's chest. His men and the opposing escorts drew their weapons, ready for confrontation.

"Hold on, hold on," spoke the diminutive, purple-eyed man. "Let's be civil. After all, Pausanias here is our guest. Behrouz, Farhad, put down your weapons."

Pausanias nodded to his men to do the same. As everyone sheathed their weapons, the little man approached Pausanias and patted him on the head.

"What?" Pausanias managed before a sudden wave of fatigue engulfed him. He turned his head just in time to witness his comrades collapsing unconscious. Battling the sensation, he turned back to Kushim. "What have you done, you bastard?" he spat, before stumbling to one knee.

He struggled to stay awake, straining to lift his head. His vision spun and darkened. Kushim's cryptic words echoed, "No one managed to stay awake this long in centuries."

Pausanias awoke with the agility of a snake, springing to his feet in a defensive stance, scanning the well-lit room for any potential threat.

He stood beside a wooden-framed bed at the far end of a sparsely furnished stone cave. Spotting a sturdy wooden door at the room's end, he made a dash towards it.

"Relax," a voice from the left side of the room advised. Pausanias swiftly spun and crouched. It was the little man.

"Bastard, I'll kill you!" Pausanias roared. Before he made a move, the man raised both hands and knelt. *Is he surrendering?*

"Please, I mean you no harm, truly. I had to be sure of who you are, you understand? I have much to tell you if you'll calm down to listen. Before you bombard me with questions, consider your position. You are my guest here and in no place to make demands."

"Sure, sure, you have me at a disadvantage," Pausanias said, gesturing to his near-naked body. He had been stripped down to his loincloth.

"Trust that I will not harm you. If I wanted you dead, you would already be. I have ensured your men are safe, awake, well-fed, and free to explore the town. After explaining myself to them, they are at ease, as you should be. They await your return. You seem to be someone they deeply trust and care for. As for me, my name is Kushim of Sumer. I can see your Spartan mind is filled with questions. Sit, and let's talk," Kushim requested.

"I'll stand, thank you," Pausanias declared, crossing his arms.

"Ah, yes, the little victories add up, I suppose. Have it your way. So, what do you know of magic?"

"Shit all. My army was attacked by demons, my king killed, and I received some relics and diplomatic papers to go looking for answers. I've been attacked by wandering tribes twice on my way to India and was ambushed by a Persian Dev Demon. I came here because I learned more about the safest way into India, and that the people of these mountains had intimate knowledge of demons."

"Ignorant, then. I thought the Greeks sought knowledge," Kushim sighed.

"Listen, little liar, some Greeks might like to keep their heads in books all day, but Spartans are real men. We do one thing better than anyone."

"Ah, killers, then. I didn't think I would ever see the like again."

"Now who's the ignorant one, PSEUDO," he challenged, using the Greek word for liar.

The little man was up from his chair with a balled fist in Pausanias's stomach before the Spartan reacted. *Men don't move this fast.* As Pausanias doubled over, he oversold it, leaning down and grabbing Kushim's ankle. He pulled with all his might, bringing the man down.

However, before Pausanias mounted him to start pounding on him as planned, Kushim's arms fell over the back of his head as he went down.

Instead of crashing to the floor, those arms landed palm down, elbows up by his head, allowing Kushim to roll in a backflip and escape back to his feet. *Gods, what am I fighting?*

He ran in to land a punch but met with an invisible wall of force that knocked the wind from him. Before he made sense of it, he felt it again, a strong wind pushing him back.

Pausanias screamed as he tapped into the Minis, the Spartan battle rage. Unlike most, who feared battle, Spartans thrived on it. The Minis drove men to incredible feats but often led to exhaustion and loss of control. Pausanias, however, mastered his rage from a young age, thanks to his mother's teachings. He used this mastery now, pushing against Kushim's magical air wall with controlled thought. He pushed, kicked, and searched for a breach with his hands.

A flash of insight struck Pausanias. Instead of resisting, he leapt backward, using the wall's force to propel himself. Tucking his legs, he rebounded off the wall at an angle, away from Kushim's reach. Tumbling across the room, he rolled to his feet and launched into another roll, anticipating Kushim's counter. Surging up, he struck at Kushim's head.

Kushim's hand rose to deflect the blow, but Pausanias's punch landed, making Kushim recoil. Suddenly, pressure built in Pausanias's head, a sign of Kushim's attempt to render him unconscious. But Pausanias's Minis resisted.

"That's not going to work this time, fucker."

"Okay, Malaka," Kushim conceded, releasing the spell. "So, before I get really angry, and I end up killing you, let's sit and talk?" he proposed, looking strained.

Pausanias gave in to nausea and vomited.

Amidst the chaos, both men found humor in the situation.

Pausanias, half-naked and battling a magician, laughed. "Did you call me a Malaka?" he managed to ask between laughs.

"It was the only way to get your attention."

As the laughter faded, Pausanias stood at the ready. "So, a truce then? By the way, why'd you hit me?"

"Well, you kept insisting I was a liar, and while I have been many things in my long life, being a liar has never been one. Spartans aren't the only ones who can lose their composure, you know," Kushim chortled and winked.

"So, you are at least two thousand years old, huh? And still cannot maintain your emotions?"

"Oh, yes, I know exactly who I am, and never have I been one for patience or guarding my emotions. Before I tell you my true age, I ask that you listen to all the things I have to tell you first."

"Okay, but can I have something to eat first? After sleeping all night, and waking up to a fight, I find myself quite hungry," Pausanias said with a straight face.

"Sure thing, actually you've been sleeping for three days. I had to use a considerable amount of my magic on you compared to your comrades. I may have gone a little overboard."

He went to the door, ignoring Pausanias's shocked expression, and knocked four times. His personal bodyguard opened it.

"Have food brought to my room," he said to his guard while pointing down the hall. The guard rushed to make it happen, and Kushim gestured for Pausanias to follow.

"One more thing, ancient grandfather, could we stop by a latrine? I haven't had a shit or piss in days, apparently," Pausanias said vulnerably.

CHAPTER 10

Pausanias and Kushim entered the latter's room, adorned with practical furnishings. The wooden floor exuded warmth.

Kushim, noticing Pausanias gawking, explained, "Underground springs bring up warm water that's carried through a series of pipes to some of the rooms. It raises the temperature in winter and runs under the latrines to keep the cavern clean and save people from having to endure latrine duty."

After motioning for Pausanias to sit in one of the chairs, a maiden arrived with Pausanias's food. He thanked her as she exited. His stomach growled at the sight of food, and Kushim told Pausanias, "You do the chewing, and I'll do the talking. Please take your time. Your stomach may not be used to eating so much after a couple of days without."

"Isn't the first time; Spartans are trained to hunt and gather their own food and are often left out in the wilderness alone without supplies from a young age. I'll manage," Pausanias replied while he tucked into his food.

"Well then, enjoy and listen carefully. I don't like to repeat myself, but perhaps I will have to, seeing as catching you up on the happenings of the world over my lifetime could well take several decades. Suffice it to say, I will have to give you an outline at best. Please save your questions for the end, and reserve your shock at the door. I don't want to have to stop every couple of minutes to say 'Yes, really.'"

Pausanias tore off a piece of bread and dipped it into a bowl of hot soup. Kushim sat down next to Pausanias and paused to collect his thoughts.

"Where to begin, I wonder, where to begin," Kushim pondered.

"At the beginning," Pausanias said, letting out a burp.

"Yes, yes, of course. Well, I'll start with myself, I suppose. To answer your earlier question, I am much older than two thousand. I believe myself to be about ten thousand, six hundred and sixty-two years old," Kushim said, pausing for dramatic effect.

Pausanias whistled and carried on eating.

"I was eighty-five when the world ended," Kushim said casually enough to get Pausanias to raise an eyebrow and look around.

Kushim explained, "Well, my world, anyway. You see, I belonged to a time before a cataclysm struck this planet. What followed was over a thousand years of never-ending winter. Most life was demolished—plants, animals, humans, and demons alike. I am a citizen of the greatest empire that ever roamed the earth, and have the honor of being its only remaining citizen. I said I was of Sumer because that is the area where I was born, and it remains close to where we sit today. The name of my Empire was I, and I know it sounds strange."

"I? As in me I or eye like the things we use to see?" Pausanias asked through mouthfuls.

"Just I like me. The word I is the oldest word in the world. It is the origin of language itself, but more importantly, of identity, of complex reasoning. This word was sacred to my people, and we brought it and spread it to every person on the planet.

"Still with me?"

Pausanias grunted.

"Remember when I asked you what you knew of magic?"

"Yes, I thought you were supposed to be telling the story without interruptions," Pausanias shook his hands for Kushim to hurry up.

"Magic or energy shapes the world itself. If you had a greater understanding of magic, I could gloss over more sections of my story, but alas. My empire ruled for some two thousand years.

We were a people of enchantment; everyone was born with it. Of course, as we spread throughout the world, we loved and had children with humans we met from different tribes, villages, and countries. Our magic was passed on to our offspring regardless.

No one knew or ever bothered to tell me where our magic came from. Most theories suggested a woman was blessed by a god, and her baby carried that power, and it divided into each subsequent generation. The magic we had was our special way of communicating with the earth, seeing the spirits in all things, contacting our deities, and learning. We created a lot to be proud of. This very mountain cavern is one such example," Kushim explained, spreading his arms wide.

"Ah yes, the walls, I thought as much," Pausanias mumbled under his breath, adding, "No regular men moved those stones. So where—"

"Continue stuffing your face. Please try the cheese; it's most excellent, a variety I came up with myself, combining milk from cows, goats, camels, and donkeys. I know, I know, it's a weird thing, but I consider myself quite a culinary expert.

So, as I was saying, those walls were indeed built with magic, and no, there is not any other structure left to be found above ground. We built many grand buildings and palaces, but we built simple, strong, and sturdy structures that would last forever. Or so we thought. As I said, the world faced a catastrophic event when I was young. However, that wasn't the only reason for my empire's collapse. In hindsight, it was the final blow. We would have survived if not for another reason."

"Demons."

"Yes and no. Demons are negative energy gathered and manifested onto our realm. But there was one thing worse than the demons. Hubris."

Pausanias raised an eyebrow. Kushim elaborated.

"I've studied the nature of men: despite our enlightened minds, great magic, and strong positions, we are still prone to petty conflicts. We were winning the war against demons until we turned against each other over politics and religion. Civil wars erupted, forbidden magic was used, and we ultimately created the greatest horrors on the planet."

"You made new types of demons, didn't you?" Pausanias accused, clenching and unclenching his fists.

"I didn't. Playing with demons was dangerous, but others thought it was worth the price. People added their magic to demons, hoping to teach them rudimentary tasks like attack dogs. This was largely successful, but rivals soon adopted and enhanced the technique.

Mixing demons with animals yielded varied outcomes. Some became intelligent leaders and strategists in battles, while many emerged mindless and uncontrollable, often destroyed. Then, a dreadful event occurred."

Pausanias crinkled his face and sat up straighter.

"Mixing humans with demons was disgraceful. Initially, non-magical humans were used as they were seen as expendable. Later, our own people were sacrificed to create powerful demon lords who combined human intellect and magic with demonic strength, making them nearly invincible. The problem was we did not understand them. They reasoned and lived like men, but they were driven by a desire for greater carnage."

Kushim pointed to a tome behind Pausanias, "I will show you something. This is the diary of a demon lord," Kushim said casually. Pausanias grabbed it, opened it, and couldn't read a word. The glowing words startled him.

"Don't worry, the words can't hurt you. They reveal the true intent of these demons. They seek to destroy the world, returning all life, including themselves, to the void. They believe the earth will be remade in darkness—no life, no strain, no love or hate, just oblivion.

This book belonged to a demon lord who tried to turn on his human masters. He and most of his kind were destroyed, but at a terrible cost. Whole armies were lost. On average, ten magic users were needed to defeat a second-type demon, and double or triple that to bring down a demon lord.

Here is where the story gets more complex," Kushim said, taking a quick break to pour himself a glass of water.

Pausanias felt sick, the food he ate threatened to come up again. He forced away the feeling and waved Kushim to continue.

"I assume the cataclysm was your people's fault as well. Some terrible overuse of magic," Pausanias said.

"Not really. We learned from our mistakes and united all the peoples of Earth to fight and defeat the demons. We were winning. Then a meteor fell. Our greatest astrologists predicted it. Seen almost a thousand years earlier, it appeared every two hundred and thirty-five years, growing larger each time. We tracked its probable course but didn't know its exact size or where it would strike.

It landed in the ocean, bringing doom. Tsunamis swept over most of the planet. Only high mountain points like this stayed above water. The meteor's explosion sent huge plumes of ash into the sky, blotting out the sun. I was lucky enough to be in a safe subterranean spot when it happened," Kushim said, his voice thick and slow.

"And then?" Pausanias pressed, unwilling to let Kushim off easily.

"And then, everything ended. No more empire, no more

demon army. Half the humans and animals died instantly. The other half faced worse predicaments. The sun was blocked, causing global temperatures to fall. Without the sun, crops wouldn't grow. Herds had nothing to eat. Birds fared little better. It looked like the demons won; the Earth was going to die a slow, miserable death," Kushim asserted, taking another swig of water.

"Apparently, recalling the end of the world makes one thirsty," Pausanias remarked.

Clearing his throat, the oldest man in the world continued, "There were other terrors. The meteor somehow damaged magic. I know it sounds strange. How could something damage energy? Before the meteor fell, I could lift one of those stones you saw outside with magic. I was a strong user. Now, I can barely levitate a man-sized boulder.

To our people, magic was life and death. We couldn't fathom living without it. It sustained us, helped us achieve miracles, and connected us in every conscious moment. Now, I scramble for power like a drunken thief, stumbling to remember how to crawl when I once flew.

Many took their own lives, unable to bear the severance from thaumaturgy. Others went mad. Some fell to the hands of fellow humans, who rightly blamed us for the catastrophe. From an original population of about fifteen million, only a couple of thousand of us remained.

Our true cities lay underground. With magic, we created light, mimicking night and day, and accessed fresh water in the consistently warm depths. Most above-ground settlements were mere symbols of our power and rule. Almost all our underground cities survived the meteor blast, buried deep and sealed with giant stones and magical wards," Kushim explained.

"Sealed?" Pausanias interjected.

"Yes, to keep demons and other human tribes away. How did we come and go? That was our greatest achievement. We created portals of pure energy, doors to other places. It took centuries to develop, the loftiest mechanism we ever built."

Pausanias banged his fist on the chair, "Holy Hades."

Kushim continued, "These flash portals allowed us to travel from, say, Athens to Thebes instantly. Construction was arduous, requiring builders to travel the old-fashioned way to a new location, build a new door, and spend years gathering enough energy to activate it. They were our most guarded secret."

Pausanias stood up and started pacing. He thought better when he paced. "Continue, continue," he said, waving his hands.

"Once up and running, a person named the place they wanted to go to and walked through."

"How many were there?" Pausanias asked.

"Five hundred and twenty-two portals, in total. About a hundred were either destroyed in the meteor blast or lost to us. We, of course, tested all the portals, but there were problems.

Magic persisted, but some locations became deadly as underground sites filled with water. I remember one quick-thinking man who, upon stepping through a door, swam back soaking wet. Superstitious, he always held his breath when crossing. After that, we checked other sites more cautiously. Few remained intact.

As we regrouped, reality hit: our survival as a people, as an empire, was unlikely. Our losses were staggering, and worse awaited. Yet, in our darkest hour, a glimmer of redemption emerged. Those with strength and purpose devised a desperate plan.

We couldn't save ourselves, but perhaps we could rescue the world. A clandestine league formed, uniting men from across the globe. Our mission: defeat the demons and pull the planet back from the brink. In part, we succeeded. We safeguarded seeds and animals, storing them in caverns away from the relentless cold.

With help from others, we laid the groundwork for future generations. We tracked the outside world and any demon activity. Still, the thousand-year winter weighed heavily. Rare forays beyond our refuge revealed a desolate landscape.

"What did you subsist on?" Pausanias blurted out.

"The cavern lighting helped us grow food. Meat became scarce, but we had abundant fish from underground lakes. We watched regular humans live passionate, purposeful lives and pass away quickly compared to ours. Our people had only the culmination to look forward to.

We weren't truly immortal; we could die from physical harm like anyone else. Our numbers dwindled over time, while human tribes grew. Despite some tribes turning against us, we continued our mission to preserve life on Earth.

After centuries of winter, we emerged to rebuild. Tribes spread across the globe, laying the foundations of new civilizations and overcoming natural disasters.

As nations developed, minor demon sightings occurred, but the fate of the greater demons remained uncertain. Some of my kind, believing their purpose fulfilled, chose death.

However, not all demon lords were destroyed. We discovered some humans had allied with demons, lured by promises of power and wealth.

Through interrogations, we gleaned insights into the demons' nefarious plans. Ever wondered why demons have been elusive throughout most of your life?"

"No."

First, our network uncovered that the demons fared even worse than humanity after the meteor strike. Their numbers were decimated. As civilizations like Egypt, Samaria, India, China, Greece, and Persia emerged, humanity collectively drove most demons away.

Second, real stories morph in the retelling; legends blur the lines between truth and fantasy over time. Take your country, for instance. The Minotaur—merely a tale to spook children? Absolutely not. These were formidable demons capable of strategic planning, wielding weapons, and instigating terror in grown men.

The last reason for the scarcity of demons here remains an enigma. The decline of magic in certain areas seems linked to fewer magic users and fading magical energy. Some regions still hold strong magic, possibly less impacted by the meteor. While Earth prospers without magic, demons rely on it. They must amass magic quickly to threaten the world before it dissipates."

"So, they've been tailing the magic, migrating to those lands," Pausanias deduced.

"Yes, precisely. Reports from eastern China, Korea, and the Land of Wa strongly suggest this," Kushim affirmed.

"What's Korea and the Land of Wa?" Pausanias asked, confusion etched across his face.

"Far-flung countries, my friend. The Greeks have likely never heard of them. Hence, it is crucial for someone to venture there and thwart their plans. However, that someone needs a particular set of skills—magical abilities, to be exact. And this, my dear Pausanias, is why I brought you here," Kushim concluded.

"What do you mean brought me here?" Pausanias questioned, sitting back down. "I ventured here on my own, a mere emissary on an assignment. India is my ultimate destination, as per my instructions. I'm not versed in magic. I've never crossed paths with you. What makes you think I'd undertake such a task, even if I had the ability—which, let me reiterate, I don't."

"I've witnessed your royal rites of passage and conversed with your comrades. Don't you find it peculiar that you traveled thousands of miles, arriving precisely where you uncovered almost all the answers you seek? Spartans may be dim, but put two and two together, man."

"I... well, I mean..., wait, what, how?" Pausanias fumbled over his words.

"You forgot who, where, and why. I'll address your simple-minded questions first. The what—your perceived mission and the mission I just assigned you—are one and the same. The how is easily explained; I leveraged my connections in Greece and Persia through my agency. The who will remain my secret for now.

"The signatures speak for themselves. I assume your influence and power extend to the highest echelons in most countries," Pausanias replied.

"That it does, at least for influence. Power, I have no interest in, and probably couldn't seize it even if I wanted to. One man can only do so much."

"So, you want me to enroll in your order?" Pausanias asked, his eyes narrowing, and his voice taking on a sharp edge.

"Of course, but first, you'll have to stop denying your use of magic. I know you recognize you have it, and you don't really understand how to utilize it."

Pausanias caught on lightning-quick, "Eneas, your contact in Athens is Eneas."

"One of."

"My magic, is there any way I can learn to command it?"

Kushim grinned. "Come now, before the question left your mouth, you already knew the answer. You can start training with me tomorrow. We've both had enough excitement for today. And before you say you haven't agreed to anything yet, I'll let you ponder the following: Don't you want to be stronger? Don't Spartans appreciate a challenge?"

Pausanias, leaning forward with his eyebrows raised but keeping his hands clasped in his lap, asked, "How long would it take?"

"Learning the basics could take a month, give or take. Your magic is unique and will evolve unpredictably. I'll teach you some basics and tricks, then you'll learn on your own. Once you know your magic type, I can recommend specialized teachers," Kushim replied.

"I'm in, damnit, but if I'm in, I am going to need a lot more information. You joke about the density of the Spartan mind, but I know my talents. I was on the fast track to being a general before I got thrust into this new life. I can lead men in battle, plan, tend to logistics, and strategize better than any man I've ever met. Consequently, if you are going to use me, you better use me to my full potential."

"Oh, I will, and if you think your Spartan training prepared you for the hardships of my training, well, 'Fuck no,'" replied Kushim.

They both chuckled.

The ensuing morning, the training commenced in earnest.

CHAPTER II

299 B.C.E. Kazuno, modern-day Kazuno city, Akita, Japan.

Magumi's brow furrowed as she tried to meditate, her keen wolf senses assaulting her with every subtle rustle. A fleeting glimpse of a swift fox triggered memories of strategic maneuvers and swift escapes; tales woven through the artistry of survival. She closed her eyes and remembered when dear Saoka had to use every ounce of strategy to survive her first battle.

Urgent screams of watchmen heralded the unexpected arrival of the demons. Bells rang out. Thanks to her foresight in bathing and sleeping in her clothes the night before, Saoka sprang from her bedroll and darted from the tent, armed with her bow and quiver.

Reaching the ramparts, Saoka took a firing position. Morning fog obscured the tree line below.

What's in there?

Birds erupted from the trees, causing them to sway. From the fog emerged a grotesque ten-foot-tall aberration. Saoka, having encountered bears, read about tigers and lions, and crossed paths with huge boars, tried in vain to stop her hands from trembling. She took an irrational step back, as did many other gap-mouthed soldiers around her.

Singing emanated from the center of town, growing louder with each moment. Though Saoka couldn't discern the words, the melody, imbued with magic, bestowed courage. She turned back, swallowing her terror.

The demon, beyond its immense stature, bore a semblance to a man. Its body was adorned with unexpected iron armor. The demon's face, though vaguely human with a beard, had yellow eyes, horns, pointed ears, and sharp fangs. It radiated potent crimson magic.

Following the first demon, others emerged. Some resembled bears or boars, others appeared as giant spiders or insect-like creatures. The smallest among them stood at an imposing six feet tall, muscled and formidable.

Other demons were grotesque amalgamations with exposed intestines and organs. Tentacles and scales adorned some, while others sprouted horns from unusual places—elbows, shoulders—accompanied by an excessive number of eyes or none at all. The grotesque spectacle overwhelmed many spectators. Amidst the chaos, a silent resolve took hold. Eyes locked forward, hands gripped weapons with white-knuckled intensity, and feet planted firmly on the ground. Not a single soul turned their back to the menace; instead, they stood immovable.

Half of the demons sported poorly crafted armor, wielding giant iron clubs or claws as long as a man's forearm. As the last one emerged from the tree line, Saoka anticipated ferocious roars and terrible animal sounds.

Moving almost in unison, the demons organized themselves into five blocks of twenty to thirty, staying out of bow shot and remaining silent.

IN THE LAND OF NI

Hundreds of mercenaries advanced. Each mercenary bore a patchwork of battle scars and trophies. Black robes draped over mismatched armor pieces—wooden bracers paired with iron greaves, leather cuirasses alongside bronze pauldrons—each telling silent tales of conquests past.

Their towering presence among the shorter locals spoke of northern lineage, their armor a mosaic of many battles. Most bore webbed tattoos on exposed flesh, indicative of their unique identity.

The mercenaries aligned into five groups in front of the demons. A hundred horsemen burst from the forest and formed a distinct group to the right of the main formation. Saoka noticed a creature at the rear.

An Akuma, a demon man, rode a horse with grace, adorned in exotic armor resembling leather scales. Devoid of a helmet, his human-like face suggested an origin distant from the lands near Wa—too tall, too bronzed in complexion. His menace was heightened by his eyes, glowing an unsettling purple that locked onto Saoka. In his hand, he carried an unassuming spear.

The sheer power emanating from him created an aura of scarlet magic, fierce and blinding. It dwarfed anything Saoka had ever witnessed. Her psyche might be playing tricks on her. This Akuma, this abomination, appeared from his aura to have a strength equivalent to nearly fifty of her sisters combined.

The unexpected appearance of this formidable figure elicited cries of shock and disbelief across the ramparts. A fellow soldier to her right exclaimed, "Why the fuck is he glowing? Oh shit, what's happening?"

Saoka's throat tightened as she felt the man's terror mirror her own. Pushing down her unease, she asked the soldier, "Can you see his magic?"

"Can't you? He's glowing like a torch. Holy fuck, we are all gonna die," he responded.

Ordinary people couldn't perceive magical energy. If the Akuma's radiance was visible to ordinary people, it meant he either deliberately showcased it or possessed such overwhelming power that even the uninitiated sensed it.

With a casual raise of his hand, the Akuma commanded one of his minions to advance toward the town. The figure guided his horse up the hill along a footpath, breaking into a gallop. The man intended to parlay, a rare occurrence.

Demons sought death and destruction, not negotiations. In a matter of minutes, the man reached the walls, dismounted, and called out, "I wish to speak to the leader."

Mocking remarks from the defenders echoed down the walls. "Wasn't sure demons' dogs spoke," someone shouted.

"Sit, boy, who's a good boy," another jeered, triggering laughter from all around.

A voice boomed, "Stay right there; I and my advisor will be down shortly." It was Mayuki, and Saoka couldn't help but wonder who her advisor might be.

Moments later, a breathless sister with a shaved head approached Saoka. "Blessed Mayuki wishes to see you," she conveyed through labored gasps.

Saoka's heart skipped a beat as it dawned on her—Mayuki was tapping her to serve as an advisor. Hurriedly making her way to the gate, Saoka found Mayuki pacing.

"Follow me, write down everything you hear, and don't say a word," Mayuki commanded.

A ladder and a gangplank were brought up for the ladies to cross the moat. Mayuki climbed down without hesitation, Saoka followed, wiping sweaty hands on her shirt.

The demon's pet stood six feet tall, with a patch over his left eye and a scar on his forehead. His black hair was unwashed and wild, and wearing all charcoaled leather armor, he looked every bit a mercenary.

"Speak," Mayuki spat.

"My master would like your name," he said.

"I'm sure he would, tough shit."

"No need to be unwholesome. I am simply a messenger. I

bring an offer that would save the lives of everyone in this town."

"So, all of you are going to just commit suicide right here and now. Thanks, that would be great."

"Tell us what we want to know, and we will be on our way."

"Well, anything of course. I mean, it's not like I'm dealing with an army of demons and demon lackeys at the gates. How long does this deal last?"

"My master is patient. He would give the citizens here twenty years to live peacefully, move on, or join his new empire."

"Well, you do have my interest. What is this empire called? Does your master even have a name to go by? And what if we say no?"

"The empire is the empire. If you won't give me your name, why would I give you mine?"

"Not very original, 'the empire.' Are you getting all this down, dear?" Mayuki glanced at Saoka, who nodded.

"To answer your last question: death, for everyone in this town," he grinned, revealing horribly cared-for teeth.

"And there it is, some honesty from the dog who licks the boot of a demon. I guess that coward you call master doesn't have a name," Mayuki said.

The mercenary started shaking. "You underestimate the power of the Akuma. Our master's empire is unstoppable. You can't win this war, and your recalcitrance will only bring suffering."

Mayuki smirked. "Empty words from a lackey. I won't betray my people, and I certainly won't surrender to a faceless tyrant. If your master wants a fight, he'll get one. Now, leave before I change my mind about sparing your pathetic existence."

"Of course, he does, you bitch. Maybe he'll tell it to you as you bleed out. Think, sister, you could save all these people with a simple bit of information. Or doom them all," the mercenary said, standing straighter. "You can witness his power, can you not? How many blessed, how many sisters do you have hidden away up there, I wonder. Will it be enough to stop him?"

"He and him are used for men. Not even man enough to give a name or come up here and talk," Mayuki shot back.

"You should show some respect to Iry—" he stopped mid-sentence before continuing, "You will not get anything else out of me. So here is the question: where is the gate? Answer, and they all live; refuse, and they die," he screamed the last word.

"The gate is behind me, fool."

Mayuki's tone of voice was off, noted Saoka.

"Not that gate. Do not play dumb; you know the gate of which I speak. Wa is supposed to have two. One is located somewhere close by," he said.

"I do not. Sorry, Iry—came here for nothing. Tell him if he leaves now, we'll let him live." With that, Mayuki walked back toward the gate, leaving the mercenary seething. She crossed back over the moat, Saoka following closely.

As they returned to the safety of the ramparts, Mayuki whispered, "Make sure you capture every detail in your notes. We may need this information later. The empire's arrogance might be their undoing."

Mayuki shouted orders, "Blessed and sisters, I need a magical shield around these fortifications now. Nothing too strong; only a handful of you should maintain it. I want a rotation set up so it is maintained at all times. If you see a blue flag raised from the watchmen, redouble your efforts and use twice the number of forces.

I pissed that fucker off something terrible, and the demons aren't going to like what I said much more. Remember, everyone, your orders and colors. Brown flags for arrows, red flags for assault magic, green flags to call healers, black flags for signaling fire brigades. If those things breach the walls, white flags mean switch to spears, swords, and axes. Why we fight."

Saoka raced to catch up. "What shall I do?"

"Don't leave my side unless ordered. Record everything,

don't stop writing. You will want to pick up your bow, maybe use your magic. But what I ask of you now is the most important thing. Do you understand?"

Saoka nodded.

"Good, now watch. That commander nears his master," Mayuki said, spitting over the wall.

The man on horseback approached his master and had a short conversation with him. The whole affair was eerie because the soldiers and demons in formation remained silent. An occasional stretch of the leg, a movement of the head from side to side.

The demon lord threw back his head and laughed. He rammed his spear through the mercenary's torso with appalling speed. He raised his spear above his head with the mercenary still attached and squirming.

The man, armored, had to have weighed almost two hundred pounds, but the demon lord moved him over his head one-handed without much visible effort. He reached back, taking aim at the town, and threw. The spear flew toward the wall, the man still attached. It battered an outer blue wall of magic, sizzling and spinning on its point. Saoka saw the women strain to hold the magic. The spear lost momentum, exploding upon the magical blue wall. A bloody smear dripped down.

A horn rang. The demons and the mercenaries screamed.

Saoka felt their skin crawl.

The enemy started forward at a trot.

Archers on the walls notched arrows, took aim, and fired.

Shields of magic ascended over each of the five columns of the foes, deflecting every incoming arrow. Saoka discerned the points from which the magic emanated, realizing that the demons had eight among their ranks of the second class.

"Archers, fire in threes," the command echoed down the line. Saoka's fingers worked in harmony with her breath, writing in her book in a steady cadence. Under this tactical approach, every third person fired and started reloading, then the next one fired two seconds later, and finally, the third person shot last.

The cycle continued, compelling the demons to sustain their magic shields, which drained their energy faster. However, the downside was a reduction of two-thirds in the total number of arrows striking the enemy.

As the demons and mercenaries crested the hill, Mayuki's voice pierced the din, her flag slicing through the air. "Spells! Magic! Do it now!" Elemental fury rained down, fire and ice sculpting the battlefield, wind howling its wrath.

The sky itself seemed to tremble, and with a resonant boom, a demon's shield faltered. Arrows, hungry for flesh, found their home.

Saoka's heart raced as the front line crumbled, human and demon alike falling before the onslaught. Most of the fallen were human, though a couple of demons continued to walk despite multiple arrows sticking out of their hides.

Another wave of magic followed, pushing the demons' barriers back. Saoka saw three more demons gathering energy, bringing the count to eleven second-class demons.

On the wall, the signal for barrier magic was called, and Saoka braced herself. The three demons unleashed fireballs at the wall, larger than those sent downhill.

Nearly thrown from her feet, Saoka gasped, the world reduced to the roar in her ears and the pounding in her chest. *If any of those fireballs had penetrated, they would have devastated a ten-meter section of the wall.*

The volleys of magic from the sisters persisted, as did the arrows. Some projectiles found their way through the demons' lines, causing explosions that threw both man and demon to the ground. Bodies burned or frozen in place fell, shattering into numerous pieces.

The demons advanced, their magic clashing with the defenders'.

Saoka's gaze flicked to the barrier, noting its spiderweb fractures. Around her, the air was thick with screams and the scent of blood.

Traps claimed lives on the hillside. Saoka saw a demon pull itself from a pit, a spike impaled through it.

The command changed to "Arrows in twos," as demons neared the moat's defenses. An air blast tore through a demon's flesh, exposing bone just moments before a flurry of arrows brought it to a silent end.

The mercenaries, shadows among the chaos, returned fire, their arrows whispering death. The town's barrier quivered under the assault. An arrow thudded near Saoka, and Mayuki yelled, "Stay down and shield yourself!"

But Saoka's spirit rebelled; she was no mere bystander in this dance of war. She watched as the enemy breached the moat, their ladders a bridge to destruction.

A magical onslaught from Kazuno's mages broke enemy barriers, exposing them.

"Target those columns," Mayuki's voice was iron as she pointed toward the exposure.

Death entered the gaps.

Saoka, her reluctance a fading shadow, wove a shield of magic around them both.

The middle columns lay in ruin, the ground littered with the fallen. Fireballs shattered the wall, chaos blooming like a deadly flower.

Mayuki, a statue of resolve, called for reinforcements.

Another fireball tore through homes, and Saoka's heart clenched for those unseen, their fates a silent scream in the din. The defenders' magic intercepted further attacks, thunder echoing with each block.

Magic and arrows poured onto the invaders, breaking their shields. The defenders' magic clashed with the invaders', a symphony of thunder and light. Saoka's hope surged as their barrier held.

The enemy suffered heavy casualties, their dead a carpet of

gore. Fierce fighting erupted at the breach as mercenaries and demons attempted to lay ladders across the moat. Some demons swam in the water, striving to climb the walls or hack at them.

All the second-class demons expended their magic or perished. The magical barrier was now used to deflect arrows from bowmen further down the hill.

Occasional arrows found their way through small holes in the barrier. Saoka's voice rang out, a clarion call of concern. "The magical barrier must be at its limit." Her eyes searched the battlefield, and there, at the tree line, stood the Akuma, an observer to the carnage. No guards, no fear. Saoka's shout cut through the chaos, "Mayuki!" Her arm outstretched, pointing to the distant figure.

Mayuki caught on and ordered a volley of magic to be directed at the Akuma. Three small fireballs and two ice balls raced toward him, but he blocked them all with a subtle hand. Saoka roared, "How strong is he?"

Mayuki tisked and reordered the sisters to refocus their magic on the demons and men closer at hand.

The moat churned and bubbled, its waters turning an angry red, as demons and men alike met fiery and watery graves.

Saoka gagged.

Demons were getting through the breach with a handful of mercenaries. Mayuki ordered all available attack magic to eliminate the enemy archers.

The flag for close-in fighting went up, hundreds unsheathed their swords and brought spears to bear. The soldiers, fierce, jumped to the breach to defend their town.

The fighting grew fiercer.

Saoka witnessed a demon attack berserker-style, slashing and jumping into a line of men. It killed everything in its path. A brave man barreled into it from behind, burying his sword into it, and paid with his life.

The demon, distracted, whirled around and used its claws to decapitate him in a blur of blood.

IN THE LAND OF NI

Other combatants drove their weapons into it, bringing it down.

Mercenaries poured in behind the slain demon. *Cowards! Easier to attack from behind a ten-foot monster.*

Of the original hundred or so demons on the battlefield, only a dozen remained in the fight. Saoka estimated that half of the mercenaries had been incapacitated. Saoka's breaths came in sharp bursts, her mind racing—victory was within grasp. She sought Mayuki's steady presence for reassurance, but the sight of her mentor's grimace sent a jolt of panic through her.

Mayuki's eyes were distant, locked on a new threat gathering like storm clouds at the tree line.

Saoka's voice tore through the air, "Magic incoming!" as fireballs, like falling stars, hurtled towards them. The sisters' shield, a gossamer veil, shattered under the onslaught, and Saoka felt the world spin, the ground rushing up to meet her.

Some sisters still possessed magic and cast a new shield, though it appeared weak. The shield shattered in a thousand places, allowing much of the blast force to penetrate, creating two new holes in the wall and claiming lives.

Time blurred as she lay there, the battle's roar a distant echo. Pain lanced through her. But as the darkness beckoned, Saoka's spirit rebelled. With a guttural cry, she surged to her feet, her fear transmuted into fury.

"Fuck that shit!" Saoka screamed as she dropped her magical shield, preparing to unleash a fireball at the demons, only to be interrupted by a soft hand on her shoulder.

"Don't do that, girl," Mayuki's voice was a lifeline in the chaos.

Saoka's anger simmered, but obedience won.

"I gave you an order; put that spell back up around yourself right now. If you want to see some dead demons, watch this shit," Mayuki said.

She watched, awestruck, as Mayuki summoned magic so

potent it seemed to tear the very fabric of the sky. Mayuki launched a beam of light towards the heavens.

Then, from behind, a symphony of war drums and horns sang of reinforcements. Saoka's heart leapt as the cavalry, a tide of iron and determination, swept around the town and crashed into the enemy's flank.

A signal!

Magic cascaded from the walls, a futile but distracting rain.

The cavalry's charge was a thing of brutal beauty, a dance of death that left the demons crushed beneath their hooves, trampled into red pulp. The cavalry had been perfectly timed.

How had Mayuki known there would be more enemies?

Mayuki's knowing slap on her back was a benediction. "Told you I'd put on a show for ya," she said, and Saoka's tears were a mirror of her own—tears of relief, of triumph.

The cavalry's horns sang victory as they encircled the enemy. The townspeople, a vise of vengeance, closed in. The demons' end was a foregone conclusion, their fate sealed by the relentless press of the defenders. Caught from all sides, the demons and mercenaries were overwhelmed by the iron grip of the townspeople, bleeding them into oblivion.

"Keep some of the mercenaries alive. Kill every last demon fuck," Mayuki ordered with a flick of her wrist.

The first order was necessary, slowing the townspeople's bloodlust. The second wasn't. It was over. A handful of prisoners were the only remnants of the enemy.

"Saoka, dear, you can let go of your magic now," Mayuki said.

Saoka tried to respond, but her vision was fading. *What's happening?* She had overused her magic. "Oh," she managed before falling unconscious into Mayuki's arms.

CHAPTER 12

Magumi let her thoughts wander back to the previous day. The discovery of a hidden cave echoed with tales of sanctuary and reflection, where profound truths emerged in the shadows of an earthly womb. Saoka herself had once found an even greater cave, with grander truths. Magumi allowed her mind to wander.

Saoka's eyelids fluttered open, revealing the dim confines of the tent. The discordant sounds of hammers clanging, saws buzzing, and a medley of human voices—cries, laments, and unexpected laughter—bombarded her. Confusion clouded her mind as discomfort anchored her firmly to the bedroll. Struggling to rise, her body rebelled, heavy and defiant, plunging her back with a jolt of frustration.

Eyes cracking open again, she turned toward a rustling to her right. Mayuki's voice, deep and textured as unrefined honey, sliced through the tumult. "Don't move; that's an order."

Saoka's spirits plummeted. "Did we win?"

A tired chuckle tinged Mayuki's response. "We wouldn't be

talking if we hadn't. But you, asleep while there's work to be done? That's a shame."

Saoka's shoulders slumped under a heavy cloak of remorse, her eyes tired and distant. "I'm sorry, I pushed too hard. I'll be up soon," she vowed, her body protesting vehemently.

Mayuki's snort carried a blend of irritation and grudging respect. "You went beyond 'pushing too hard,' Saoka. Didn't they teach you restraint at the Order? Still, I owe you thanks."

"Are you angry or happy with me?" Saoka asked, her voice trembling with uncertainty.

"Well, a little of both. You don't even realize what you did. For one, holding a spell for so long is draining," Mayuki admonished, her voice softening. "You put your spell around me as well, which was in violation of my command. However, that decision saved my life. I can see by the look on your face you don't understand. You blocked a demon fireball. A demon fireball," Mayuki repeated, louder this time.

Shock widened Saoka's eyes, and tears started to brim as she grasped the reality. "You're our leader; I had to protect you. You see the battlefield like no other. Your strategies, like the surprise cavalry, are our lifeline. I may be young and impulsive, but we can't afford to lose you," she sobbed.

Mayuki's stern expression softened. "Well, you sure know how to compliment a girl. Anyway, the fact is I'm impressed and a little concerned. Not too many people would dare defy me, and even fewer can block a direct blast from a demon on their own. I mean, you saw how many sisters and Blessed it took to hold those shield walls. It just shouldn't be possible."

"I've always had a knack for magic. I'm not a freak. I just acted in the heat of the moment. But the others—how are they? And the town?" Saoka's voice trailed off, consumed by guilt.

Mayuki silenced her with a gentle finger to her lips. "The men fought like lions. Still, those lions were fighting demons. We've gone from two thousand able-bodied men to six hundred.

About a hundred villagers perished. Of the enemy, only ten men remain.

They have been given food and water and are only being allowed to sleep if they tell us everything. Some spilled out anything they knew right away; a few are proving more troublesome. We now know that the demons under the Akuma have firm control over the entirety of Hokkaido.

They are gathering arms men from as far as Korea, China, and Mongolia. We don't know their exact numbers, either of men or demon, but what we fought here was just an advanced expedition. Word has been sent back to all three mothers, but it will take some time to reach them all.

We dealt them a blow. We need to set up more outposts, clear more roads, consolidate into a more manageable position. There's a lot to do, and not a lot of time to do it. We will remain here for a week and help Kazuno rebuild and take a necessary rest. Then we will travel back to Inawashiro. I also have a very important task I must take care of."

"The gate?" Saoka interjected, her mind racing.

"Yes. You'll join me there after a couple of days' rest. It's vital, and I'll brief you then. Keep this between us," Mayuki instructed, her tone absolute. Saoka nodded, secrets swirling in her thoughts.

"Rest now. I'll send sisters with water and food."

"And a chamber pot?" Saoka requested candidly. Mayuki's laughter, a rare comfort, filled the space. "Work awaits. The pot's behind you—be careful."

A lone chuckle escaped Saoka's lips, quickly smothered by a rising tide of guilt. "Laughter feels wrong amidst such sorrow," she whispered, tears stinging anew. Overcome by fatigue, she succumbed to sleep.

Later, a gentle shake roused her. Ramona and Akiho stood there, their smiles and tears a balm to her soul. With their support, she rose, her legs shaky.

"May I have some privacy?" she asked, a blush coloring her cheeks.

The women returned with food, and Saoka's hunger roared to life. She devoured the meal, the others watching, astonished.

Ramona and Akiho recounted the battle's horrors. "I saw a sister explode," Ramona confessed, her voice cracking as she hid her face in her hands. Saoka's heart tightened, her hands falling to her lap as she inhaled sharply, her breaths ragged in the struggle to hold back tears.

Having eaten and conversed with her companions, Saoka felt the tug of weariness again. She reclined, kneading her aching muscles, seeking solace in the bedroll's embrace. Noting only bruises, she drank deeply and surrendered to slumber.

As dawn broke, the early morning light washed over the landscape, softening the edges of the night's shadows and breathing a gentle vibrancy into the weary camp. Despite aches, Saoka ventured out, only to be greeted by an acrid odor. Smoke columns billowed in the distance. A passerby shared the grim task at hand: the pyres for the fallen.

Saoka whispered prayers and expressed her gratitude as she walked through the town.

That night, Saoka sat by the fireside with her sisters, sipping rice wine brought over by some admiring men. The girls giggled, the bonds forged in battle loosening the usual restraints between the men and women of the Order. Saoka, however, found solace in listening to her comrades and admiring the stars as she drank.

Mayuki's abrupt awakening jarred Saoka. "It's still dark," she mumbled, drowsy. With a grunt, Mayuki handed Saoka her bow and quiver, signaling an unspoken urgency. They navigated the camp to their horses, ready for departure. Without a word, they set off into the forest's embrace.

They stopped at the base of a broad hill. Dismounting,

Mayuki tied her horse to a tree and did the same with Saoka's horse. They climbed the hill to a man-sized pile of rocks that resembled a grave. Mayuki began pulling at the smaller rocks, and Saoka joined in, her thoughts racing. Grave robbing sent a chill down her spine.

As they cleared the rocks, they revealed a colossal, smooth rectangular stone buried in the dirt. "Can you levitate things?" Mayuki asked.

"Only a little, it's one thing I was never good at," Saoka admitted reluctantly, feeling a pang of inadequacy.

Mayuki didn't seem surprised. "It's one of only three spells I can do, but I am rather adept; come sit down and help. We need to lift this stone out of the way."

Saoka was taken aback. While elder sisters often specialized in two or three spells, most Blessed used five or six, some even more. What was the other spell? She sat down, gathering her magic. The rock, about two feet wide and six feet long, loomed large and intimidating, its thickness hidden beneath the earth. Saoka pushed aside her thoughts, focusing intently on the spell.

The rock began to glow as the two sisters poured their energy into it. Slowly, it started to rise. Levitation required convincing an object that it should push itself off the ground, a feat only possible with inanimate objects since living things inherently understood their connection to the earth. The rock continued to rise, one foot clear, then another. *How damn big is this rock?*

When the rock had risen six feet, Saoka gasped, sweat pouring down her face from the strain. She and Mayuki shifted the rock to the side, finally setting it down and releasing their magic. Saoka realized Mayuki had done most of the work. Saoka, still growing into her magic, had never levitated anything more than a knee-high rock. She sat there, mouth agape, as Mayuki panted and sweated beside her.

"What, if you think that was something, you should see me in my underwear," Mayuki joked, breaking the tension.

Saoka laughed, the sound surprising her. "I already passed out this week, thank you. Best not to make it a habit."

"Shall we uncover the world's greatest secret?" Mayuki prompted, standing tall.

Saoka, reminded of their quest, hurried to the now-exposed staircase leading into the earth's depths. What lay below?

Mayuki pulled a torch from her bag, lit it, and touched the flame to a small piece of red rock embedded in the staircase wall. The wall glimmered faintly, casting light down the staircase and beyond. Saoka whistled in awe. Magically powered lighting, here in the middle of a forest, far from any settlement. What was this place?

"Let's go," Mayuki said, and Saoka eagerly followed her commander. They walked down three hundred and fifty-five stairs, by Saoka's count. The effort required to dig this far underground seemed impossible.

Just as Saoka was about to speak, they reached the bottom, and she gasped. A simple iron door stood before them. Mayuki pushed it open, revealing a vast cavern with orange and yellow walls. The cavern was ball-shaped, with a domed ceiling and a bowl-like floor two hundred feet down and a mile across. Another staircase to their left led down further, with tunnels fanning out in multiple directions from the bottom level. The scale of magic needed to create this lighting was unfathomable.

"Who crafted this sanctuary? Its age must span eons. How long have you known of its existence?" Saoka's inquiries cascaded forth, her mind alight with curiosity.

"Twenty years ago, the Mother unveiled this place to me," Mayuki began, her voice echoing the cadence of a tale often told. "She spoke of an empire named 'I,' whose people wielded magic beyond our wildest dreams, now lost to the annals of time. Their dominion spanned the globe, their power dwarfing ours."

Saoka absorbed the revelation, her mind a whirlwind of wonder. An ancient empire, its magic potent and pervasive, vanished without a trace. What mysteries did this cavern hold? What was its true purpose? Awe and anticipation surged within her as she delved deeper into the subterranean enigma with Mayuki.

"Do you think they were here before the meteor struck? You know, the one Mother told us about?" Saoka asked, her voice tinged with curiosity and a hint of awe.

"Yes, it would make sense. Hurry and follow, I have more to show you and will explain as we walk." The two started their descent down the second staircase. Mayuki picked up her story where she left off, "Mother explained to me that this was one of two such locations in the land of Wa. Here and at Nara, directly under the Order's Headquarters.

These two were part of a network of cavern cities all over the world. While she didn't say how many, she made it seem as if there were quite a number of them. What she did say was why they were so important, and what I would have to do if the time came."

Reaching the labyrinth's nadir, a web of tunnels sprawled before them. Mayuki, propelled by a silent imperative, chose a path. Saoka's gaze darted, her footing uncertain.

Sensing her companion's disquiet, Mayuki reassured, "Fear not, we are alone, and time is short. The secrets of this forsaken place will soon be yours to behold."

Turning her attention to the wall, Saoka discovered a fresco depicting deities amidst flora, its colors faded yet striking. Their eyes a haunting purple—akin to the Akuma's.

Mayuki paused, following Saoka's gaze.

"Their eyes... they mirror the Akuma's," Saoka said, a chill tracing her spine.

"A curious connection indeed," Mayuki's eyes narrowed. "Could it be mere coincidence, or something more?"

Saoka hastened to Mayuki's side, her voice urgent. "Is it possible for a demon to track us here?"

"The Mother assured me of the caverns' protective enchantments, impenetrable barriers. Yet, it's the gates that render these sanctuaries invaluable—and perilous."

"Gates? To where?" Saoka's arms wrapped protectively around herself.

"Conduits of magic, capable of instantaneously bridging vast distances."

Saoka's skepticism was palpable. "Such a thing... it can't be real."

But the sight that greeted them next dispelled all doubt—a stone archway, pulsating with arcane energy. Saoka stood, transfixed by the spectacle.

Without hesitation, Mayuki approached the gate, tools in hand, intent on its destruction. "The Akuma mustn't learn of this," Saoka lamented, understanding the necessity of their grim task.

Mayuki hesitated only a second before walking over to the gateway. Pulling a chisel and hammer from her satchel, she began to dig at an inlaid gem in the stone. There were several more.

Saoka stated, "You are going to destroy it. The demons aren't supposed to know about them, but that Akuma did. It is too dangerous to leave this one here. Such a waste."

"Yes, but it couldn't be helped," Mayuki said, pulling the first gem from the stone. In a matter of minutes, she collected all the gems and used her hammer to smash them into dust. Mayuki gathered the dust into a small handkerchief and tucked it into her bag. Saoka turned to go. The two women didn't say another word until they were back out in the forest.

"Well, it's done. I need you to record this in your notes, but show no one. Are you familiar with how to write in code?" Mayuki asked.

"Absolutely, and I already have been. I developed my own code over a year ago. I gave the cipher to Mother during a lesson she was teaching on the subject. She is the only one who knows it besides me," Saoka answered. Talking about something she was knowledgeable about lightened her mood momentarily. Mayuki laughed.

"Well, it seems even immature brats have secrets," Mayuki teased.

"And they're usually juicier than old, ripe, mature brats' secrets," Saoka shot back. "Except for the whole fight to save the world thing, demon-man hybrids, and gates of an extinct ancient race of people."

They both grinned and went to work resealing the door. It was easier to plug up because once it was about halfway levitated in, they dropped their spells and let gravity do the rest of the work. Saoka helped Mayuki pile some rocks and branches on top, and once satisfied, they walked down to their horses to set out for Kazuno.

As they mounted their horses, the grove's mystical aura enveloped them. The paulownia trees whispered ancient secrets, their leaves rustling with the wisdom of ages past.

A hush fell as a divine creature emerged, bathed in the sunset's glow—the Hōō, a symbol of serenity and celestial grace. Its plumage, a kaleidoscope of the elements, danced in the fading light. Saoka, recalling tales of such beings from the Order's archives, watched in silence as the creature moved, the very air around them bending.

Compelled by a force beyond their understanding, Saoka and Mayuki approached the Hōō, a guardian whose very presence bridged the mortal realm and the divine. Its eyes, deep wells of ancient knowledge, mirrored the tranquility of a world untouched by strife. The Hōō, a symbol of rebirth, cast an aura that defied the passage of time.

In a dance of celestial grace, bamboo seeds fluttered from the Hōō's beak, each a covenant with the soil below. Its wings, a canvas of fleeting beauty, captured the day's last light, splashing the grove with a spectrum of colors. The air hummed with a hallowed frequency, a chorus praising the virtues of honor, decorum, faith, and compassion.

Silent reverence enveloped them as the Hōō ascended skyward.

On their way back to Kazuno, Saoka and Mayuki rode in silence, each lost in their thoughts, occasionally glancing at the sky where the Hōō had flown, their minds replaying the moments of their mystical encounter.

Days in Kazuno blurred into a montage of activity.

Saoka sat cross-legged with scrolls spread around her, scribbling furiously in a code only she could decipher. Between her writings, she practiced her spells, her hands weaving intricate patterns in the air, her brow furrowed in concentration as she sought to perfect each gesture and incantation. She spent evenings in the company of her sisters, eager to expand her repertoire of spells.

Mornings were dedicated to martial training—sword, staff, spear, knives, and bow. She varied her sparring partners, embracing adaptability. The town bustled with reconstruction, and Saoka admired the swift progress. On the fourth day, the Order set forth for Inawashiro. Throughout the journey, Saoka's rigorous routine left her weary yet fulfilled.

Inawashiro's embrace was that of heroes returning. The town's jubilant cheers were a balm to the soul. "Never have I felt such bashfulness," Saoka confided to her companions.

"Attribute it to nerves, compounded by the recent ordeal," Rimona consoled.

Dismounting, a messenger hastened to Saoka with news of

Mother's summons. Ayana, brimming with worry and eagerness, rushed to her side. "Were you safe? What wonders did you witness?" Ayana implored, her eyes alight with fervor.

A maelstrom of emotions churned within Saoka—hope, affection, grief, pride, and remorse entwined in silent chaos. Words failed her, so she laughed instead, embracing her sister with a promise to share all later. Hand in hand, they made their way to Mother's abode.

Saoka bid Ayana farewell and ascended to Mother's quarters, where a council awaited. Mayuki, the blessed, and the Egyptian were present. Saoka joined them, settling into the gravity of the stone table.

After hours of debriefing, Saoka prepared to depart with the others, but Mother beckoned her to stay. Mayuki and the Egyptian remained as well. Saoka pondered the significance of their gathering.

Speaking for an hour, Saoka then entrusted her diary to Mother, who received it with reverence. Mother's bibliophilic nature was evident as she perused the initial pages, then paused, weighing her words.

"Brethren, we stand at a precipice I had hoped to avoid. The demons stir, and among them, an Akuma. We've dealt them a blow, but their resurgence is inevitable. The Akuma's knowledge of the gates, his eyes a telltale purple—could he be of the Empire of I? We must unravel these mysteries. Your mission is clandestine, and haste is paramount. Departure is at dawn," Mother declared, her voice heavy with the burden of command.

"Where does our path lead, Mother? To whom are we bound?" Saoka inquired, her mind awash with questions.

"The details will come through coded messages. The guardians of Nara's gate must remain oblivious to our endeavors," Mother instructed, her resolve clear.

Mayuki, silent until now, voiced her concern, "Will Himiko be privy to our mission in Nara?"

"She forges alliances afar and will not be present. Yet, she will be informed through means I cannot disclose," Mother assured, her eyes glinting with secrets.

With the council concluded, Saoka sought Ayana in the mess hall for a final meal before embarking on the unknown.

CHAPTER 13

299 B.C.E. The road between Inawashiro, Fukushima, and Nara City, Nara Prefecture, Japan

The subtle fragrance of wild roses transported Magumi to a moment suspended in time, where love's essence lingered amidst petals exchanged in whispered promises. Her thoughts drifted to Saoka, finding herself out of the Land of Wa, to a place where she would first meet Pausanias, and they would make their first whispered promises.

Dawn's first light had barely touched the horizon when Saoka slipped out to the stables, finding Mayuki already there, a silhouette against the waking sky.

"You never seem to sleep," Saoka said.

"What delayed you?" Mayuki countered, her tone teasing.

With a snort, Saoka swung onto her horse and set off at a trot, leaving a mock-exasperated Mayuki to follow.

"That was hardly fair; we're meant to wait for our escort," Mayuki said, catching up with ease.

"Fairness isn't my style lately," Saoka tapped her chest, "and if you'd listened, you'd know our escort is meeting us by the lake."

Mayuki snorted.

"Like a battle of two princess pigs," Saoka said.

Their banter faded as they reached the lakeside, greeted by the sight of their escort—ten formidable men clad in black and blue armor, a blend of leather, straw, wood, and bronze. Their helmets, simple yet functional.

Introductions were brief, and soon they were underway, the day's journey unfolding under a clouded sky. This smaller band, unlike the larger force that had headed to Kazuno, made swift progress through the countryside.

As evening approached, they halted to rest. Saoka, dismounting with a grimace, lamented, "I fear my backside is beyond saving."

"Endure the saddle's trials, and you'll emerge a seasoned rider," Mayuki replied, her smile a glint in the fading light.

"How do you all manage this?" Saoka groaned to Sota, a young soldier whose chuckle was a balm to her aches.

"You'll grow accustomed," Sota said, his tone light, "though I'll spare you the timeline for such an adjustment."

Saoka's attention drifted from Sota's words, his handsome features a pleasant distraction. "Thank you, Sota. Have a good night." She made for the tent she would share with Mayuki.

Upon entering, she found Mayuki already engrossed in a hot meal.

"Saoka, grab some food and come on back," Mayuki said between mouthfuls. Mayuki was already cocooned in her bedroll by the time Saoka returned.

"Taken with the young soldier, are we?" Mayuki teased, her voice betraying no real interest.

"He's undeniably gorgeous, but a little dense. Anyway, now

isn't the time to entertain such thoughts," Saoka's cheeks reddened.

"Ah, dense and hard, just the way I like them. So, you don't have to marry the man; why not have a little roll in the straw? Get it out of your system."

Saoka, unaccustomed to hearing such words from a lady, blushed.

"Oh, shit, you're still—I mean, sorry," Mayuki stumbled.

"Do shut up, please, nitwit," Saoka said. "My backside already feels like it was rolling around in the straw all day."

The next day brought rain and discomfort, but Saoka immersed herself in her journal, spell practice, and much-needed stretches. The downpour lasted until the fourth day, and even when it ceased, the dampness clung to her.

On the fifth day, the escort leader, a man as steadfast as iron, slowed their pace to spare the horses. Saoka took a moment to breathe, absorbing the beauty of the valley they traversed, the rice fields bathed in golden morning light.

"The sun holds its own magic," she said, halting her horse as a shadow danced across the light.

The procession stopped, all eyes turning skyward.

A dragon soared in the distance; its slender, white form adorned with nine heads. Saoka and Mayuki, tapping into the sight of nearby birds, enhanced their vision with a spell of clarity.

"It's not a demon," Mayuki said, the group exhaled.

"Should we avoid it?" Saoka asked, eyes wide, moving her head from side to side, hands raised, palms up.

"Not a chance," Mayuki grinned. "It's not every day one encounters a dragon."

With a collective groan, the escort leader steered them toward the creature. They followed the stream eastward, the waterway widening into a river as they neared the rocky hill where the dragon circled.

Thirty minutes into their journey, they had only covered half the distance. Saoka's brow furrowed. "Mayuki, I fear I've misjudged the scale. On horseback, the dragon looms far larger than expected."

Mayuki cast a wary glance at the dragon. "Indeed, we must proceed with caution. The land here is unforgiving."

As they neared a rocky hill, the sound of cascading water intensified. "Look there, atop the hill," Saoka pointed out. "The dragon rests by a waterfall."

Mayuki pondered, "But from where does the water spring? No nearby hills could house such a source."

"It must be subterranean," Saoka said, gesturing eastward. "The water's journey begins beneath us."

At the hill's base, they dismounted, Mayuki's stare fixed on the dragon. "It observes us with half its heads."

"And now we climb this path, etched into the stone," Saoka said, her head tilted, as she examined the rocks.

Halfway up, a gust from the dragon's descent swept over them. It opened its many mouths, releasing a scent as sweet as fruit. *Wasn't expecting that.*

"What, what, what, do, do, do, you, you, you, want, want, want?" echoed three heads in a haunting chorus.

"We seek peace," Mayuki projected her voice over the waterfall's roar.

"Peace, peace, that, that, is, is, good, good," two heads now spoke, the dragon's posture easing.

"My name is Saoka. This is Mayuki, our leader. We are on our way to Nara, and we saw you flying. Curiosity got the better of us as we sensed no evil aura coming from you." Saoka forgot all her sheepishness. *Did dragons eat sheep?*

The dragon snorted as if annoyed.

The closest head grinned and spoke by itself, which was a relief; the more heads that spoke, the stranger it was to listen to. "First time seeing a dragon, I gather. Well, little Saoka, my name is Kuzuryu. If it pleases you, I, as well, sensed no evil in you and your comrades."

Mayuki, now having caught up to Saoka, laughed and said, "So where did you come from, dragon? Your kind is rare to begin with, and most don't talk, or so I've heard."

"Oh, nonsense, we can all talk. It's just that most of us are too arrogant to think that humans would have anything interesting to say. As to your question, I come from right here, this very spot. I was born here, and I shall die here as well, I hope," Kuzuryu said.

Saoka took a liking to this dragon.

He gestured with his massive forearm and told the group of still slightly nervous men to take a seat.

"Before this conversation goes any further, can I assume that two dominant members of the Order are traveling for ominous reasons?" Kuzuryu asked.

Both ladies looked baffled but nodded their acknowledgment. Before they asked, the dragon spoke again, "Do not be so shocked. Dragons such as I have lived a long time, and, well, we like to collect information. A few from your order have come across this place in my long life. Like you, they are curious. Runs throughout the lot of you Order girls."

"You'd be surprised," responded Saoka.

The dragon laughed—a strange but pleasant bird-like sound that vibrated the very air.

"Please, you are welcome here, and your secrets are safe with me. I know some of the dangers you face. Demons steer clear of this place. I don't care for their kind, you see," Kuzuryu said.

"We would take a rest here for the day if that's amenable to you? We have many questions, and we can trade in knowledge," Mayuki said as she paced in front of the dragon.

The whiskers on Kuzuryu's face twitched in amusement. "Fine by me, the water here is fresh and delicious if I do say so myself. Please help yourselves, although perhaps your men would make camp at the bottom of the hill; your horses look as if they might run away at any moment."

With a respectful salute, the men retreated, leaving the women to converse with the dragon under the stars.

Mayuki spoke of Kazuno's demons and their broader conflict, careful to withhold the Order's deepest secrets.

Saoka, meanwhile, was captivated by Kuzuryu's stories—tales of ages past, his miraculous birth, and his rare confrontations with demons. Despite his size, the dragon bore a gentle spirit, reluctant to resort to violence.

"How did you come to speak our tongue?" Mayuki asked.

Kuzuryu's eyes gleamed. "Shall I reveal my most treasured secret?"

At their eager nods, the air pulsed, and in a blink, the dragon was gone. In his stead sat a man of elegant poise, his hair a pristine white, his attire simple yet regal.

The transformation left Saoka and Mayuki speechless. Such shape-shifting was unheard of among the larger Yokai.

"It is our greatest safeguard," Kuzuryu explained, now in human form. "To the world, I am but a man, avoiding the hunts and accusations that follow my true kind."

Mayuki found her voice. "Such modesty in your guise, yet I suspect many would be charmed by your appearance."

Kuzuryu chuckled. "This form was crafted after much observation. Beauty, it seems, can unlock secrets as swiftly as gold."

"Could you teach me this art?" Saoka asked, her eyes wide with wonder.

Kuzuryu shook his head. "Transformations such as mine are beyond human capability," he explained, addressing Saoka's earlier question. "And perhaps that's for the best. The world might be a bit too chaotic if everyone were as striking as I."

Mayuki, ever curious, steered the conversation. "What have you gleaned from your time among humans?"

Kuzuryu pondered, his gaze drifting to the stars. "I've witnessed the creation of tools, the rise of buildings, the birth of books, music, art, and fashion. Yet, the greatest treasures I've

IN THE LAND OF NI

discovered are the boundless capacity for love and the simple pleasure of a ripe pear."

"Pears?" Mayuki raised an eyebrow. "Of all things, pears?"

Saoka's eyes lit up, and a warm smile spread across her face as she leaned in closer. "He mentioned love too, which is quite endearing."

The dragon chuckled at their banter. "The night grows old, and you mortals need your rest. But before I leave you to slumber, I must warn you. The demons will return, and I believe I can offer guidance that may aid you in the coming battle, Mayuki. And for you, Saoka, a gift."

With a gentle sweep of his arm, Kuzuryu unveiled two treasures: a map for Mayuki and a small white flute for Saoka.

"I'm afraid I can't play this," Saoka admitted, her head dropping.

"Fear not," Kuzuryu reassured, "crafted from my scale, this flute carries a fragment of my essence. When played, it will summon me, but use it sparingly—only in dire need, for I will arrive ready for battle."

Saoka accepted the flute with a humble nod. "I am grateful, Kuzuryu. I will honor your gift and call upon you only in desperation."

Mayuki, studying the map, added her thanks. "This is invaluable, dragon."

Kuzuryu merely smiled, his gaze joining theirs on the celestial canvas above. Silence enveloped them, a shared reverence for the night's beauty.

Breaking the quiet, Saoka inquired, "Have you ever tasted pear jam?"

The dragon's human lips parted in a smile. "I have not had such a pleasure."

"Then I shall bring you some upon our next meeting," Saoka promised.

With that, they bid Kuzuryu goodnight and descended the hill to rejoin their companions. After a brief exchange with the guards, Mayuki led Saoka to their tent, where sleep claimed them swiftly.

Saoka woke to the bustling sounds of camp disassembly, the clanking and shouting wrenching her from sleep. She blinked against the morning light, her heart sinking as she realized the activity had started without her. *How could I have slept in?* she berated herself silently, scrambling to her feet.

Her movements were hurried and flustered, as she began packing up her own gear. After a quick wash in the stream, she returned to find a rice ball awaiting her in Mayuki's hand.

"He's vanished," Mayuki observed, noting the dragon's absence.

Saoka mounted her horse, half a rice ball stuffed in her mouth. "Hurry up, Mayuki. I've been waiting all morning."

The following days passed without incident, the road populated by caravans and travelers. Saoka greeted each with a nod and a wave, embodying the Order's benevolence.

Then, amidst the tranquility, chaos erupted. Children from a nearby village, no taller than three feet, burst from the trees in a playful ambush. The guards, momentarily startled, quickly sheathed their swords as laughter filled the air.

A young girl approached Saoka with wide eyes. "Are you a sister of the Order?"

"Yes, sweetheart," Saoka replied.

"But you don't look like an old witch; my mother said the sisters like to eat children," the girl said.

Saoka grinned. "Only the naughty ones. Have you been good?"

The girl giggled and scampered away, leaving the guards' leader unamused.

"Let's not let our guard down again," his tone firm.

Caravans and travelers populated the road as they moved

through the days, each passing without incident. As they approached the city, the number of villages increased, each one a marker of their progress. On the eve of their arrival, they found shelter in a stable, where Saoka took the opportunity to update her diary and maintain her meditation and combat skills.

The journey had sculpted her body into a vessel more attuned to the rigors of the road. "My legs have adapted to the saddle, and my arms have grown stronger," she boasted to Mayuki, who offered only a noncommittal grunt in response.

"Nitwit," Saoka said.

When they finally laid eyes on Nara, the sight was staggering. The city, nestled in a valley and cradled by mountains, was a testament to the grandeur of Wa. Its population neared half a million, and its architecture bore the unmistakable influence of Chinese design.

Five concentric walls spiraled out from the city's heart, where the grand palace stood—a colossal structure dwarfing all else. The streets, paved and orderly, formed a labyrinth of perfect squares, each a neighborhood unto itself, fortified by its own set of walls. The Saho River and twin moats bolstered the city's defenses, creating a fortress of unparalleled complexity.

Every newcomer's face lit up with big eyes and open mouths as they beheld the city. Mayuki, familiar with the city's splendor, remained unimpressed.

"Looks can be deceiving," Mayuki whispered as they dismounted, her voice barely audible over the city's cacophony.

Inside, the din was overwhelming. Saoka marveled at the sheer density of life, the variety of shops and eateries, and the kaleidoscope of colors worn by the bustling crowd. Patrols of fifty men marched through the streets, a vigilant presence amidst the chaos.

It took an hour to reach the palace gates, which opened to reveal an edifice even more magnificent than Saoka had imagined. She looked up at the palace towering above, its five stories standing as a beacon of authority and power.

Mayuki, ever the leader, commandeered the palace guards to attend to their horses and presented her documents. Recognized seals granted them passage, and they bid farewell to the guardsmen who had accompanied them.

Inside, Saoka yearned to explore, to drink in the splendor of each room and corridor, but Mayuki's pace allowed for no dawdling. They descended a staircase and entered a nondescript room, where a bolted door awaited, guarded by a contingent of men and sisters.

Saoka's curiosity was piqued. How many knew of the secrets that lay beyond? She inquired, only to learn that few had ever passed this threshold. Mayuki, too, sought information, confirming the addition of extra security.

"Yes, blessed," a young sister confirmed. "Three blessed and two men now guard the next door."

"Men?" Mayuki asked, her arms folded and face stern.

"It's unusual, but we honor our duty," the sister replied.

"As you should. Thank you, sister, that will be all," Mayuki said with a small bow of her head. She motioned for Saoka to follow. Beyond the door was another staircase, illuminated with oil lamps.

Down, down they went, eighty-three steps this time, spilling out into a larger chamber that was much brighter than the staircase and lit by the same magic that lit up the cave near Kazuno.

Again, at the end of the room was another door and the five people they expected to see. Mayuki recognized one of the blessed, her face lighting up. "Iruru, you dirty bitch, what are you doing here? I thought you were stationed at Lake Biwa?" Mayuki shouted in glee, as she bounded over to hug her friend.

"Well, I was, stinky breath, but these Nara girls needed some muscle, so here I am. Who's your little friend?" Iruru asked, pointing towards Saoka.

Introductions were made all around. Iruru was the first to speak, "We received word that you and an acolyte would be coming. You are allowed passage, and here is a sealed note from the mother for your eyes only."

Mayuki thanked her friend and the other people guarding the Order's largest secret in all of Wa. She opened the note, read it twice, committing everything to memory. She held it out in front of Saoka and said, "Be a doll and burn this, please."

Saoka used her magic and created a very tiny but very hot fire in her hands. Mayuki stuck the note in the mini furnace.

Beyond the final door, a wooden tunnel obscured the cave's vastness, guiding them through the darkness. Saoka's magical flame flickered, casting shadows as they ventured deeper. Soon, they reached a fork, and the path ahead promised secrets yet to be unveiled.

Following Mayuki's lead, Saoka entered a sub-chamber illuminated by the same magical light they had grown accustomed to. Before them stood a gate, its design mirroring the one in Kazuno. Mayuki approached, her fingers dancing over the lavender stones in a sequence that seemed almost ritualistic, infusing each with a trace of her magic. With the final touch, the stones blazed with light, and the air rippled like the surface of a disturbed pond, revealing a room within a cave.

"You coming?" Mayuki called, stepping through the gate with the ease of routine, her figure instantly appearing in the room beyond.

CHAPTER 14

Saoka hesitated only for a moment before following Mayuki through the portal. The transition was seamless, devoid of the sensations she had braced for—no tingling, no blinding light. A simple step through a doorway.

"See, nothing to it," Mayuki said, noting Saoka's disoriented expression.

"Easy for you to say," Saoka retorted. "Wasn't this your first time too? How are you so unfazed?"

"I've been briefed by the Mothers," Mayuki replied, her composure unshaken. "Besides, I prefer not to dwell on apprehension."

Their exchange was interrupted by the creak of a door and the entrance of an older man, his eyes a striking shade of twilight purple. Saoka's breath caught at the sight; she froze.

"I was not expecting visitors," he stated in Chinese. Then, noting their confusion, he switched to the language of Wa. "Who are you, and what brings you here?"

"I am Blessed Mayuki, and this is Sister Saoka. We come bearing urgent news for you, Kushim," Mayuki declared.

Kushim raised an eyebrow. "And how do you presume to know my name?"

"Your purple eyes betray your lineage—the last of the Empire of I," Mayuki responded with a smirk.

Kushim's laughter filled the room. "You speak boldly for one so young. And what of you, Sister Saoka? Do you share your companion's audacity?"

Saoka met his gaze. "I am fluent in three languages, including Chinese. I've mastered twelve spells and am learning five more. My skills are many and varied."

Kushim chuckled. "Apologies, but at my age, I forget the arrogance of the infants around me. I've forgotten more than three languages because they're dead. I speak close to a hundred. Spells, of course, are another thing entirely. The magic was so abundant when I was young that we did almost anything that came to our minds. Thousands of what you would call spells."

Saoka's retort was swift. "And yet, despite your years, you share in our arrogance."

The room fell silent, Saoka wondering if she had overstepped. But Kushim's laughter soon dispelled the tension. "Arrogance? Perhaps. But what have I to boast of?"

Mayuki interjected, "Well, you did establish an order that spans the globe, only to seclude yourself like a sage."

"Don't worry about her, Master Kushim. She's the worst of us all; see, she already forgot to tell you something super important," said Saoka.

"Yes, about the demon attack on Kazuno, and their collusion with the human tribes in Hokkaido. I already know. The Nara Mother came here a little over two weeks ago to inform me. She was a little short on details, but I have the ability to see between the lines. She also told me of the destruction of the Kazuno gate at the hands of a lady named Mayuki," he stated, turning to stare.

Mayuki shrugged.

In the presence of Kushim, Saoka grappled with her hesitation. The secrets he held, the motives behind his actions—were they as pure as they seemed? She pondered how he might react to what she knew.

"Speak up, girl. It's written all over your face," Kushim urged, his previous disinterest replaced by a piercing gaze.

Taking a deep breath, Saoka revealed, "You're not the only one with purple eyes."

Kushim's demeanor shifted instantly, his casual air replaced by a stern intensity. "Repeat that," he demanded.

Saoka repeated herself, and Kushim gasped.

"How in the, where, when, a name? Tell me everything, every small detail right now," Kushim said while putting his hands on Saoka's shoulders and shaking the girl.

"Release the youngster if you please," Mayuki warned.

Moments later, he relented. He didn't, however, stop glaring into Saoka's soul.

Saoka gulped. Then she went about recounting every modest detail of the Battle of Kazuno. How the demon-human hybrid who was the leader of the demons had purple eyes and used spells with ease. Then she went back further and gave up half a name. Iry-H, she remembered.

"That is impossible," he whispered. "He and all the others are dead."

"Who, what others?" Saoka asked.

Kushim had a far-off look on his face but began to recount his thoughts. "Iry-Hor is his full name. He was once like an older brother to me, one of the mightiest magic users of my people.

Like me, he survived the cataclysm. Also, like me, he believed, or it seems, used to believe in the cause of protecting this world and helping humanity to rebuild. He was even the first ruler of—"

"Egypt, about three thousand years ago," Saoka said, finishing Kushim's sentence for him. She learned everything from the books gathered by the Order. There were still great gaps in her knowledge of history, but wherever she could, she would try to plug those gaps.

Kushim tilted his head, and his eyes widened a fraction. "I had heard he was killed along with his wife and child in a terrible accident. If he's a demon now, then we are in more trouble than I thought."

"He knows about the gates. He knows all your secrets because he's one of your people," Mayuki interjected.

"We are in trouble because he's powerful and cunning, but actually he does not know much about the gates. It was common practice among our leaders to keep the locations of gates secret. We were an empire, but at times, a fractured one. When new gates were made, they weren't always reported.

Someone got around to accounting for them all; that information wasn't common knowledge. Of course, everyone knew of the gates that led to our major cities, but the more backwater locations were kept from the public.

While a powerful magic user, Iry-Hor was not a politician of the empire, nor did he hold any position within the government. He was a merchant. Adept at trade, negotiations, and—"

"Information?" Mayuki asked.

"Well, yes, I suppose anything is possible. Still, you said he knew of the gate but didn't know its exact location. Also, a majority of the gateways were destroyed or flooded, thus rendered useless. Most of the other portals are well protected, with those protectors having explicit instructions to destroy the gate if it was in threat of being captured.

The real threat is not his use or knowledge of the gates. No, he has a far deadlier tool at his disposal. He knows how to make demons of the third tier. Demons of the second kind don't have the life-creating magic to help him in that task. Otherwise, the Earth would have already fallen. He himself can't do it either, as he's now a demon himself."

"He needs humans with magic," Saoka reasoned out loud.

"Yes, and a lot of them, and preferably ones who know how to use magic," Kushim added.

"He's after the women of the Order. That's his next target," Mayuki said.

"How can you be so confident?" Saoka asked.

"Well, that's what I would do. We know the magic is fading faster in other areas. There are not many countries with a high enough concentration of magic users for him to harvest from. Wa is his best bet. The magic is still strong there. He already controls Hokkaido. He may have what he needs already," Mayuki stated.

"Yes and no, the magic it takes to perform such a thing is often dangerous to the caster. An uncaring demon in a haste might kill many magic handlers just to produce one demon-human hybrid. You also have to use a magic user in the process, so you lose a person there. Not to mention the failure rate. Sixty-five percent was the recorded number from the empire's records. If you tried to make ten of the bastards, six are going to die," Kushim said.

"Wouldn't it be easier to produce more of the second type of demon? We saw quite a few at Kazuno," asked Saoka.

"Yes, you are correct. Still, the success rate isn't great," Kushim answered.

"We have to make sure his access to any magic user is limited. I believe I must return to Wa and inform the Mothers at once. We should start rounding up any women who aren't members of the Order who use magic, as well as round up boys and girls who haven't yet shown an ability in magic.

It runs in the family, so we can narrow down the numbers that way. The Order in Wa does keep fairly good records. With your permission, Master Kushim, I'd like to depart now," Mayuki said.

Kushim nodded his agreement.

Mayuki turned to leave, and Saoka made to follow before he laid a gentle hand on her shoulder. "I think Mayuki is up to the task, dear. I have another task I'd like you to start training for."

"You can borrow her, but only for a month. She has duties to fulfill with me as well," Mayuki stated with a hard stare.

IN THE LAND OF NI

Kushim assured her, "One month, and then she's yours again."

Mayuki stepped through the gate back to Nara.

Saoka's lips pouted as she watched Mayuki's retreating figure, her shoulders slumping and her fingers clenching at her sides, feeling like a pawn in their plans.

Once alone with Kushim, Saoka's curiosity got the better of her. "Where exactly am I?"

"You're in Persia," Kushim revealed with a chuckle at her wide-eyed wonder. He promised her a tour and a meal before retiring to her quarters for the night.

The caverns of Kushim's abode were a labyrinth, and Saoka struggled to remember the twists and turns. Her room was simple: a bed, a desk, a chair, and a pile of books. Her stomach, however, dictated her priorities, and she devoured the meal brought by Kushim's assistant before sleep claimed her.

Saoka woke early, dressed, and headed toward the door. She opened it at the same time a stranger made to knock.

What a stunning stranger. I could eat him up; he's so damn cute. And strong-looking. The man had bronze skin and blue eyes.

Saoka did not know anyone with blue eyes. She found them lovely. He was wearing some strange golden breastplate and something akin to a skirt. He had a sword buckled at his waist.

He tried to speak to her, but she couldn't understand and gestured as much. He switched to another language. Still, she didn't understand. He switched to Persian.

"Yes, I can understand you now," she said.

"Great, my name is Pausanias. Kushim told me yours is Saoka, is that correct?" Pausanias asked.

Why does my name sound so good mispronounced on his lips? "Oh, yes, although the first part is pronounced 'sa.' Um, Pausanias, is there any way to get breakfast around here? I'm really hungry."

He laughed and said, "A woman after my own heart."

More than you might suspect.

He gestured for her to follow.

"Kushim said that he would like us to train together. You are to try and teach me how to use magic, and I'm supposed to teach you some history and how to fight," Pausanias stated.

Saoka raised an eyebrow. She had never taught anyone how to use magic before, and certainly not a man. "I already know how to fight, thank you very much," she answered.

Pausanias looked a little distraught before saying, "Excuse my presumptuousness; I was only following directions. I hope I haven't offended you."

Saoka, for her part, blushed and said, "Sorry, no, I get cranky in the mornings before I eat. I'm new to Persia and have never been outside my own country, Wa, so I'm a little on edge, I suppose. Also, I am competitive and try to learn everything I can. So, I have read many history books, and I have honestly never taught anyone to use magic. I'm a little more than a newcomer to the Order. I just became a sister a little over a month ago, and I—wait, you don't know what a sister is, do you?"

"Never heard of it, sorry. Until about two weeks ago, I didn't even know that there was a country called Wa. In any case, Kushim must have his reasons. I am sure he saw some potential in you; he said as much. I would consider it a kindness if you taught me what you know, and I will teach you what I know. Consider it a trade," he said, while holding out his hand.

Was she supposed to take it? In Wa, people bowed; was this some sort of courting ritual, Saoka wondered.

Pausanias must have recognized her hesitancy and said, "In my country, we extend our hands like so and grip the forearm of the other person as a greeting or when reaching an agreement."

"Ah, I see. After careful consideration, I have agreed to your

IN THE LAND OF NI

terms, Mr. Pausanias. Here, let me try this forearm gripping," Saoka said, seizing his arm. His hand seized hers back, and while a calloused one, it still felt smooth and gentle. Pausanias then realized he lingered in his touch a little too long and released his grip. He blushed.

Over breakfast, Saoka inquired about his origins. "I hail from Sparta, in Greece," Pausanias shared.

"Greece? I've never heard of it," Saoka admitted between bites.

His laughter filled the canteen, prompting her to frown. "Is my ignorance amusing to you? Am I to be laughed at for not knowing your tiny unimportant country?"

"Not at all," Pausanias assured her. "Tiny?" He placed his hands close together and started spreading them out in increments as he talked.

"The Greek empire's influence stretches across the Mediterranean, the western coast of Persia, Egypt, northern Africa, Macedonia, and beyond. And my laughter was not at your expense—it was the irony of our situation. We're united against demons, yet we're strangers to each other's lands."

Saoka nodded, her interest piqued. "I'm familiar with Egypt, at least through books."

"But you can't speak the language," he teased.

"Point taken. So, where does your mighty Greece lie on a map?"

"Directly north of Egypt, across the sea," Pausanias explained.

"Tinayu, the Egyptians' name for your country. Keftiu, perhaps?" Saoka ventured, recalling her studies.

"Indeed, Keftiu is what we call Crete, part of the Greek isles. I'll show you the maps later," Pausanias offered.

"I'd like that. Perhaps I can share about Wa and its neighbors in return," Saoka replied, her voice tinged with excitement.

"Shall we begin our training then? Magic or combat first?" Pausanias asked, eager to start.

"Magic, since it's not your forte," Saoka decided.

Pausanias's attempts at magic were dismal, despite his strong aura.

Saoka learned he hailed from a world where magic had faded into myth. They spent hours daily on meditation, making slow progress. Saoka admired his Spartan determination.

In turn, Pausanias found teaching history to Saoka effortless.

She devoured texts and filled gaps in her knowledge with ease, impressing him with her voracious intellect. During training, her arrows hit the target with impressive accuracy, but when she switched to swordplay, her strikes lacked precision and her footing was unsteady. She fumbled with the spear, struggling to maintain balance, and her knife throws often missed the mark. Pausanias's rigorous training sessions pushed her to improve.

One day, curious about his prowess, Saoka inquired about his combat experience. Pausanias suggested sparring with his Spartan comrades. The following day, he stepped onto the training ground, ready to face them. His movements were fluid and precise, each strike and parry reflecting a life dedicated to battle. He outmatched them all, his prowess evident in every motion.

As Saoka watched, she noticed that meditation wasn't the key to Pausanias's magic. His true essence revealed itself in the heat of combat. During a particularly intense sparring session, she saw his aura flare to life, a radiant display of his inner power. She raised her hand, halting the duel with a sudden realization.

"Your magic—it's unlocked through battle!" she exclaimed, attacking him playfully. In an instant, he disarmed her, his wooden sword tapping her backside.

Over the course of the following week, Pausanias woke extra early to train with the other Spartan men and a group of male magic users. "It is only with men such as you that I am challenged. I ask you all to do something that I realize is extremely stupid, but I could think of no other way. I asked you to train with live blades," Pausanias said.

IN THE LAND OF NI

Those wonderful bastards grinned in response.

Through the course of an hour, he felt his blood pumping as he fended off the attacks of an Indian man he had met recently. The Indian had experience fighting as a magic user. He used his magic much like Kushim, to speed himself up. This put Pausanias on the back foot. Still, he was catching up.

Was it due to the Indian tiring or him gaining some control of his own magic, Saoka was not sure. The whirl of blades was amazing. Pausanias kept sparing glances at his feet to make sure they were keeping up with the brutal pace. It was dangerous, and the Indian man started to notice, lunging the next time Pausanias looked down and scoring a glancing blow to Pausanias's breastplate.

One of the Indian's friends, who was observing from a corner of the training room, started laughing.

Saoka watched Pausanias's jaw tighten, his eyes narrowing as he faced his opponent. She could almost hear the echoes of laughter from his past training sessions in Sparta, where being mocked was just another trial to endure.

But now, seeing the non-Spartan's derisive smirk, she noticed a flicker of something different in Pausanias's eyes—a flash of anger. His fists clenched at his sides, and his movements became sharper, more aggressive. She realized this taunt had struck a deeper chord, riling him up.

Pausanias snarled and planted his back foot with force. The wooden floor under him snapped, but he didn't notice. He was all over the Indian, cutting, feinting, twirling, slashing. Saoka saw the change in Pausanias's demeanor as he fought.

His eyes blazed with an intensity she recognized—the Spartan battle wrath. It was like a drug, coursing through his veins, driving him to fight harder, faster. Each clash of swords seemed to feed his hunger for more, pushing him to the edge of his limits and beyond.

He took another step forward and swung his sword so fast and hard that he barely had the control to stop at the Indian man's neck. A thin line of blood dripped down, and Pausanias dropped his blade, making a loud clang on the floor of a now completely silent room.

He issued his apologies in Persian. The Indian man waved them off. "Finally, a warrior worthy of hearing my name, although still dawdling as a slug," the Indian man said while pulling Pausanias in for an embrace. "Aadi is my name. And I have much I would like to teach you about your battle magic."

"And I have much I would like to teach you about fighting. Stop telegraphing your left-handed slashes," Pausanias whispered back. Aadi bellowed. The rest of the day, with Saoka listening in and watching, Pausanias was able to reach his magic twice, but both times lost control of it and couldn't find it again.

By the end of their month together, both learned many things. Saoka started studying Greek and had been able to examine a plethora of new books.

Saoka told Pausanias, "I am grateful for your fighting lessons, I feel stronger than ever and I have gained a true understanding of my abilities with weapons. I still have much to learn, and a lot of practice to do, but with time—"

"You will become a competent swordsman soon, I have no doubt," Pausanias cut in.

"I, for my part, haven't made much progress in the ways of enchanting, but at least I found out the secret to getting there. Now it's simply a matter of putting in the work, something I am very comfortable with. I am also thankful for my time with you," he said in her tongue.

Saoka enjoyed the moments she spent teaching Pausanias her language. She saw the way his eyes lit up with each new word, their minds equally sharp. Though nothing had happened between them yet, she felt a growing connection, a mutual attraction simmering beneath the surface.

On their final evening together, Pausanias approached her with a gleam of determination in his eyes. "So, within the next year, I will come to Wa. Kushim told me that he sends a messenger once a month to Nara. I will include messages to you when I can. However, I will be leaving for India, and then to China. Once in China, if possible, I will use the gate there to get to Nara. Then I hope to be able to come and find you."

"Whatever for?" Saoka said.

"Well, I had fun; I hope you did too. Plus, I never finished training you, and you're still pretty incompetent with that sword of yours," Pausanias said, sticking his tongue out.

"Not nearly as bad as you with magic. Would Kushim allow you to do that? Come all the way to Nara, to Wa?"

"Yes, I already asked him, plus I don't take orders from him. I agreed to join, not be a slave. He holds a lot of cards, that one, but he can't be everywhere all at once. Also, he admitted to grooming the both of us."

"Grooming? For what?"

"Wa is where I would eventually go anyway, along with most of the Order. That's where the big battles will be conducted. Kushim needs generals. Smart ones, with magic, able to communicate with many peoples, think for themselves. We're both young, but he knows what we do and…" Pausanias said.

"That we are coming into our own, grand, important pieces on his game board," Saoka finished the thought for Pausanias, who smiled and made to leave. She put a hand up to stop him. She gave him a quick hug, nothing too intimate, just enough to let him know she cared.

"I'll be waiting for those letters. See you within a year, Spartan."

CHAPTER 15

299 B.C.E. Father onward to India

A sudden gust of wind conjured the camaraderie of long journeys, where laughter and banter echoed against the backdrop of vast, rolling landscapes and thick forests. Pausanias had also found himself on such a journey.

Pausanias, Sabas, Aadi, and Dilios made their way through a thick jungle, led by ten guides Aadi had hired.

Pausanias wiped the sweat from his brow, his breath coming in labored puffs. "This jungle is nothing like what I expected. I thought India was supposed to be scorching and arid."

"That's just what you learned in books," Aadi replied, cutting away a vine.

"Hot and dry is something any Greek appreciates. This area of India is blistering and not dry. This damn jungle—wet, humid, and miserable. Everywhere I look there is green," Pausanias said, waving his arms.

Moss carpeted the jungle floor, and every step squished underfoot. The ferns, a hundred shades of green, towered over them, and even the mist seemed tinged with green, blending seamlessly with the canopy above.

"It's as if nature had grown wild and lazy at the same time," Sabas added.

Thick vines hindered progress, streams and swamps were abundant and covered with algae.

"One is almost happy to see a member of the local wildlife because it's not green," Pausanias said.

"Not really. Most of the local life is dangerous. Snakes, wild elephants, tigers, poisonous frogs trick you into believing they are cute because of their out-of-place colorful bodies—oranges, blues. Their bodies don't care about blending in. They're the masters of their realms," Aadi said.

"Shit," grumbled Sabas.

"Rain should have brought some comfort. In Greece, precipitation drops temperatures rapidly and clear skies follow. Here, it only makes things worse. The plants gobble up rain, churning the jungle mists incessantly on. Dampness penetrated everything," Pausanias said through gritted teeth.

"Even your female undergarments?" Sabas asked.

Everyone laughed.

Aadi moved to the back of their group. "It's impossible to keep dry for long, and if you march too much in one day, that moisture only helps ensure your clothes stick and chafe your body."

A week passed since they ventured into the heart of the rainforest. The two-week descent from the mountains of Bactra challenged them with cold and dry conditions. The abrupt climate shift hit Pausanias hard.

He paused, his breath ragged, then continued beside Sabas, determined. "I've been grappling with recent events in Persia; I wasn't mentally prepared for a mere change in weather. A Spartan should never be caught off guard by such simplicity."

"Learn from it," Sabas answered.

They followed the jungle guides, slashing at intrusive vines, and placing one foot ahead of the other.

Months in the mountains taught Pausanias much, but uncertainty lingered about the demons' plans and whereabouts. He met ancient mountain tribes, fire worshipers who balanced agriculture with nomadic life, absorbing their wisdom but finding few concrete leads. Mud-brick huts and caves were their homes, reflecting the resilience of a simple yet robust people.

"How far are we from clearing the rainforest?" Pausanias asked.

"Two days away," answered a guide.

"Sabas, my brother in arms," Pausanias said, his voice heavy with concern, "the road ahead is fraught with unknown peril. I cannot bear the thought of leading more of our kin to their end."

Dilios walked over. "We know. That's why, before entering Kushim's mountain palace, you sent the rest of the Spartans back home. Not willing to risk more lives on what could be a one-way journey. And that is why I refused to leave."

"Thank you, my friend. I say a prayer for Pleistarchos and Polydorous, named after kings of Sparta. Both fought bravely, and I vow to recount their tales to their families upon returning to Greece. They died honorably in the same ambush that killed Ardeshir after starting out on this insane quest," Pausanias said. He looked down, his shoulders sagging and his eyes clouded with sorrow.

"Hey, my Indian," Pausanias shouted behind him.

"Much to my chagrin," Aadi replied. "The persistent use of the nickname entertains you in a peculiar Spartan way."

"Aadi, you have proven to be an exceptional fighter, aiding me in unlocking more facets of my magic. I can now maintain it for a considerable duration—five minutes. Moreover, I occasionally summon my magic without succumbing to a battle rage."

"What you need is reassurance that your ability to call upon your magic at will is imminent."

IN THE LAND OF NI

"You read my mind. I find myself questioning how best to utilize it."

"Through speed boost and enhanced strength."

"While potent, I struggle to integrate them seamlessly into my combat repertoire."

"Give it time, my Spartan."

They stopped for lunch in a small clearing, sitting down to eat.

Pausanias gazed into the distance. "The thought of Greece is a balm for my weary soul. Kushim, against all odds, has granted us a communication line to our homeland."

Sabas stopped chewing. "Your words bring warmth, Pausanias. To set foot upon Grecian soil, to breathe its air... it is a dream I dare to nurture. Would you bring Saoka?"

Pausanias smiled. "Yes, I would."

A guide interjected, "My lords, the flatlands will offer respite, but be wary. The jungle awaits our return; the flatlands only stretch so far."

Pausanias nodded. "We shall face what comes with the strength of our forebears. Let us prepare for the journey ahead."

Pausanias and his companions pressed on through the flatlands beyond the rainforest's edge. Though less dense, the vast expanse tested their endurance and resolve. The guides led the way, their familiarity with the land evident as they maneuvered.

Pausanias's thoughts turned to Saoka daily. He had intended to travel directly to Wa through the gates, but Kushim persuaded him to detour to India for recruitment before venturing into China.

There, Pausanias and his men would gather materials crucial for the impending battles against the demons. Kushim remained tight-lipped, yet Pausanias, ever the obedient Spartan, stood ready.

A day into their journey across the flatlands, an unsettling tension cut through the air. The jungle's usual symphony fell silent. The guides shot each other anxious looks, and the stoic Aadi picked up on the atmospheric change.

Pausanias tightened his grip on his sword. Sabas and Dilios flanked him, their senses heightened, ready for whatever awaited them. The guides halted, their eyes scanning the horizon.

A guttural growl echoed through the air. The ground trembled beneath their feet as a creature emerged from the shadows of the flatlands. The Nawarupa, a mythical amalgamation of nine different animals, stood before them—an abomination of nature, a creature of nightmares.

Its body, a grotesque patchwork, bore the head of a lion, its eyes ablaze with an otherworldly intensity. Serpentine coils writhed in place of a tail, and feathers adorned its back like a macabre mantle.

Each limb belonged to a different creature—a bear's claw, an elephant's leg, a tiger's paw, and more. The air crackled with a dark energy, and the Nawarupa emitted an otherworldly growl that reverberated through the flatlands.

Pausanias's instincts kicked in, and without a word, he signaled to his companions.

Sabas and Dilios flanked the creature, swords drawn.

Aadi, beside Pausanias, focused his magical prowess, ready to unleash its power.

The Nawarupa lunged forward, its movements a chaotic dance of mismatched limbs.

Pausanias met its charge, his sword clashing against the creature's head, and bouncing off.

Sabas and Dilios attacked from the sides, aiming for vulnerable joints amidst the creature's disparate limbs.

Ferocity and desperation painted the battle as the Nawarupa lashed out at strange angles. Its limbs, each a separate beast's strength and agility, thrashed independent of the others.

Pausanias, his Spartan discipline in full display, weaved through the barrage, each dodge a dance of death.

Aadi's spells wove seamlessly into his ally's steps, lending supernatural swiftness and sharpness to Pausanias's reflexes.

Sabas and Dilios struck in harmony, their blades seeking the creature's limbs.

The Nawarupa spewed venomous fumes while shadows writhed around its form, rendering it a phantom in battle. The toxic cloud claimed two mercenaries and a bow-wielding scout who ventured too close.

The clash crescendoed, steel sang against the roars and the sinister hiss of dark magic.

Pausanias, alongside Sabas and Dilios, fought with a warrior's grace, their shared battle rhythm essential in the fray.

Aadi, tapping into his arcane wellspring, conjured shields and hurled energy bolts, disrupting the Nawarupa's relentless assault.

Pausanias discerned a rhythm in the Nawarupa's chaos.

Each disparate limb bent to one sinister will.

A spark of strategy ignited in his mind, a plan to turn the creature's fused nature against it.

"Everyone, aim for a different creature," Pausanias yelled. They adjusted their tactics.

Sabas and Dilios focused on disrupting the Nawarupa's coordination.

Sabas targeted the serpent-like tail, aiming to sever it and hinder its mobility.

Dilios concentrated on the limbs, aiming for joints and weak points.

Aadi intensified his magical support, creating illusions and flashes of light to disorient the Nawarupa.

Pausanias seized the opportunity. His sword became a blur as he aimed for the lion head.

The Nawarupa, caught off guard by the change in strategy, staggered under the relentless assault.

Pausanias's strikes, fueled by his Spartan discipline and magical enhancements, targeted the lion head's eyes and throat.

The creature roared in agony, its disjointed limbs momentarily losing their predatory coordination.

Sabas and Dilios exploited the Nawarupa's vulnerability. Sabas severed the serpent tail, causing the creature to thrash in pain.

Dilios, with a precise strike, disabled one of its mismatched limbs.

As the Nawarupa weakened, Pausanias pressed the advantage. He delivered a final, decisive blow to the lion head, severing it at the neck.

The battle cries of victory echoed through the flatlands as the Nawarupa's dismembered parts convulsed and then lay still.

CHAPTER 16

Magumi felt the caress of the wind from atop Mt. Akiha. It carried whispers of ancient secrets, inviting her to meditate on the interconnected threads that bind all living things across time and space. Such a wind reminded her of the mysteries of life and of a grand mystery awaiting to be uncovered by Saoka in Kusatsu.

Saoka stepped through the magical gate into Nara, feeling the energy swirl around her like a warm embrace. Sisters welcomed her with bows, and a guard led her out to the city.

Ancient temples rose amidst rustling leaves, and distant temple bells added a backdrop to the peaceful air. The sun cast a warm, golden hue over the city.

As she walked, Saoka admired the grand temples and vibrant red shrines. Locals greeted her, recognizing her as a Sister of the Order. Children waved, their eyes wide, while elders nodded.

The guard led Saoka to a modest lodge tucked away from the bustling streets. *Mayuki sure does like her privacy.* The lodge was surrounded by a garden of blossoming cherry trees, their petals drifting gently to the ground like soft, fragrant snow.

Inside, a young woman dismissed the guard and guided Saoka to Mayuki's cozy room, filled with plush cushions and soft, inviting furniture. The room exuded warmth and comfort. Soft lantern light cast a gentle glow.

Saoka barely had a moment to settle before Mayuki approached her with a solemn expression, a parchment bearing the seal of the ancient order in her hand. Saoka's heart raced, but then Mayuki's serious face broke into a grin. "Had you going there for a second, didn't I?" she said with a playful wink.

Saoka laughed, relieved. "Hello to you too. How's everything here in Wa? I have so much to tell you about my month away." She hesitated, thinking of her budding romance with Pausanias. *Would Mayuki approve?* She felt a flutter in her breast.

Mayuki's playful demeanor faded, her lips pressing into a thin line. "We have a new mission—an expedition to ancient Kusatsu in search of a mysterious magical relic. It's said to possess powers lost to the annals of time. Recent disturbances in the balance of magical energies suggest the relic's dormant power might be reawakening."

Saoka furrowed her brow. "Aren't relics supposed to just do their thing? What's this about reawakening?"

Mayuki huffed, her eyes rolling. "I don't know all the details. There was a relic from Kushim's time, buried near the magical Kusatsu hot springs. It's been emanating magic, attracting yokai to the area. The dense magic makes pinpointing its exact location difficult. We sent a message to Kushim, and he believes it's a reaction to the waning magic surrounding the area. He says the relic is both dangerous and useful, so we need to retrieve it."

"What can we do that the other sisters in the area can't?"

"Maybe a fresh set of eyes. Apparently, Kushim had it buried by his subordinates when the Order first came to these shores. The exact location was lost due to shifting topography, and the only written record was destroyed in a monsoon eighty years ago."

Saoka shook her head, a slight smile playing on her lips. "Can that guy ever stop being so mysterious? Seems like an oversight to have only one written record."

Mayuki chuckled and took Saoka's hand, guiding her to the western-facing balcony. "There's an onsen bath waiting for you. You need it. You've been spending too much time with the boys."

"You're a goddess."

Saoka cooed in relief, feeling the tension of her journey melt away. The chrysanthemum-scented water refreshed her.

After washing thoroughly, she returned to find dinner laid out on a low-sitting table. The aroma of freshly cooked rice and delicately seasoned vegetables filled the room. Mayuki gestured for her to sit.

"Say, Mayuki, does this relic have anything to do with that map the dragon gave you? I confess I forgot about it, which I admit is crazy."

"No, dear, that's for me alone. Now tell me about your month away."

They talked for hours, sharing stories and laughter, before deciding to sleep.

The next day, Saoka and Mayuki met their escort near the city gates. They mounted their horses and set off from Nara, the rhythmic beat of hooves echoing through ancient forests. The air filled with the fragrance of blooming sakura, their petals drifting lazily like confetti.

Mayuki led the way, her chin held high. Saoka rode a step behind, her gaze shifting between the towering trees and distant mountains.

As they traveled, Mayuki recounted tales of Kusatsu's ancient past. "Legends whisper that this land was touched by the divine, and its very soil holds echoes of forgotten epochs."

Saoka, eager to impress, recited poetry while they rode. "The landscape unfurls before us like a living tapestry. Emerald valleys stretch beneath the azure sky, and crystal-clear streams meander through the meadows. Deer graze peacefully, and butterflies dance in the sunlight."

"Boring," Mayuki teased with a smirk.

Two days from Kusatsu, the journey took a turn.

They traveled on a narrow mountain trail that wound through thick forests and steep slopes. The crisp breeze refreshed Saoka. As they ventured deeper into the mountains, the dense vegetation thinned, revealing a serene valley bathed in dappled sunlight.

A massive figure emerged from a thicket of bamboo, capturing their attention and eliciting a collective gasp.

An ijū stood before them; it had a mane of long, flowing hair and a gentle gaze. It resembled a man-like monkey, hairy all over with long claws.

The group gaped at the living embodiment of Wa folklore. The creature stood twice the size of a man.

Mayuki offered a respectful nod and a soft smile. Saoka, though surprised, sensed the creature's benevolence in its slow movements and bowed head. It radiated natural earth magic.

The soldiers watched, hands close to their weapons.

Following tradition, Mayuki retrieved food from a provision bag and extended a portion of rice to the ijū. The creature's eyes gleamed as it accepted the offering, devouring it calmly. Its movements were graceful.

It stood still for a moment, then gestured towards the mountain pass ahead. Mayuki interpreted the silent communication, whispering to Saoka and the soldiers that the ijū granted them safe passage.

The travelers, as one, bowed deeply.

With a final nod, the ijū retreated into the bamboo thicket, disappearing.

IN THE LAND OF NI

Two mornings later, emerging from the pass, they found Kusatsu Onsen. Thatched roofs and wooden facades against rolling hills, lantern-lit streets warming the cobblestones. Cherry blossoms adorned the thoroughfares, their petals dancing in the zephyr. Saoka squealed and sighed.

The hot springs' sulfur scent mingled with the mountain air. Locals in traditional attire walked along roads, their wooden sandals clapping off the stones. Saoka followed Mayuki past the Yubatake, where hot spring waters flowed down seven long wooden conduits into a huge turquoise pond.

Entering a quaint teahouse, Mayuki exchanged polite greetings with the proprietor, a wise elderly woman in a traditional hemp robe. The air inside was fragrant with green tea, and the straw mat floor invited the group to sit and partake in the age-old ritual. The setting was serene, offering a moment of peace and reflection.

As they sipped the steaming tea, Mayuki asked the elder, "We're seeking information about the ladies of the Order?"

After a brief respite and their questions answered, Saoka and Mayuki resumed their journey. Venturing a couple of miles east of Kusatsu, they entered a secluded area where the sisters of their order resided.

Sunlight filtered through the lush canopy, casting patterns on the forest path. Birds chirped, their melodies blending with the rustle of leaves.

Approaching a clearing, soft murmurs reached their ears. Emerging from the woods, they discovered a group of women clad in flowing robes of muted earth tones. Some tended a communal garden, others sat in meditation or practiced martial arts.

Saoka and Mayuki, recognizing the Order's garb, were met with warm smiles from the sisters and their leader, a salt-and-pepper aged Blessed. They exchanged respectful bows. "Welcome, sisters. My name is Yoko."

Seating themselves on woven mats, Saoka said, "We're here to help find the relic."

"Yeah, we heard help might be coming. The sisters here are trying to tap into the spiritual energy that flows through Kusatsu. It's deeply connected to the elemental forces, and we need to keep that balance," Yoko said, her hands on her hips. "I can see that fate brought us together. Your help is definitely welcome. Stay with us tonight, and we'll get started in the morning."

Mayuki, always the one to lighten the mood, chimed in, "So, Yoko, where can a good girl like me find a stiff drink around here, or anything stiff really?"

Yoko laughed, the sound a light, musical note.

At dawn, the sisters commenced their quest. Yoko led them to a cliff. Yoko, glowing with an otherworldly light, channeled the mystical forces, orchestrating the group's ceremonies.

Despite her status, Saoka felt disconnected, her recent magical practice lacking. She focused, determined to bridge the gap.

The ritual, a symphony of chants and symbols, connected the sisters to the earth's energies. Saoka and Mayuki delved into the mystical performance, searching for the hidden relic. The air hummed with energy, the ground beneath them pulsing with life.

Yoko explained, "The sisters of Nara go deeper into their mystical practices than most. We use creatures living underground to help us see, to feel, a network of passages. Most of these routes are too small, made by worms and moles. We can ignore those and focus on finding a larger passage leading to a hidden chamber."

Saoka and Mayuki moved in unison, their hands clasped, eyes closed, breathing in the earthy scent of pine and moss. A soft glow emanated from their intertwined fingers. The ground vibrated underfoot. Blue light swirled around the sisters, lifting their hair in a silent breeze. The fabric of reality thinned, and for a moment, the barrier between the physical and the mystical blurred.

"This is exhausting," sighed Mayuki after a fruitless day.

The following day, they tried again. Two hours later, the combined force of all the sisters revealed the relic's hidden chamber.

"We found it," exclaimed a sister, discovering a cavern filled with artifacts from an older Wa.

The rest of the morning, the sisters of the order dug earth and removed rocks until they found a passage. Inside, amidst the relics, lay a pulsating artifact, its glow casting eerie shadows on the cavern walls.

Yoko moved a clay pot aside, revealing a simple necklace with a purple gem. "No idea what that thing does, but it reeks of magic," she said, tossing it to Mayuki.

With heartfelt thanks and quick goodbyes, Saoka and Mayuki began to make their way back to Nara.

The very next day, trouble appeared.

The sisters of the Order and their guards encountered a pair of yokai.

The yokai appeared by the side of the road, startling the group. One was a raccoon in priestly robes; the other, a female yokai with a snail's head, wore a beautiful multi-layered dress.

The guardsmen prepared to attack, but the yokai raised their hands in a gesture of goodwill.

The raccoon spoke, "Strange magic you're carrying. It would be wise to get it somewhere safe."

Mayuki and Saoka dismounted and approached the yokai.

"Greetings, travelers. I am Shukaku," the raccoon said, gesturing to his silent companion. "This is Shumoku Musume." He motioned to a log that appeared out of nowhere. "Please, have a seat."

Saoka eyed the log but sat, feeling the solid wood beneath her.

Shukaku produced a pot of tea and cups from his robe. "It's just tea, no tricks," he assured.

Mayuki and Saoka exchanged a glance. "We sense no malice," Saoka said, and they both took a cup, sipping the warm brew.

Saoka felt revived and alert.

"Yes, beloved, it is a healing draught of my own creation. I hope you like it. My snail friend and I will help you escape harm on the road back to Nara. We will go in the other direction, using our magic to distract any foul creatures."

Shumoku Musume bobbed her head and smiled, her eyes big, soft saucers.

Mayuki refused. "I don't want to put you in danger."

"Not to worry. Demons and other yokai aren't interested in us. We taste too much of good magic," Shukaku explained, his voice soothing.

"The tea was delicious, thank you, Shukaku," Saoka said.

"You're welcome, but it's Shumoku's recipe," he replied.

Saoka hugged the snail lady.

Shumoku Musume blushed and turned her head.

The ladies of the Order thanked the yokai and continued their journey. Saoka kept a wary eye on the sides of the road, but no more oddities appeared. Her thoughts drifted to more mundane things, the scenery blurring as she focused on the task ahead.

They reached Nara and passed through the magical gate to Persia.

Kushim awaited them, seated at his desk, his back straight and shoulders squared.

Mayuki and Saoka stood in front of the desk. "We found your relic," Mayuki said, as she tossed it to him.

"Good. Now, I need you to go through the gate to Nara and

IN THE LAND OF NI

deliver messages to the Mother. Afterwards, use the gate again to go to China and wait for Pausanias. He has made fantastic progress in reaching Pataliputra and convinced a large contingent of the Indian army to join with the Order. They are marching for the gate in China," Kushim said. He gazed at them and folded his hands.

Saoka's heart fluttered. She tried to suppress her emotion under the watchful eyes of Mayuki and Kushim.

"What about this relic of yours? What is it, and what does it do?" Mayuki asked.

"Well, it's a necklace. It's damaged. I can fix it, but it will take time and energy. It allows the user to collect latent magic from the surrounding area, amplifying their magic by multiples," Kushim said.

"Aren't you strong enough as it is?" Saoka asked, her brow furrowing.

"It's not for me. No, I'm never strong enough. Are you? We all seek to become stronger. Now, before you ask any more questions, I refuse to answer. I have much to do today. See yourselves to the gate," Kushim said, waving them away.

Mayuki nodded to Saoka, and they left. Before stepping through the gate, Mayuki stopped at a storage room and pilfered an old bottle of wine. She gestured for Saoka to keep silent.

Saoka giggled all the way through the gate.

CHAPTER 17

In the ancient forest of Ni, Magumi marveled at leaves caught in a whimsical dance. Their erratic journey symbolized the unpredictability of travel, where each turn may reveal unforeseen wonders or challenges. Not unlike the wild, unpredictable nature of Pausanias's trip into India, and on through to China.

Pausanias and his allies approached the ancient city of Pataliputra, a bustling metropolis along the banks of the Ganges River. Towering structures of wood and stone adorned the cityscape, showcasing the architectural prowess of the Mauryan Empire.

"The city's grandeur tells a rich history through its ancient walls and bustling streets," Aadi said, spreading his arms wide.

The group entered through the city gates, where intricate carvings depicted scenes of mythical conquests and divine blessings. Aromas of spices and incense filled the air, mingling with the myriad sounds of the bustling market.

The streets teemed with people from all walks of life. Stalls lined the thoroughfares, adorned with colorful fabrics and intricate jewelry, creating a kaleidoscope of vibrant hues. "What's that?" Pausanias asked, pointing at a towering structure.

"The city's heart, the magnificent palace complex. Its spires reach towards the heavens. The palace grounds below sprawl over a vast expanse, adorned with manicured gardens, reflecting pools, and pavilions dedicated to various aspects of art, culture, and governance," Aadi explained.

Clad in their distinctive Spartan armor, Pausanias and Sabas drew curious glances from the locals. The denizens of Pataliputra, familiar with their city's diversity, raised their eyebrows and offered close-mouthed smiles to the newcomers.

City guards, wearing ornate armor with symbols of the empire, saluted formally as Pausanias and his companions passed through the main thoroughfare.

"They sure know how to impress," Sabas whispered under his breath, eyes wide in admiration.

One of their guides gestured to the right. "You should stay at that nice stone inn over there."

Aadi perked up. "Oh yes, I forgot. That inn's specialty is two drinks produced from sugar cane. One is a simple juice, and the second, a liquor produced from fermentation. Let's book some rooms."

The travelers refreshed themselves upon entering the establishment, which smelled faintly of herbs and wood smoke. The distant chatter of patrons and the clinking of pottery filled the air. "Oddly, it isn't as sweet as I expected," Pausanias said.

"The liquor is sweeter and packs quite a punch. Promise to wait to consume it until I return from my duty," Aadi said. He took his leave to seek an audience with the King.

Aadi returned with a spring in his step and informed Pausanias and Sabas, "The king will see us in two days."

With nothing else to do for the day, the group started drinking.

"Ah, that's good," Aadi delighted.

"Aaahh, it burns going down," Sabas said through a burp.

"Gggwwwaaaa," Pausanias replied, grimacing.

Two days later, within the heart of Pataliputra, the group stood in awe of the imperial court. Courtyards, filled with musicians and dancers, wove tales of love, valor, and the divine. The air vibrated with the melodies of sitars and the rhythm of drums, while the scent of sandalwood and jasmine filled their nostrils.

Inside, opulence reigned supreme. "Do you see these tapestries? They depict conquests and prosperity," Aadi said.

"And those golden censers?" Sabas asked with a grunt, pointing to the ornate vessels.

"They carry the fragrance of sacred herbs," replied Aadi, taking in the rich, earthy aroma.

"They stink," Sabas said, holding his nose.

Emperor Bindusara waited within the throne room. His vibrant silk garment, gemstone-adorned bangles, and an antariya signified Pataliputra's rich heritage.

"Emperor, it is a pleasure to meet you. My name is Pausanias, and this is Aadi and Sabas. As Aadi already told your men, our purpose here is to seek knowledge and forge alliances in an effort to destroy the demons. We have traveled from Greece to meet you," Pausanias said, bowing deeply.

The emperor gazed at Pausanias before speaking. Aadi translated, "Welcome to Pataliputra, a beacon of enlightenment. I do indeed have answers to what you seek. Within these majestic walls, let Spartan valor meet Mauryan sagacity. You are invited to address the city council tomorrow. While Emperor, our laws state that I must get approval from the council for important decisions."

"Thank you, Emperor," Pausanias said, bowing and taking his leave.

They made their way back to the inn. Aadi explained along

IN THE LAND OF NI

the way, "The intricacies of governance are entwined with the threads of various belief systems, creating a delicate balance that veers between unity and discord. Pataliputra, a thriving hub of trade, spirituality, and power, harbors a mosaic of political factions, each vying for influence and control."

He pointed out temples dedicated to numerous deities. "The priests wield both spiritual and political authority, a formidable force rooted in the age-old customs that shaped the city's identity."

"However," he stopped beneath a canopy of trees and sighed, "beneath the veneer of religious unity, fractures emerge. Sectarian divides simmer, with various religious groups advocating for their distinct beliefs and practices. The competing voices of Brahmins, Buddhists, Jains, and followers of other spiritual paths create a cacophony of ideologies that often clash."

That night, Pausanias lay on his bed, staring at the wooden ceiling of the inn, his mind churning with the day's revelations. He wrestled with his thoughts, the weight of the impending mission and the city's complex dynamics pressing down on him, straining his chest.

The next day, Pausanias found himself an outsider navigating this complex web. The Brahminical establishment, wary of foreign influences, viewed him with narrowed eyes and upturned corners of pressed lips.

The Buddhist communities, seeking solace in the teachings of Siddhartha Gautama, questioned his motives.

Pausanias, seeking alliances against encroaching demons, navigated a challenging terrain. Political factions, aligned with specific religious affiliations, vied for supremacy. He had to tread carefully on religious fault lines as the city's leadership grappled with tradition versus change.

As the city's leaders debated, whispers of dissent and clandestine alliances filled the air. Frustrated by his inability to understand the various factions' arguments, Pausanias stood up and threw his sword to the ground. The echoing clang captured everyone's attention.

"Aadi, translate what I'm saying," he shouted, before continuing, his voice trembling with a mix of anger and desperation, "Listen, all of you, you won't have a future if you don't decide to help. I've seen more demons here than in my homeland, yet you act like they are a sideshow. They are so much more, and they will come for you and everyone else until all life is dead. No more debates, no more delicious sugar cane spirits. Nothing."

Pausanias's eyes burned with intensity as he paused, taking a deep breath to steady himself. "These demons are not just myths or stories to frighten children. They are real, and I have witnessed their destruction firsthand. Villages razed to the ground; people slaughtered without mercy. If we do not unite and act now, this city will suffer the same fate. I am leaving tomorrow, towards China. If you have a spine at all, maybe you'll take a second to think about saving the world and not just your reputations," he said, his voice now firm with unwavering resolve.

With that, he turned to the Emperor, bowed, and left the palace, his comrades close on his heels.

Thankfully, an hour later they were called back to the palace. Evidently, the council wanted to hear more.

Pausanias, with heartfelt sincerity, warned, "A cataclysm threatens our very existence. Aadi can tell you himself about his time with Kushim and our plight." His words, drawing agreement from divided leaders, emphasized the need for unity.

Sabas, at Pausanias's side, shared tales of their battles, highlighting the strength of their alliance and the urgency for a united stand. The leaders, inspired by their valor, saw the importance of overcoming their differences.

A consensus formed: Emperor Bindusara stood. "The leaders commit their armies, recognizing unity as the key to victory. We

IN THE LAND OF NI

agree to send emissaries and magicians, to reinforce Kushim's outpost, aid Wa, and accompany you to China. Pausanias, you will receive ten thousand soldiers, including one hundred magicians for the journey."

The assembly ended. That night, Sabas laughed, appreciating Pausanias's charismatic storytelling. Their camaraderie lightened the burden of their grave mission.

"Hey, Pausanias, I've got a joke for you!" Sabas said through slurred words.

"Is it another dad joke?" Pausanias groaned.

"How many Spartans does it take to change a torch?" Sabas asked and answered his own question. "None, Spartans don't fear the dark!" It was a terrible joke, but it made Pausanias laugh. He didn't remember falling asleep at the communal table. Awakening the next day with a terrible headache but a sense of happiness, Pausanias gathered himself for the trip into China.

A few days were required to muster the needed men and goods. It took Pausanias a moment to adjust. Aadi told him, "With well-provisioned men and horses, our destination is still some two thousand two hundred and fifty miles away." It was a daunting journey. "We will have to cross mountains, skirt through part of a desert, face more jungle, dense forests, and rolling plains."

Tracking back to Kushim's outpost was not an option due to distance and security concerns.

CHAPTER 18

Pausanias led a small army on a two-month journey to their destination, knowing that bad weather or delays could extend the trip. As they traveled, he pondered the challenges ahead, the potential allies they might encounter, and how to maintain contact with his order.

Accompanying him were skilled Indian guides and advisors. The Pataliputra council had sent messenger birds ahead to secure resources and local guides for the journey. During the nights, Pausanias immersed himself in learning languages and local customs, while his mornings were dedicated to training in combat and magic.

One night, after entering southern China, Pausanias joined Sabas by the campfire. "This journey through these new lands is a test of endurance and diplomacy. I'm exhausted," Pausanias admitted, rubbing his temples.

"Ha, try having these old bones," Sabas said with a chuckle, adding a log to the fire. "We encountered the Pyu people, a civilization rich in culture, and we didn't even know it existed."

Pausanias nodded, a smile tugging at his lips. "Their irrigation systems put Greece to shame. This world is so vast."

Sabas looked up at the stars, his eyes reflecting the flickering

IN THE LAND OF NI

flames. "And in return, you shared our ways, the spirit of Sparta."

Pausanias poured them both a drink. "Now we're meeting the diverse peoples of southern China. Coastal communities the last two days, and today, inland settlements practicing agricultural methods we don't even understand," he said, swirling his cup.

Sabas grunted in agreement. "And there's still so much more out there for us to discover."

Two months into the journey, things took an unexpected turn. Still three weeks from their destination, Pausanias stumbled upon the remnants of a once-thriving Chinese village, now reduced to a grotesque tableau. The air reeked of death. The wooden structures lay in ruins, charred remnants testifying to the brutality that had unfolded.

Pausanias, attuned to magic, felt the lingering stench of demon-wielded powers.

The ground beneath his feet was stained with the blood of innocents, both human and animal. Lifeless bodies lay scattered, limbs twisted in unnatural angles, faces frozen in agony. The merciless demons had left nothing untouched.

"Oh Zeus," Sabas muttered as he dismounted, his eyes wide with horror.

Pausanias moved through the gruesome scene, his boots slipping in slick, coagulating pools of blood. The stench clung to every breath, a putrid miasma that seemed to permeate his very soul.

"This... this is beyond savagery. It's a massacre of the soul itself," Sabas said, his voice trembling.

Pausanias' gaze hardened. "They've not only slain the body but sought to desecrate the very essence of life. Look there—"

He pointed to a grotesque spectacle: a circle of decapitated heads, eyes wide in terror, mouths agape in silent screams. At the center, a blackened heart impaled on a spike, its dark blood spilled onto the white petals of a lone, untouched flower.

Pausanias moved forward, vowing to avenge the fallen and bring justice to those senselessly slaughtered.

Han, his tutor in rudimentary Chinese and a skilled woodsman and tracker, ran up to him. Han pointed to a trail leading away from the village, his eyes darting frantically from shadow to shadow, his hands trembling with rage.

Pausanias clasped his friend's shoulder and ordered, "Men, mount up. We have some revenge to exact."

For two nights, they found no sign of their quarry. At night, Han shared everything he knew about the local demons, mostly legend.

"There's the Aoyin, an appalling beast with long, deadly claws that likes to eat human brains. They look somewhat like upright hyenas," Han explained, his voice low.

"Sounds like a nightmare," Pausanias said, his head cocked to the side in surprise.

"Yes, then there's Daolao Gui, terrible four-legged beasts with short arms on their chests, like a mix of a green and black dog-spider hybrid. They can attack by shooting poisonous projectiles," Han said, glancing around the dark forest.

"Damn, I hate spiders," Sabas said, inspecting his body for any unwelcome creatures.

"I forgot the Duoji, a wolf-like creature with red eyes and a white tail," Han added with a smirk.

No one slept well.

On the morning of the third day, they spotted the demons. Scouting parties from Pausanias's force went out with strict engagement rules. Each party consisted of twenty men. Han and other trackers estimated the fiends numbered around a hundred. "It's difficult to tell as some tracks slither like snakes, while others might belong to monsters with more than two legs," Han summarized.

Pausanias gave the scouting parties simple orders: if spotted by demons, lure them to where Pausanias's main force waited atop a large, wide grassy hill with a small clearing near the edge of the woods that formed a natural curve.

Pausanias addressed his troops, "Dismount and hide the horses behind the hill."

He and Sabas had learned Indian battle tactics. "The Indian army excels in archery and guerrilla tactics and usually uses chariots or elephants. We left them behind in India due to the vast distances we've traveled. I suggest using our archers," Sabas told Pausanias.

"I was thinking the same. Keep twenty percent of the army in reserve to protect the rear, the horses, and the noncombatants traveling with us."

"Right away."

Close to midday, the first riders appeared, galloping at breakneck speed. On their heels were the stuff of nightmares. Pausanias recognized some of the creatures from Han's descriptions.

A boar-like creature with a snake for a tail rounded the corner in the blink of an eye. The riders closed in on their position, riding hard. Pausanias saw the horses' nostrils flared. Damn it all, but the demons were almost as fast.

With a signal, his troops revealed themselves out of the long grasses.

Some demons stopped in their tracks, while others, driven by bloodlust, charged.

Arrows flew as line after line of men let fly. At Sabas' suggestion, they kept their valuable magic users back, having them work together to create a barrier against incoming projectiles.

Some of the more cautious demons began to blast magic toward the hill.

The barrier held, though Pausanias still jumped when colorful explosions rippled in the air mere yards from the front lines.

Sabas grinned and yelled, "More arrows!" Demon hide was tough, but the sheer number of arrows overwhelmed them.

Within minutes, the battle was over. A cheer went up as orders were given to stop firing.

Pausanias called for his most senior magic user to join him near the front. Anahita, a lanky Indian girl with green eyes, stepped forward. "Is it safe to drop the barrier, or can some magic users direct battle magic at the demons to make sure they're dead?" he asked.

"We can maintain a strong barrier while some mages handle the grim business," she assured him.

Fire and lightning crashed into the clearing. A couple of beasts squirmed, thrashed, and died.

As the fires burned out, the wind picked up, covering the surrounding area with the stench of dead demon. It stunk of sulfur, hair, and excrement.

The day was theirs. That night, they honored the dead villagers with a bonfire.

With deliberate caution, the army continued toward the Longyou Caves of China. Two and a half weeks later, a full day out from the caves, they encountered a sizable Chinese army on edge. The Chinese sent messengers to Pausanias to parley.

"We mean no harm. We represent the Order. We only want to kill the demons. General Kushim sent us. Here are our documents," Pausanias said, handing them to a Chinese officer.

Pausanias and his men were quickly accepted and ushered toward the caves and the city surrounding them. Word from Kushim had arrived, and they had been expected.

Outside the caves, a vast Chinese city on water stretched before them. Pausanias halted his horse, mesmerized by the labyrinth of interconnected canals and arching bridges. As he approached the town's edge, the gentle lapping of water against stone created a soothing melody that welcomed him.

The canals, woven like intricate threads, crisscrossed the town, providing both transportation and a lifeline for its inhabitants. Narrow boats glided along the waterways, guided by skilled oarsmen. These vessels, adorned with vibrant silk banners, carried goods, produce, and passengers, creating a bustling and lively scene on the liquid streets.

Arched stone bridges spanned the canals, their elegant curves reflecting in the rippling water beneath. Each bridge had intricate carvings and statues adorning their surfaces. Hanging lanterns, suspended from bridge railings, imbued the town with a warm, golden glow as daylight waned.

The buildings lining the waterways showcased traditional Chinese architecture. Wooden structures with upturned eaves and intricate lattice windows stood along the canal banks. Ornate doorways beckoned visitors, inviting them into hidden courtyards adorned with potted plants and delicate sculptures.

Merchants lined the canal edges, displaying their wares on floating platforms. Colorful silks, exotic spices, and fragrant teas enticed passersby. The air carried the aroma of sizzling street food – skewers of grilled meat, steaming dumplings, and aromatic rice bowls.

Residents and visitors alike meandered through narrow alleys, creating a vibrant tapestry of movement. The constant hum of conversations, laughter, and the occasional musical notes from a street performer contributed to the lively symphony that enveloped the water town.

Pausanias, a stranger in this water world, watched the narrow lanes with curiosity while being led by an entourage of the Chinese army. He caught glimpses of locals practicing ancient arts – calligraphy, martial arts, and traditional live performances.

Pausanias, absorbed in the magic of this ancient water town, couldn't help but marvel at the harmonious coexistence of nature and human ingenuity.

He arrived at the entrance to the caves. Pausanias knew that at the bottom of the cave system lay one of the magical gates that could instantly transport him. He hadn't yet had the opportunity to use it, and if he were honest, the idea made him nervous. The city outside buzzed with activity, but near the cave entrance, it was eerily quiet.

"Why isn't there anyone around?" Pausanias asked. His escort, the elderly General Shang, explained, "For secrecy, only those with high enough rank among the Order are allowed into the caves. Entry to the bottom levels is even more restricted."

Pausanias ventured deeper into the darkness, his steps echoing against the cavern walls. The flickering torchlight illuminated the vast expanse before him.

As he delved further, the silence became palpable, broken only by the distant echoes of water droplets. The caves' architecture created a testament to the ancient craftsmanship of the people who carved them. Massive pillars adorned with ornate patterns supported the expansive chambers.

Pausanias's senses heightened as he navigated the cavernous halls. The air smelled damp, the earthy musk of the caves. Stalactites and stalagmites formed natural sculptures, casting eerie shadows as he passed by.

Mystical symbols adorned the cave walls, depicting scenes of ancient rituals and forgotten stories. Pausanias, unfamiliar with the local scripts, marveled at the artistry and wondered about the tales they told. The flickering torchlight played tricks on the carvings, making them seem to come alive in the shifting shadows.

As he progressed, Pausanias noticed side passages leading to hidden chambers. These enigmatic spaces contained relics and artifacts from bygone eras, offering glimpses into the lives of those who once inhabited these caverns. Dust-covered pottery, remnants of ancient textiles, and tools lay scattered.

Deeper in, the temperature dropped further, and the sound of flowing water reached Pausanias's ears. He followed the subterranean stream, leading him to a cavernous chamber filled with an underground lake, its waters reflected the dim light like liquid silver. Pausanias marveled at the natural wonders hidden beneath the earth's surface, realizing these

IN THE LAND OF NI

caves held not only the secrets of the past but also the key to the future.

As he passed several layers of doors and guards, he entered a room where the ancient gate rested upon a stone wall. At the center of the room stood Saoka, looking impatient but more beautiful than he remembered.

"Pausanias," she greeted him, her voice a mix of relief and irritation. "You're late."

"I've been a bit busy, Saoka," he replied with a grin, stepping closer. "You look well."

"Flattery won't get you out of trouble," she said, though a smile tugged at her lips. "We have much to discuss."

Pausanias nodded, his expression growing serious. "Let's not waste any time, then. Lead the way."

"Finally, what, did you just stroll down here?" she spoke.

"If I had known you were down here, I might have run the other way."

Saoka grinned and ran up to him, kissing him. Pausanias tried to return the favor, but a sound and a flash of light from the side of the room stopped him. Another beautiful woman entered from the gate.

"Saoka dear, I hope I'm not interrupting something," the lady said.

"You wish, bitch," Saoka replied with a laugh.

Pausanias blushed. It took him a moment to realize he was looking at Mayuki, one of the members of the Order, of which Saoka had spoken numerous times. Another moment later, he understood he was being carefully analyzed by Mayuki's gaze. For some reason, he stood straighter, as if being examined by a field marshal of a Spartan regiment.

Mayuki said something to Saoka in their native tongue that Pausanias couldn't understand. He cocked his head to look back at Saoka, who grinned wider. "She said it looks like I found a prize bull," Saoka explained.

Pausanias blushed deep cherry, gathering his wits. Facing

Mayuki once again, he used what little he knew of Saoka's native tongue to say, "Nice to meet you, Mayuki."

She was pleasantly surprised, but before Pausanias could speak further, Saoka interrupted, "We can exchange pleasantries later, Pausanias, we need to go. You've done great work here, but more is needed of us back in Persia. I'll have word sent to your men to follow when they can." Without waiting for him to reply, Mayuki stepped back through the gate, while Saoka started pushing Pausanias from behind.

"Wait a minute now, does, I mean... is this thing sa—" He never got the chance to finish his sentence.

One second, he was in a cave in China; the next, he was back in Persia, staring at an irascible-looking Kushim. *Is everyone I know always this impatient?*

For two days, he updated his associates on recent events, and they reciprocated. "We discovered a powerful artifact," said Saoka, bobbing in her chair.

"And oversaw Wa's affairs," Mayuki added, flicking her hair behind her.

"I have gathered magicians and soldiers globally, leveraging centuries-old favors. The task was immense, involving resource negotiations, feud resolution, and strategic ally placement, all while minimizing demon intelligence," Kushim added, head held high.

Pausanias, elbows on the table, leaned down and rested his chin on curled hands. "What of the demons?"

"There's been an increase in demon attacks in Wa and fewer sightings in the West. I believe the demons are regrouping for bigger conflicts. I insist you, Pausanias, go to Wa for language and magical training, while instructing the people of Wa in large-scale warfare," Kushim said, sipping wine from a golden goblet.

"Who will teach me?" Pausanias inquired after Kushim's lengthy exposition.

"Well, Saoka, of course. I couldn't think of anyone else more qualified and less occupied with matters of rank and state. Plus, I thought you two hit it off," Kushim said matter-of-factly.

Mayuki laughed while reaching for a bottle of Persian wine, before opening her mouth to say, "Oh, I'd say he'd like to hit it alright." She had a way of making people blush. Kushim was unaffected.

Anxious to change the subject, Saoka jumped up. "We can leave anytime, sir. I am keen to get to work."

"Oh, I bet…"

Saoka threw a ball of rolled-up parchment paper into Mayuki's mug. Everyone smiled.

"You can leave tonight if you wish. Pausanias has already supplied me with all his relevant information, and Sabas and Aadi have already arrived. Mind you, I need them to stay here for the time being. They both have skills that are vital for getting some of our newer recruits up to speed," Kushim stated.

Saoka tugged at Pausanias's shoulder for him to rise. He did so, bowed, and bid Kushim goodbye. Mayuki rose as well, nodded to Kushim, and started after the two lovebirds.

CHAPTER 19

296 B.C.E

The distant call of a nightingale mirrored the melody of a time when songs harmonized with the beating hearts of comrades around a campfire. The memory evoked a feeling of joy in Magumi, recalling her first meeting with Pausanias and Saoka in these very woods. Pausanias had arrived on Wa's shores two years earlier and had been traveling the lands ever since, learning. Saoka was ever at his side, and they had married after only a year together.

Entering a concealed position among the brushwood posed no challenge for Magumi. After nearly a millennium, she knew every nook and cranny of the forest. With an innate sense of balance and an ability to shift her weight, she moved as a master of the hunt.

Prowling with a rhythmic crisscross of her paws, Magumi's heart raced with anticipation. As a magical being, she had no need for the same amount of sustenance as the animals she pursued. The thrill of the hunt captivated her—the tension, the razor-sharp focus, the sensation of the wind through her fur. It was an inherent aspect of her nature.

This particular section of the forest held a unique appeal. Nestled on the lakeside of Akiha Mountain, about halfway down, was a flat clearing that provided clear sightlines. To the left, a cliff face served as her hiding spot among the dried-out, leafless brushwood.

Subtle signs of the impending season change were evident. The cloudy sky hinted at rain. Magumi sensed her target approaching. However, a disturbing realization struck her—too fast and accompanied by humans. A male and a female were attempting to pilfer her prey.

A young doe bolted from behind the tree line and flashed across the clearing. Not to be outdone, Magumi dropped all pretense of stealth and ran to intercept the deer, executing a quick, clean kill.

She turned, snarling in the direction from which the deer came.

Two figures emerged from their run.

"Oh shit, a wolf! It's huge! Quick, shoot it!" the man yelled, hastily notching his bow.

"No, wait!" the woman interjected. "Look, that's no normal wolf."

The man hesitated, lowering his bow. "Let's move back slowly. It looks angry."

"Oh, she won't hurt us. Look, she's glowing. She's a spirit, perhaps a Goddess," the woman explained.

"Don't be so sure, human," Magumi replied, causing both humans to stop in their tracks, dumbfounded.

"It can talk, oh holy hells," the man whispered.

"It can hear you too," Magumi added through bared teeth.

"My apologies, Wolf of Ni. We shall not attack; we were startled, is all," the lady responded.

There was something strange about them, Magumi decided.

What were they doing here, and why could they see her? Most people couldn't see her unless she wanted to be seen. Wait, did the girl say "glowing?" Who are they? As if sensing her newfound curiosity, the man took a step forward.

He looked peculiar, dressed in armor she had never seen, carrying a huge gold and red shield, quiver, and a spear across his back. He was donning a helmet that screamed magic. A sword and dagger adorned his waist.

He carefully lowered his bow. "My name is Pausanias, and this is my wife, Saoka. We are here scouting for a place to live. We come in peace and on an important mission. May we have your name?"

"I will decide if you ever get the chance to do either, not that I care for the work of man."

"Oh, silly wolfie," the girl interjected. "We aren't here on any mission from man. We're here to stop Mokushiroku."

Magumi's head spun with questions—why, how, when, where? All she managed to say was, "Magumi. You may call me Magumi."

Magumi observed them with penetrating, glowing eyes. The mention of Mokushiroku stirred ancient memories, like ripples on a tranquil pond disturbed by a sudden gust of wind. The wolf spirit hesitated, her mind delving into the depths of what she knew about this ominous force.

Mokushiroku—the very utterance of the word echoed with foreboding. A term that resonated through the spiritual realms and the natural world alike. Magumi's thoughts intertwined with the ethereal energy that surrounded her, a silent language that only the spirits comprehended.

The humans know of Mokushiroku? Magumi pondered. What twisted path led them to confront this malevolent force?

In the threads of her lupine consciousness, Magumi sifted through prophecies and whispered warnings shared among the spirits. Mokushiroku was not merely a cataclysmic event; it was a convergence of dark energies, a cosmic imbalance threatening the delicate harmony of existence.

Humans, fragile and fleeting, yet embroiled in battles that transcend their ephemeral lives. They seek to halt the encroaching tide of Mokushiroku. Can they, with their mortal strength, withstand the torrent of malevolence?

Pausanias and Saoka, she projected her essence into the spiritual realm. What tale of destiny binds you to the impending darkness?

Pausanias and Saoka exchanged glances, their expressions a mix of wonder and apprehension as they stood before Magumi. The air was heavy with anticipation, and the verdant surroundings stilled in reverence to the unfolding encounter.

"Pausanias and Saoka, seekers of the unseen, bearers of a mission entwined with the threads of fate. Mokushiroku looms on the horizon, casting shadows. Why do you tread this perilous path, and what power guides your steps?"

Pausanias stepped forward, a glint of determination in his eyes. "Magumi, we venture not for conquest or glory but to thwart the encroaching darkness. Our mission is one born of necessity, driven by the encroachment of demons. Mokushiroku threatens all that is sacred, and we aim to defy it."

Saoka, her gaze unwavering, added, "We seek allies. Will you join us on this quest, lend us the guidance only a creature attuned to the whispers of the earth can provide?"

Magumi lowered her head. "Mokushiroku is a force that transcends time and realms. Its tendrils weave through the very roots of existence, threatening the delicate balance crafted by the unseen hands of destiny."

She lifted her gaze once more, locking eyes with Pausanias and Saoka. "I, Magumi, guardian of the ethereal tapestry, sense the gravity of your quest. The ancient pact between spirits and the living binds us. I shall accompany you, not merely as a guide but as a sentinel against the encroaching shadows."

The couple exchanged glances, a mixture of gratitude and realization lighting up their expressions. Magumi's decision carried weight, and the alliance formed in the heart of the verdant wilderness held the promise of destinies intertwined. Together, under the guardian gaze of the wolf spirit, they embarked on a journey to defy the looming darkness of Mokushiroku.

The New Beginning

The morning sun stretched its golden fingers over the clearing, casting long shadows that danced around Magumi. She watched Pausanias and Saoka work tirelessly. They had chosen a spot near the top of Mt. Akiha, where the view stretched for miles, encompassing the vast forests and serene lakes. The humans had begun building their hut, a humble structure made from the sturdy timber of the mountain.

Magumi prowled the perimeter, her keen eyes scanning for any signs of danger. She had agreed to accompany them, yet the decision still felt strange. These humans, with their earnest determination, had a way of drawing her in, and she found herself curious about their lives and their mission.

"Pass me that beam, Pausanias," Saoka called, her voice cutting through the stillness of the morning. Pausanias, his muscular frame glistening with sweat, hoisted the wooden beam, his arms steady as he set it in place.

"You two work hard," Magumi remarked, surprising herself with the casual tone she used. She had grown accustomed to speaking formally, a habit from centuries of solitude and ancient rituals.

"We have to," Pausanias replied, his voice straining under the weight of the beam. "This place will be our home, our sanctuary from the world and its troubles."

IN THE LAND OF NI

Saoka nodded, wiping her brow. "And with Mokushiroku on the horizon, we need a safe place to plan and prepare."

Magumi's ears perked up at the mention of Mokushiroku. Despite the growing familiarity, the word still sent a shiver down her spine. "Tell me more about Mokushiroku," she said, her curiosity getting the better of her.

Pausanias set the beam down and took a deep breath. "Mokushiroku isn't just an event; it's demons and human mercenaries joining forces to plunge the world into darkness. We've fought them and heard their sinister plans."

Saoka added, her eyes serious, "We can't fight it alone. That's why we need allies, like you, Magumi. Your knowledge of these lands and your strength are invaluable."

Magumi nodded, absorbing their words. She had felt the imbalance in the natural world, the unsettling disturbances that hinted at something larger and more dangerous. Yet, hearing it from the humans made it all the more real.

As days turned into weeks, Magumi began to feel a sense of camaraderie with Pausanias and Saoka. They shared stories by the campfire at night, their laughter echoing through the forest. Magumi found herself drawn to their tales of far-off lands and ancient battles, her formal speech gradually giving way to more relaxed, conversational tones.

One evening, as the trio sat around a crackling fire, Pausanias spoke up. "Magumi, have you ever wondered about your own origins? Where you came from, why you are the way you are?"

Her gaze lost in the fire, Magumi recounted her tale. "I have lived for nearly a millennium," she began, her voice soft. "I was once like any other wolf, bound by the laws of nature. But something changed. I was granted a gift—or perhaps a curse—that made me what I am today. A guardian, a spirit of the forest."

Saoka leaned forward, her eyes wide with fascination. "Who granted you this gift?"

"I do not know," Magumi admitted. "The spirits of the forest spoke of an ancient pact, a binding force that connects all living things. But the details are lost to time, like whispers."

Pausanias nodded thoughtfully. "Perhaps our paths were meant to cross."

The months passed, and the hut began to take shape. Magumi watched as Pausanias and Saoka worked together, their bond growing stronger with each passing day. The structure was modest but sturdy, built into the ground to withstand the harshest elements of the mountain.

Near the base of Mt. Akiha lay a small human settlement, the village of Ni. The village consisted of sunken huts with thatched roofs, encircled by a protective moat. Wooden bridges allowed access across the water, and fields of crops surrounded the settlement, a testament to the villagers' hard work. Pausanias and Saoka often visited Ni to trade and gather supplies. They would return with stories of the villagers' warmth and generosity, but also tales of their struggles and fears.

One afternoon, as they finished securing the roof, Pausanias turned to Magumi. "We've made good progress. Thanks to your vigilance, we haven't had any major setbacks."

Magumi felt a strange warmth at his words. "I'm glad to help," she said, almost shyly. "It's... nice to be part of something again."

Saoka smiled warmly. "You're more than just a guardian, Magumi. You're a friend."

Magumi's heart swelled at the sentiment. She had spent centuries alone, her only companions the spirits of the forest. Now, she had found something she hadn't realized she was missing—companionship, a sense of belonging.

Yet, despite the bond she was forming with Pausanias and Saoka, Magumi still felt uneasy about the village of Ni. The scents of so many humans and their activities were overwhelming, mingling with the earthy smells of the forest in a way that made her nose twitch.

The rhythmic thud of hammers, the laughter of children, the

murmur of conversation—were a cacophony compared to the forest.

As the days grew shorter and the air turned crisp with the approach of autumn, Magumi found herself looking forward to each new day. She hunted not out of necessity but for the joy of it, sharing her catches with Pausanias and Saoka. They, in turn, taught her about human customs and rituals, their laughter and stories filling the once-silent forest with life.

One evening, as the first frost of the season coated the ground, Pausanias and Saoka unveiled a surprise. "We made this for you," Pausanias said, holding out a beautifully crafted pendant. It was made from wood and stone, intricately carved with symbols of protection and strength.

"For me?" Magumi asked, taken aback.

"Yes," Saoka said, fastening the pendant around Magumi's neck. "It's a symbol of our friendship and our bond. We face Mokushiroku together."

Magumi's heart beat faster, something she hadn't experienced in centuries. "Thank you," she said. "I will wear it proudly."

As winter approached, the trio settled into a comfortable routine. The hut provided warmth and shelter, and their bond grew stronger with each passing day.

Pausanias and Saoka continued to prepare for the looming threat from the demons, their determination unwavering.

In the heart of Mt. Akiha, a new alliance was forged—one of friendship, trust, and shared purpose. Together, they would confront the darkness and protect the delicate balance of their world. And in doing so, Magumi found a new sense of purpose, a reason to fight, not just for the forest but for the bonds that now tied her to these remarkable humans.

CHAPTER 20

295 B.C.E. Modern-day Niitsu, Japan

Magumi had spent a year deciphering the human heart through the eyes of her new pack. In the village of Ni, where whispers of magic danced with the rustle of leaves, a pivotal moment was about to unfold—the birth of Eurotasu.

D*estiny?* Magumi pondered, watching Pausanias and Saoka, soon-to-be parents, preparing for the arrival of their child. *No, it's simply the natural course for them, expanding our pack.*

Saoka, clad in the village's pure white garb, stood with Pausanias. Her face, a canvas of fatigue and joy, shimmered with a magical luster. Pausanias, a pillar of resolve, mirrored her intensity, his eyes alight with pride and the weight of new fatherhood.

As Saoka cradled the end of her maternal journey, Magumi kept a protective eye. The villagers, having embraced this unusual family, understood the gravity of this birth. They had seen many births, but none as significant as this.

In Ni, where every new life was a treasure, the birth of a child born of two magic wielders was a celestial event. Their faces beamed, reflecting the joy of welcoming such a rare soul. Elders whispered blessings, and children peeked curiously from behind their parents, sensing the extraordinary nature of the moment.

With Eurotasu's first cry, the air itself seemed to pulse with his latent power. The village, no stranger to the mystical, greeted him with a reverence reserved for the extraordinary. The bond between Saoka, Pausanias, and their son, woven with love's strongest threads, shone like a beacon in the night.

Magumi stepped forward, her vow resonating with the force of her commitment. "I will shield and mentor him on the path that lies ahead."

The magic within Eurotasu responded, the wind carrying its silent agreement.

Pausanias, wordless with emotion, finally cradled Eurotasu. He lost himself in the wonder of his son's gaze until Saoka's voice, tinged with humor and warmth, broke the spell. "Unless you've discovered a way to nurse, I believe it's my turn again."

"Right, sorry," Pausanias chuckled, reluctantly handing Eurotasu back. "He's just so... captivating. So cute. You've done something truly miraculous, Saoka."

Saoka laughed softly, exhaustion evident but joy unwavering. "We both have. And Magumi will help guide him. We're not alone in this."

Magumi smiled and nuzzled Saoka. "He will be a beacon for us all. His presence already strengthens our bond."

One of the elders approached, his voice filled with awe. "Magumi, you have been with us for a year, but today, you are truly one of us. Your wisdom will shape Eurotasu's path."

Magumi nodded, her eyes meeting the elder's. "I will do my best. We all will."

As night descended, the village lay awake, caught in the tide of their collective elation. Even the stars seemed to twinkle, the world around them suddenly filled with more wonder, more worth defending. The villagers gathered in small groups, sharing stories of their own children and the magic that seemed to flow more freely tonight. Laughter and murmurs of excitement filled the air, blending with the gentle rustle of cedar leaves.

CHAPTER 21

285 B.C.E. Modern-day Niitsu, Japan

As the leaves rustled in the evening breeze, the shadows they cast morphed into memories of fear. The tranquility was a mere veneer, hiding the concealed menace of an unseen enemy. Magumi remembered well when Eurotasu had first shown signs of magic and the evil presence that had been attracted by such magic.

Eurotasu lay asleep under a pile of furs in the dead of winter. He had been sick for a couple of days and was running a fever. His parents, Pausanias and Saoka, worried and talked by candlelight.

"Is it food poisoning? Perhaps an infection? What would so afflict an otherwise healthy boy?" Pausanias asked.

"No, I've checked his body more than once. I've studied all manners of medicine and magical healing, but the cause eludes me," Saoka replied, squeezing Pausanias's hand.

In the realm of dreams, Eurotasu fled. Phantoms, shapes shrouded by mist, gave chase. He scampered and hid, yet the shapes always found him. They were getting closer. Terror clawed at his mind, stripping away all semblance of reason. His voice rose in a silent scream, lost in the void of his fevered nightmares.

In the waking world, the nightmare was all too real. Magumi had woken ten minutes earlier and entered the house in a panic. "Where is it? Don't let it near the boy, dear gods, is it too late?"

Pausanias and Saoka were confused until it dawned on them. Something malevolent stalked the boy through his dreams. Both mother and father had the gift of spirit sight.

"I don't see anything out of the ordinary," Saoka said.

Magumi, on the other hand, smelled it. "Wake the boy. Hurry, he must face this demon. It is a Kanashibari, a sleep demon. Saoka, you start a demon warding spell. Pausanias, shake the boy. He may not wake up right away, but keep trying, call to him."

As the urgency of the situation unfolded, Saoka wasted no time. She began gathering magic. The air shimmered as she wove a protective barrier, a spiritual fortress aimed at repelling the insidious Kanashibari.

Pausanias scowled and approached Eurotasu's sleeping form. He shook the boy gently. "Wake up, Eurotasu, please wake up."

The boy's restless slumber showed no signs of relenting, trapped within the clutches of the Kanashibari. Magumi's white fur bristled with an otherworldly energy as she circled the room, nose twitching, eyes narrowing at invisible shadows that escaped the sight of Eurotasu's parents. The Kanashibari's influence tightened; its ethereal tendrils ensnaring the boy's dreams.

IN THE LAND OF NI

As Saoka's incantations intensified, the room flickered with an ethereal glow. Light blue bubbles materialized in the air, forming an intricate web of protection. The warding spell took shape, creating a sanctuary that the Kanashibari struggled to penetrate. Pausanias, undeterred, continued his efforts to rouse Eurotasu. The boy's thrashing intensified. Magumi, her keen senses alert, directed her focus toward the epicenter of the spiritual disturbance.

With a sudden burst of spectral energy, the Kanashibari materialized—a shifting, shadowy figure.

Saoka's protective barrier glowed with a divine radiance, pushing back the dark tendrils of the sleep demon.

Seizing the moment, Magumi leaped forward, her form merging with the Kanashibari. In the realm beyond dreams, a struggle ensued—an ethereal battle between the wolf and the malevolent entity. The room reverberated with unseen forces.

Pausanias screamed, "Wake up, boy!" With a sudden jolt, Eurotasu awoke, gasping for breath. The nightmare's hold on him dissipated, and the Kanashibari recoiled, forced to retreat into the shadows.

The room returned to a tranquil stillness. Saoka's warding spell lingered. Eurotasu, now wide awake, gazed at his parents and the magical wolf with a mix of confusion and gratitude, unaware of the supernatural battle that had just unfolded. "Mom, I'm sleepy. Is it already morning? Why is everyone staring at me? Did I fart in my sleep or something?" Eurotasu lay down and started slumbering almost immediately.

This time, it was a peaceful slumber.

The adults paced anxiously, their movements erratic. Laughter came, but it was forced and fleeting, a thin veil over their lingering fear. Magumi pondered deeply, her eyes narrowing. "The magic in Wa has been increasing over the last decade."

"What does that mean?" Saoka asked, dropping her hands and the spell.

"I'm not sure. Still, we should reexamine what's been happening as of late," Magumi said as she sat next to Eurotasu.

"Eurotasu's grown so fast, hasn't he? Hard to believe we've been juggling parenthood with our duties to the Order," Pausanias said, sitting next to Magumi and patting her head.

"Yes, it's been a challenge. But I wouldn't have it any other way. Our adventures were thrilling, but this—being a mother—it's changed everything," said Saoka. She joined the others by her son.

"And you've both done so much for Wa. The Order's kept us safe, especially south of Kazuno. But the demons... they're advancing." Magumi's eyes locked on Eurotasu.

"Hokkaido's lost to them, and getting intel from the north is like grasping at shadows. It's not just there. The demonic forces are on the move, attacking cities, taking prisoners. They're using humans for all sorts of dark purposes," Pausanias added.

"I've heard they're forcing captured builders and craftsmen to work for them. And that ambush near Tottori—our intelligence was spot on," Saoka reached for furs to cover herself and her husband. "Kushim's been relentless, too. And now with Sabas and Mayuki as generals, we're stronger than ever. Mayuki's leading a unit she calls 'battle crazy bitches.' Fitting, isn't it?"

"It's time we unite Wa. The rumors have spread far enough. The truth about men's magic and the Order's role must come to light," Pausanias yawned.

"The people of Wa are ready. They'll stand and fight when the time comes. We'll protect our world, no matter what it takes. Now let's get some sleep," Saoka replied, curling her body next to Pausanias.

"Her pack, her brave pack," Magumi thought. I have never felt closer to the heavens. Still, I must remain hyper-vigilant. War is coming. For the next couple of days, Magumi never left Eurotasu's side.

CHAPTER 22

285 B.C.E. Niitsu, Japan

The serendipitous sighting of a far-off rainbow brought forth memories of hope painted across the skies, reminiscent of promises sealed under the hues of a divine covenant. Magumi, Pausanias, and Saoka had all promised to keep young Eurotasu safe and nourish his talents. Magumi smiled at the memory.

Eurotasu had taken a week to recover from the sleep demon's attack, during which his parents' overprotection smothered him. He yearned for independence, finding his father's fussing, especially the chamber pot, humiliating. In a fit of anger, he threw it, eliciting laughter from his parents.

"Good thing that thing wasn't loaded," his father said with a voice full of mirth.

"Well, if you have enough strength to throw things around

the house, why don't you get out of bed and do some chores?" his mother suggested.

"Sure, what needs doing?" Eurotasu asked.

"Same things that always need doing, although I'd never thought to see the day you were happy to do chores."

He shuffled out of the shelter and spent the next hour chopping wood, sweeping leaves, and helping his father clean a deer. It exhausted him, but he felt content.

"Feels good to move around, doesn't it? All Spartan men hate being idle," his father boomed.

His mother, practicing archery nearby, retorted, "He's not a Spartan, you thick-headed moron."

Pausanias whispered to Eurotasu, "Yes, you are."

Two days later, Eurotasu had recovered enough for his mother to begin his magical training. "For the next month, the boy is mine," she told Pausanias.

Eurotasu thought his father would object, but Pausanias agreed, adding, "I still want Eurotasu to run, stretch, and practice his weapon forms every morning before training with you. Take it easy on him."

"Not a chance," Saoka replied, flexing her muscles.

Eurotasu made the mistake of asking, "What's so grueling about some magical training that requires no strength of arm or fleetness of foot?"

"If you think my training was tough, just wait until she gets her claws in you," Pausanias said, without smiling.

The next day, Eurotasu's training began in earnest. Saoka wanted to teach him two main forms of magic: the blessed sight and energy collection. "We will begin with your meditation," she said calmly.

"But, Mom, I already know how to do that," Eurotasu whined.

"No buts, Eurotasu Pausanias Lykonias." Her tone brooked no argument. "You think you do, but you're barely functional.

Show me you can do something simple, anything a girl can do," she mocked.

For the first week, he only meditated. Distractions pulled at his mind, but his mother explained, "You're always trying to just focus on your focal point without understanding what it is."

"It is a sword. What else is there?"

She sighed, "How many nicks does the blade have? Where is it most polished? How many times was the leather wrapped around the hilt? Are there any other imperfections?"

"I'm not sure; I never thought about it."

"These small details allow you to understand your focal point better. See the object in all dimensions and from all angles. If you feel your concentration slipping, re-angle the image," Saoka explained.

Two days later, he managed to stay in a meditative state for hours. Impressed by his progress, his mother decided to challenge him further. "The blessed sight is much more than seeing spirits. It connects you to animals, plants, and spirits, using their senses to do your seeing. Take, for example, a rabbit forty paces beyond the tree line. I can sense its fear of a hawk circling above and see through the hawk's eyes, all the way to the Agano River."

The revelation awed Eurotasu. "How far can you see using the blessed sight? All the way to Sparta? Can you control those animals, talk with them?"

"My range is about half a mile. I cannot control animals. The effort to take over a brain would not be safe. Talking is more about conveying feelings and emotions. For instance, I could reach out to the rabbit with warmth and love, perhaps lure it here with an image of food."

"That's amazing!" Eurotasu said. "Can you ask it to attack something?"

"No. It's not in a rabbit's nature. You might convince a bear, but it would require immense effort and risk. The blessed sight is best used for studying nature, hunting, tracking, or as an early warning tool."

"So, you always know if an enemy is sneaking up on you," Eurotasu reasoned.

"Not always. You have to actively use the magic, and if an enemy avoids detection by animals, it's ineffective."

"Oh, you only use it while meditating? Seems like a disadvantage if you have to sit and wait for the enemy," Eurotasu conjectured.

"Meditation isn't just sitting. It's calming the mind, centering breath, balance, understanding the sacred and mystical forces of life. Like flowing through a well-rehearsed sword form."

"Or like when swimming underwater, I feel a sense of calm and focus?" he asked.

"Exactly. Using it while moving requires practice. Think of it as muscle memory."

"I've got so many more questions!"

"Later. First, I'm proud you learned to meditate deeply. Now, practice projecting your blessed sight."

"How?"

"Once meditative, focus on the outside world, seeing it as your personal realm. It's not easy, but worth the effort," she said.

"I can't wait to use this sight."

A week later, he glimpsed the sight, only to recoil in excitement. Nearby, his mother's meditation broke, her eyes wide with surprise.

The second attempt astounded him. His sight, though feeble, yearned to stretch further. Yet, a mere two meters out, it vanished against an invisible barrier. Frustrated, he savored this newfound ability, bonding with the Earth. His awareness danced from creature to creature within reach and soared above, gazing down at his own form. He pushed against the barrier, visualizing a blue ethereal double of himself. The barrier remained unmoved.

"Eurotasu, that's enough. You shouldn't push so hard; your body might not be able to take it," his mother warned.

"But, but," he protested. She shook her head knowingly.

"I understand the urge; it is glorious. I felt the same way the first time. Humans want to explore. However, training takes its toll on the mind and body. Stand up," she challenged.

Confused, Eurotasu stood, his body immediately reeling at the effort. He struggled to keep his balance, wondering why he perspired so much. "Why is my body so tired? Even lifting my arm hurts."

"You were pushing against a wall for half an hour. Why wouldn't your body feel tired? I was tired just watching."

"So, the physical effort of using the blessed sight drains my body?"

"Actually, it takes double, maybe three times as much effort. You're living, heart beating, lungs drawing breath. You're using your mind to its limit and expending magical energy too. Most of us can't walk or stand for days after the first time. Many vomit from the dizziness. If you can make it back to the hut, you can eat dinner early and get some rest."

Sensing a challenge, Eurotasu put one foot in front of the other, making it to the hut before collapsing. "Ooowww," he groaned into the rug.

"Good boy, good boy," his mother teased as she dragged him to his bed furs. She left to get some stew, returning to find him deep asleep. She smiled and sat beside him, reflecting on the past three weeks. *Gods, only three weeks, what is going on here?*

The next day, Eurotasu went out jogging before Saoka had processed what had happened. She collapsed by the entrance, murmuring, "Impossible, impossible."

At that moment, Pausanias arrived with a smile. "What's impossible? My stunning good looks? I know, but you're not the first lady to remark on them," he teased. Seeing his wife's distressed look, he dropped all pretense and helped her to her feet.

"What's wrong? Where's Eurotasu?" Without waiting for an answer, he signaled Magumi, who set off to find the boy. "Is he okay? Are you?" he pressed.

Saoka, tears streaming, nestled into Pausanias's embrace. "He's jogging... will return soon," she whispered. Pausanias, puzzled by her tears, offered a comforting embrace.

Regaining her poise, Saoka urged him to sit. "You must be weary. Listen, there's much about Eurotasu's training you need to hear," she insisted.

As Saoka recounted the events, Pausanias absorbed every detail and asked, "What is he?"

"He's our son, and we love him," she answered.

"Of course, I apologize. You know what I mean. Combined, we have more knowledge than just about anyone alive about the magic in this world, spirits, demons, countless wonders, and terrors of this world. Never have we seen such volumes of power, such quick transitions in manipulating energy," he said with a frown.

"I have some ideas, but they are speculations at best. His quick learning and recovery are not what really worries me. He's a youngster. There is so much he doesn't know, so many experiences he has never had. His power will only continue to increase. What worries me most is what will that power attract? He doesn't yet have the wisdom to know when and when not to use his powers. I fear, husband, he will use them too close to dangerous forces or spirits. Others would use him for his power."

"So, we train him more, tell him of the dangers of using his power, make sure he is ready to meet the world prepared," Pausanias said with conviction.

"I'm not so sure it is that straightforward. Didn't you ever disobey your parents? Your teachers and elders? Think that you knew yourself and your skills better than anyone? Want to impress, or seek glory?" she asked. As a Spartan, he gulped. "Shit, if he's anything like me, we're in a world of trouble."

"Shut up. You are too much of a good boy to know the trouble we are in. Probably never even snuck out of the barracks to see a girl. If he's anything like me, we're in real trouble," she quipped. Their laughter broke the nervous tension.

"Do tell," Pausanias raised an eyebrow.

"Not in your dreams," she winked. "Now let's get down to discussing what we should do with our little terror."

CHAPTER 23

Eurotasu had never felt so alive. His morning jog usually left him drenched in sweat, tired, and stiff. Instead of gaining energy, he always felt it leaching away the farther he ran. But today was different; he felt like he could run forever.

He turned around, and his thoughts drifted to his family. His father, a Spartan figure of strength and loyalty, spoke with a firm voice that belied his tender heart.

His mother, fierce yet nurturing, embodied their family's resilience.

Magumi, his enigmatic elder sister, mixed ancient wisdom with youthful playfulness.

He smiled, remembering the first time he played fetch with her. Using a ball his father had made—a ju, or Chinese ball, stuffed with feathers—his father had taught them the game of Cuju, which involved juggling the ball with their feet to keep it from touching the ground.

His father had also tried to teach the family a Greek ball game called Episkyros, involving passing, throwing, kicking, tackling, and wrestling. To his dismay, the rest of the family preferred simple catch games and fetch with Magumi. She had been so excited that, if a wolf could blush, she would have.

That wonderful wolf had become his protector, another mentor, and his connection to the Earth. She made him feel that humans and other animals shared the world.

As he got deeper into his thoughts, a wild ball of white fur bounded around a bend in the track that ran through the trees. Magumi. His heart fluttered. She raced toward his direction and jumped on top of him, tackling him to the ground.

"Are you harmed, young one?" she asked, her voice stressed with concern.

"Yeah, after you jumped on me, you big fatty. What's the deal?" Eurotasu asked.

"Your father and mother sent me to find you. Your mother was lying by the hut, looking distraught and terrified. What did you do?"

"Nothing, I swear. Just jogging on my way home. We've been training hard. I passed out early last night. Maybe she's just worried I didn't get enough rest," answered a bewildered Eurotasu.

"Come, let's return you to them. Jump on my back and we'll talk more as we go," she said, lying to let him hop on.

He explained his last week to her while she moved through the forest.

Some of the cute forest sprites watched them. They would notice a human or other spirit, but never give them more than a passing glance.

Glowing blue, purple, or green, and shaped like snowmen with round bodies and heads, short stubby legs, and spindly arms, they had all-black or turquoise orbs for eyes. Curious or peaceful smiles adorned their faces; the sprites loved the forests, and the forests loved them.

"Why are they watching us?"

"They don't often see a human riding a spirit wolf. Plus, your aura is pulsating light."

"My what is what? Wait, stop, let me down. We need to talk."

"We'll be home soon; we can talk then. I have much to tell you about…," she spoke over her shoulder.

Before she finished her sentence, Eurotasu grabbed a low-hanging tree limb, swung on it in a full rotation, and landed on his feet behind Magumi.

She turned quickly and bared her teeth. "This isn't the time to play games."

"No, it isn't," he crossed his arms. "How long are you all going to baby me, not tell me things, and worry over me for no reason?"

"As long as you act like a baby. Some things are not for you. You are still a child. You may think of yourself as gifted, special, or whatever arrogant imaginations you come up with, but trust me, little boy, there is much you don't know and even more you don't understand. Now when I say move, you move. Is that clear?"

"Sure, if I was a moron," he screamed. "The only reason I don't know anything is because you, Mom, and Dad hide everything. You are a bunch of liars."

Before he could say another word, Magumi swatted him to the ground and sat on his chest, pinning him with her weight. He grew livid. He wanted to scream, lash out, cry, and mask his feelings all at once. He only managed to squirm under her mass. "Get off me," he gasped through a red-strained face.

"You are so gods-damned special, make me."

"Fine, fine, I surrender," he said after a few more moments of useless struggling.

"If I let you up, do you promise not to try any more stunts?"

"I promise."

The walk back to the hut proceeded slow and solemn. Not until Eurotasu caught a glimpse of his parents running toward him did he smile, then started wailing like a newborn.

"I'm fine, I'm not hurt, I'm sorry, I'm sorry," he said through labored sobs.

"Oh son, no, it's we who are sorry," she pulled him into an embrace.

Pausanias silently inspected the boy for wounds and bruises.

Saoka continued, "We love you and have much to tell you; we just worry, as all parents do. Come, let's sit down and talk."

After an hour of listening, Eurotasu thought he had a grasp of the situation. "So, your journey here was to uncover deeper motives and mysteries of the demons," he said, pointing towards Pausanias. "You, mother, had a similar mission, along with secret meetings with the mothers of the Order. Magic users are rare and getting rarer. Kushim, the last man alive from a dead empire that had been destroyed thousands of years ago by a meteor, is the mastermind," he concluded.

"You forgot the part about how potentially dangerous you are, and that left untrained you might attract countless dangers to you and those you love," Pausanias said.

"Well, potential is for Athenians, isn't that what you always say, Father?" he grinned.

"You got me there, horse face. Hey, have you ever thought of joining a traveling band of freaks?" his father teased, relieving the tension.

"Only if you as captain allow me to join," Eurotasu shot back.

"Enough, the both of you, this is serious. Look at Saoka!" Magumi snarled.

Both males stopped and stared.

Saoka perked up and attempted a smile. She did not hold it for long. Eurotasu, Pausanias, and Magumi huddled around her in a four-way hug.

"Don't worry, Mom; it'll be okay. I'll learn how to control this magic and keep everyone safe," the boy said.

Now his mom started to cry.

After the crying and hugging ended, Pausanias made a command decision.

"No more work today. I want all of you packed and ready to march in five minutes," he said with a smile.

"Where are we going?" Magumi asked.

"Camping by the river. I want to eat some fish. Eurotasu, grab the bedrolls and camping supplies and throw them on the back of that beast over there," he said, pointing at Magumi, who only huffed in response.

Everyone did as they were told.

The world around them seemed brighter then, as the whole family's mood lifted. They pushed bad thoughts aside and laughed and joked all the way to the river.

Pausanias caught three fish to Eurotasu's two.

Saoka and Magumi caught ten together as a team. Magumi disturbed the areas of the river where fish were hiding and funneled them toward Saoka, who used her bow with extraordinary precision.

"It wasn't fair," the boys argued.

"You boys were just too dumb to figure out the best way to catch fish. In the future, why not leave the critical thinking and planning to us ladies," Magumi said.

"You can do the cooking as well, losers," Saoka chimed in, making a face.

The father and son took it all in stride and prepared a feast of fish and rice.

Shortly after dinner, Eurotasu yawned and settled down at Magumi's side. His parents smiled.

He heard his mother speak right before he fell asleep.

"Looks like our son is still plenty human."

CHAPTER 24

The scent of dawn reminded Magumi of fire. Once feared, she now found comfort in its radiant warmth. Memories of celebrations, where laughter mingled with dancing flames, filled her with wonder at the enduring power of human connection. Funny, she thought, considering she wasn't human. Still, it was at a bonfire where Eurotasu first stepped into manhood.

After the camping trip, Pausanias watched as Eurotasu returned to their hut, where Yito and Yuda greeted him. Observing from a distance, Pausanias noted the brothers' neatly trimmed hair and deer pelt parkas. He listened as Eurotasu welcomed them with handshakes.

"Sir and Ma'am, we're here to remind you of this year's sacred bonfire," Yito said to Pausanias and Saoka. "It's in a week. Our mother sent us to ensure you'll come."

"Of course, boys," Pausanias patted Yuda on the back. "It would be our pleasure."

"Thank you, sir. Our father will be pleased. He always says

no one else in the town is as good a drinking partner as you," Yuda grinned.

Yito and Yuda questioned Eurotasu about his recent experiences. He shared tales of combat training and snippets of knowledge about the wider world.

Pausanias watched, his heart softening with a desire for a fuller life for his son. "Eurotasu, you can escort these boys home if you wish but return quickly."

"Really, Father?" Eurotasu raced away with the boys in tow.

Saoka's brow furrowed as she sat on a bench by the hut, her eyes fixed on Pausanias.

Pausanias called over his shoulder, "Magumi, please trail them from a distance but remain unseen."

"Oh, bother. Fine, I'll go," Magumi replied and rose. "Wolves, even magical ones, need plenty of naps."

Saoka's shoulders relaxed at this.

"Gods, woman, he'll be fine. He'll be—" Pausanias said.

"You don't know that."

"Yes, you're right, but we can't worry about every what-if. That's no way to live a life. Should we wrap him in soft cloth and put him away in the hut forever?" he asked, hands on hips.

"Perhaps we should."

Pausanias sought to change the subject. "What will we bring to the bonfire? Your friend Hirona will be expecting something nice."

"Hirona! She can help with our Eurotasu problem," Saoka jumped from her seat.

Pausanias frowned.

"Hirona has strong magic. Not on par with the sisters from my sect, but more than adequate. Her sealing magic is the most dynamic I've ever seen."

"You lost me again; I don't remember hearing about sealing magic before."

"I'm sure I've mentioned it. Sealing magic locks away

magical energy, which can only be unsealed by a command word laced with magical energy."

"That's amazing. Why can't they just seal away all the demons?"

"Well, it's not very strong. It's used for sealing small yokai or tiny amounts of natural magic. Larger demons generally can't have their magic sealed because their magic is greater than the sealer's."

"Generally?"

"Yes, almost always. Ninety-nine percent of the time. It once took a group of twenty shrine maidens to seal a second-class demon near our home shrine at Lake Inawashiro."

"That must have been some demon."

"Yes, and it had taken damage. Villagers and the offensive sisters kept it at bay, giving the sealers time to start their work. The sealers' spells are slow and weak, so the channelers enhanced their strength. Eventually, they sealed the demon away."

"They captured it?"

"No, it died and exploded, leaving behind only ash."

"That's too bad; much could be learned from catching a live demon. So, you plan on sealing our son?"

"Yes, to protect him until he's older and more experienced."

"He won't explode? Has this ever been done to a person? Is it safe? Side effects?"

"No, yes, yes, no," she answered. "Do you really think I would blow up our child?"

Pausanias ignored her last statement, "Wait, who was this done to and why? Were they willing participants?"

"It has been done several times. Twice against someone's will. They were driven mad by their magic. Other cases involved people begging to have their magic sealed, seeking comfort in the ordinary. Children with high-level magical potential had their powers sealed until they came of age. No side effects have been reported."

"That's a lot to take in, Saoka. I need to think this through. Will this sealing stunt his magical growth? Is this what Eurotasu wants?"

"Does it matter what he wants, Pausanias? He is a child. We are his parents. We will protect him, even from himself."

"Fine, but not today. I want him to have more training first, to become more natural with his magic before we do this."

"Agreed. He will still have all his other faculties, still be able to meditate and see spirits. Any connection to natural magic will not be affected."

"We should ask him first, or at least let him know what we plan and why. Also, teach me about this command word. What is it, and who can use it to release his powers?"

"Yes, husband, I will tell you everything. Now come, sit, let's eat some lunch and talk this over," Saoka gently patted the bench. She explained that only the people involved in the spell casting could use the command word. Saoka, as it turned out, wasn't the only one with an idea.

"Can Magumi join the process and utter the command signal if needed?" Pausanias asked.

"Of course. She is a being of considerable magic; she doesn't even need to learn anything other than the word. Magic is so natural to her being that it wouldn't be any trouble at all," Saoka said.

As they finished their talk and started on lunch, Eurotasu returned. "I'm hungry, can I have a bite?" he asked, reaching for his father's bowl.

Pausanias smacked his hand back with his spoon. "Get your own bowl, and hey, why do you smell like cinnamon?"

"No reason. I was leaving the boys' house when their mother stopped me and gave me this." He pulled out a small white bundle from under his shirt. It contained two handfuls of cinnamon, nut, and oat cookies.

Pausanias reached for one.

Eurotasu slapped his father's hand away. "Get your own," he mocked, speaking in a deeper accent.

The week before the bonfire passed quietly. Eurotasu balanced his magical training with studies.

The bonfire preparations fostered collaboration among the villagers. Eurotasu mingled with the children while Pausanias, pleased with the village's defenses, reminisced about his initial visit. *Oh, what they must have thought of me.*

Arriving in full Spartan regalia, Pausanias had been a formidable sight with his shield, helmet, and blood-red cloak. His arsenal included a sword, daggers, and a spear, complemented by a leather rig carrying throwing knives and a bag packed with supplies and additional weapons.

Exhausted from his journey from Nara, he was grateful the villagers held back from confrontation. Saoka had been talking with another traveler when she joined him, her demeanor and fluency in the local tongue further eased the tension.

Shaking off the memory, Pausanias admired the village's new fortifications: a completed moat, wooden walls, and well-placed spikes. He acknowledged the vigilant watchmen in their makeshift towers with nods.

The village's eldest man Yuman sauntered over with a huge smile to greet him.

Pausanias nodded in respect. Yuman might be old and graying, but he remained sharp.

"Pleased with the defenses, I assume?" Yuman asked, bowing his head to Pausanias.

"Better than nothing, I suppose."

"Don't try to lie to me now. I know you didn't think we would have finished the earthworks by now. You have to admit, the village has done a stellar job," Yuman yawned, turning his body and gesturing towards the mountains beyond. "Although, I couldn't understand why we'd need these defenses anyway. In all my years, we haven't faced anything bigger than an angry boar. Did I ever tell you that story? You see, I was ten at the time, and..."

Pausanias halted Yuman with a raised hand. "Yes, yes, I've heard about the boar. Stubborn and full of himself, without a hint of self-awareness," he said, and then he winked.

He took a few steps closer, lowering his voice to underscore his concern. "Just because the village has never been attacked in the past doesn't mean that it will stay that way."

He paused, scanning the village's perimeter as if to point out its vulnerabilities. "I told your elders' council last month that Saoka and I received word from her order about reports of strange magic up north."

Pausanias's gaze returned to Yuman, locking eyes with him to emphasize the gravity of his next words. "Furthermore, traders from Yamagata have spun tales of villages being raided by pirates and mercenaries. If you don't complete the other defenses, Ni is in real trouble."

"Yes, well, traders often exaggerate. They lure you in with stories and then try to peddle their goods. I don't see why anyone would bother with a village like Ni. We are far from the sea and not big enough to be of much value."

"Not big enough to defend yourselves either. But I didn't come here to argue with you about defenses, Yuman. How is the village doing otherwise? Any problems? Is your wife still trying to get children out of you?" Pausanias said, bringing out a huge laugh from Yuman.

"Every damn day. You'd think she'd know that I'd run dry years ago," Yuman joked. Some things in the village never aged, and Yuman's dirty-minded jokes were the clearest example. "Say, Pausanias, did I tell you the joke about the three sisters?"

"Maybe later, Yuman. I need to catch up with Saoka and Eurotasu, but I look forward to it," Pausanias replied before bowing and turning on his heels, striding toward where the bonfires were being lit.

The bonfire's enchantment was palpable. Pausanias, basking in the joy of his family and the village's festivities, felt its allure through rhythmic drum beats. As night deepened, a hush fell; a maiden, wings adorned with feathers, danced by the fire, embodying a bird in flight—a revered village tradition.

The ritual's origins remained shrouded in mystery, adding to its allure. Pausanias, embracing the moment, joined the villagers in celebration.

They slept in a friend's hut, sparing them the journey home. Come morning, Pausanias, nursing a headache, sought out his family and found them with a stranger by where last night's flames had burned.

As he approached, his wife looked over at him, she chewed on her lower lip, a habit that surfaced only when deep worries gnawed at her. Her eyes darted about.

"Well met, stranger. What news?" Pausanias asked, bowing, and placing a hand on the small of his wife's back.

The stranger was a middle-aged man of no particular regard except he had one good eye and one that looked off into the sky. His dress resembled that of most travelers, simple but sturdy garb that blended in with the forest. He carried a large backpack with a bedroll and donned a straw hat to keep the elements at bay.

"The name's Sosuke. You must be Pausanias, Saoka's husband, and a member of a shadowy organization," he spoke with an embellished voice and hand movements. He started fidgeting his feet and continued, "Sorry to surprise you. I have been sent to deliver a message to both of you. I as well work for the Order," Sosuke finished with another flurry of his hands.

Pausanias understood this type of guy. "Well, glad we are on the same team. Have you found yourself some breakfast in our lovely town? Tell me what message do you bring?"

"I have had some exquisite food, yes. As for the message…"

"We've been sent for. They need us in Nara," Eurotasu said.

"Who is 'us,' runt?" Pausanias said.

"Actually, the two of us, dear," Saoka said.

"Does the message say why?" Pausanias cocked his head.

"No, just to make haste. I fear we have to leave within a day or two at most," Saoka said, hugging her son.

"What about Eurotasu? He is too young and not yet ready for a lengthy trip to Nara, followed by gods know what."

"I'm ready, you guys. I can follow orders, I can…" Eurotasu tried to finish but was cut off by looks from all three adults.

"We'll be doing truly dangerous work, boy, and your training has only begun," said Pausanias.

Saoka followed with a suggestion. "I think I know how you can help everyone, my son."

"Yes, Mom, anything, tell me what I should do," Eurotasu gave a little hop.

His mom motioned for everyone to step out of the village with her while she summoned some magic.

Upon exiting the village, Pausanias saw a giant ball of white moving by the tree line. Magumi approached at speed.

Saoka said, "You have another teacher here who will drill you and make sure you are on the right path. What I need you and Magumi to do is guard the village of Ni, and to send letters by messenger once every two weeks to keep us updated."

"What about sealing the boy's magic?" Pausanias asked.

That very night, plans were made and magic woven. "What command word should we use?" Saoka bade her husband.

"I know, Agape. It means empathetic, universal love in Greek."

Magumi proposed a plan to manage Eurotasu's magical training. Understanding the sealing spell, she offered to temporarily lift it for his practice, after ensuring no danger was near. She pledged to supervise Eurotasu and reseal his powers post-training.

His parents consented.

The next morning, after heartfelt farewells, comforted by the promise of both safety and growth, his parents embraced him tightly before departing for Nara.

CHAPTER 25

283 B.C.E. Niitsu

Two years had passed since his parents left, and Eurotasu remained vigilant and dedicated to his training. Word of their well-being came occasionally through messengers bearing coded letters. The messages contained little detail of their daily activities and were more personal, filled with assurances of their safety and love.

Eurotasu sat beside Magumi in the hut, ready to explain his meditation focal point. He chose his father's sword. "This sword is wondrous, capable of terrible violence but forged to help others. It's unique, blending qualities from five empires. The hilt, a rustic leather design, comes from my grandfather's Spartan Xiphos, which broke in India. Father had this masterpiece crafted in China."

"And when did you learn the story?" Magumi prodded.

"From an early age. Father told me how he discovered a new type of metal in China, lighter and stronger than iron. This blade was forged over three days, reheated, folded, and pounded to create a crashing wave pattern along its edge. Fifteen folds for a total of thirty-two thousand seven hundred and sixty-eight layers. It has a slight curve for flexibility, and the cutting edge, though straight at first glance, is subtly curved. Perfect for slashing and thrusting," Eurotasu said, practicing a thrust.

"The pommel was a gift from your father's king, wasn't it?" Magumi asked.

"Yes, a bronze casting of Khnum, the Egyptian God of the Nile, rebirth, creation, and the evening sun. The simple, stick-figure shape holds a polished orange ivory circle, representing the evening sun.

The cross-shaped guard is of Persian origin. The original broke during Father's travels. Simple and sturdy, made from iron and coated with polished silver."

"The scabbard?" she asked, rolling onto her back.

"Of Indian design. An Indian tradesman, traveling through China, insisted on making the scabbard upon seeing the finished blade. The Chinese smith who forged the sword also demanded to make the scabbard.

Father settled their dispute by paying the Chinese man double his original price and allowing the Indian to create the scabbard. It is jet black, made from magnolia wood and covered in lacquered sharkskin. A metal fitting secures the materials. A squared ring holds a knotted rope for tying the sword to one's hip. A preserved purple maple leaf and a simple lapis lazuli stone are glued on, reminders of Mother and a unique spirit stone whose story Father never shared."

"Sounds like you know your focal point well. Maybe it's time to start training?" Magumi said.

Nodding in agreement, Eurotasu stepped out of the hut and into the early morning light.

Eurotasu stood in the training grounds next to his hut. His jaw set, eyes narrowed with focus, and every muscle in his face tensed. He began his sword practice. The rhythmic hiss of the blade cutting through the air echoed in the stillness. He executed intricate forms, transitioning between offensive and defensive maneuvers.

As the day progressed, Eurotasu diversified his training regimen, incorporating an array of weapons. From the staff, spear, and daggers to the bow, he practiced with each, adapting his techniques to the unique attributes of every weapon.

Magumi watched. "Are you dancing?"

"It's called lethal precision. Now, with the physical aspects addressed, I'll turn my attention to the magical heritage flowing through my veins. Inspired by Mother, I delve into the arcane arts. A simple spell to create a protective barrier serves as my initial foray into magic. I'll channel my intent to manifest an ethereal shield."

"Why are you talking like that?"

"Watch as I seek to understand the elemental forces entwined with my magical abilities," he released a puff of wind.

Magumi laughed, rolling on the ground.

"I recognize that a warrior's strength extends beyond weaponry and magic. I'll need to practice some agility drills and acrobatics." Eurotasu's stomach growled. "First, however, I need to eat lunch."

He went inside to gather his food. He came back outside and sat next to Magumi to eat. Two rice balls, one of brown rice and another of herbed white rice, accompanied three cookies from his mother's friend Hirona, and a heaped helping of salted fish. He gave a portion of fish to Magumi, who ate it disinterestedly. Eurotasu wondered, not for the first time, if a magic wolf needed to eat.

After devouring the food, he took a small nap. A meditation session after his nap, guided by Magumi's serene presence, allowed him to cultivate mental resilience and focus. Visualization techniques, coupled with controlled breathing, honed his ability to maintain composure amidst chaos.

"Okay, Eurotasu, we still have to practice our coordinated attacks."

They trained tirelessly, their movements synchronized with precision as they honed their skills.

As the sun dipped below the horizon, Eurotasu concluded, "That's enough for today," wiping sweat from his face.

"Good job today, little sapling. Remember, each day brings new challenges. Embrace them, knowing your journey toward mastery is a lifelong odyssey."

"Now who's talking strange." He walked inside to start a fire.

Magumi followed, "A bath would serve you well, and don't forget your chores around the hut."

"It's a lot of work keeping the hut and my clothes clean, the firewood stocked, and the vegetable garden tended. You could help."

"Do I look like a human to you? You have books that you haven't finished reading yet. Tomorrow, we must add more educational variety into your day."

"Yeah, yeah," he nodded.

"Plus, I love listening to how humans read books. The voice you use when reading is magic."

CHAPTER 26

The rhythmic hum of insects brought memories of summer nights, where laughter and camaraderie blended seamlessly with nature's symphony. The following summer was one of joy for Magumi. Regular messages arrived in Ni, reassuring her and Eurotasu of Pausanias and Saoka's safety. Eurotasu had been making progress in all his endeavors, and part of his mental training involved sharing his meditations with Magumi. One tale struck a chord with her, reminding her of the simplicity sometimes present in human thoughts and actions.

"Strange how this river rock can evoke happiness," Eurotasu mused to Magumi. "It's not a precious stone coveted for trade. Its shape is unremarkable, rounded over time, and it's not even noteworthy as a throwing stone. Yet, its color fascinates me. White on top, gray on the underside, with a straight line of red running through it. I collect things no one else has. Diving into the waist-high river to catch a glimpse of something sparkly feels like an adventure."

Magumi asked, "Does this stone's white top result from erosion, or has the bottom's gray come from sedimentation?"

"I don't know. I'll think on it," he returned to the river, grabbing another rock with a red streak. To him, this was a sign the rock was battle-tested. It felt silly, but when meditating in a river, one made up one's own rules. He took a deep breath and swam to the shore, dropping the rock onto a boar fur piled with others.

This was his time to reflect on what was precious. The Earth seemed to scream "me first" in his mind, and he never protested. Time here felt almost irrelevant, though the ever-running waters spoke to its continuity. All the problems of the human world slipped away. Underwater, his thoughts slowed, allowing him to focus as he never could on dry land.

Family and friends came second. He remembered their little details—the way his mother flipped her hair while cooking, his father's proud smirk when Eurotasu completed a difficult task, Magumi's trusting eyes when he scratched under her neckline.

After another half hour in the water, Eurotasu sought company. Finding Magumi near the stream, he invited her to tell him a story at dinner.

Magumi nestled beside Eurotasu, her voice a gentle caress as she began, "Once, in the distant mountains, there lived a fox, a monkey, and a rabbit. They roamed together, their camaraderie tested by the trials of the wilderness. One day, they found an old man, weary and weak, lying on the road."

Magumi paused, letting the gravity of the scene settle. "The monkey, nimble among the trees, plucked fruits and nuts. The fox, swift by the river, gathered fish. But the poor rabbit, feeling inadequate, found nothing to contribute."

She continued, "Undeterred, the rabbit turned to his companions, pleading, 'Help me build a fire.' The monkey and the fox, understanding his sincerity, helped kindle the flames."

In a somber tone, Magumi narrated, "In an act of unparalleled sacrifice, the rabbit leaped into the fire, offering his body to nourish the old man. His compassion knew no bounds, transcending his humble form."

"The old man, revealed as Taishakuten, a celestial lord, gazed upon the rabbit's sacrifice with profound appreciation. He lifted the rabbit into the moon, making him a beacon of inspiration for generations."

Magumi smiled softly as she concluded, "To this day, if you gaze at the moon, you may glimpse the jade rabbit. The smoke from that selfless fire still billows, a reminder of the rabbit's enduring kindness."

Magumi's tale lingered in the air, the echoes of sacrifice and compassion weaving a timeless narrative that resonated with their shared journey.

CHAPTER 27

281 B.C.E. Niitsu

Seasons shifted, and with them, three years unfurled. Eurotasu's stature and courage swelled with each passing day. This year, as autumn's breath swept through the land, nights grew colder, and Magumi found solace in the quiet vigil of the dark. A lone wolf's howl intertwined with the villagers' whispered fears, and the night air carried the distant clash of battles long past. Shadows from the rustling leaves danced like specters, hinting at horrors hidden beneath the calm. Was Eurotasu prepared for what was to come?

"Awaken, Eurotasu!" Magumi's voice, laced with urgency, cut through the silence.

Eurotasu leapt to his feet, his heart racing. Magumi's tone, so full of concern and pain, was new to him. "What's happened?" he called out.

"Raiders from the north—no time to explain. Ring the bell!" she commanded, her voice a notch steadier.

Eurotasu bolted to the bell, striking it with fervor. His blows echoed into the night, stirring the town into motion. He glanced at the moon—dawn was still an hour away.

Magumi's next order snapped him to attention. "Arm yourself, Eurotasu. We ride to Ni River."

"But the villagers..." he protested.

"We'll intercept the raiders. It's the only way," she insisted.

Eurotasu nodded, his determination clear as he gathered his gear. Magumi awaited him, her form low and ready. This ride could be his last. He had never truly fought before—his experience limited to training and scuffles, nothing with stakes this high.

"Remember your training. Keep your distance, strike with your bow. They're not men; they're targets," Magumi instructed, her eyes stern.

"Yes, ma'am," he replied, mounting her back, his grip tight with resolve.

Magumi moved with a predator's grace, bounding down the mountain, her powerful frame making the ride perilous. Eurotasu, the only one ever to ride her, held on, trusting their bond.

They reached the Ni River swiftly. Magumi leaped the expanse and halted behind an oak. To the west, smoke and screams rose into the sky.

"Let everyone be safe, please," Eurotasu whispered.

"Target, thirty paces, right side," Magumi stated, her voice calm.

Eurotasu turned, his arrow finding its mark in the silhouette that dropped in the distance.

"Another, ten yards right. And one more, twenty left, elevated on the embankment," she directed.

His response was mechanical, precise. They were shadows in the night, unseen, unheard, save for the thud of falling targets.

Then Magumi's warning came. "Down!"

IN THE LAND OF NI

Eurotasu catapulted off Magumi, landing in a splash of mud as an arrow whistled through the space he had vacated. Six raiders bore down on them.

The first raider barely managed a step before Magumi's paw struck, severing his jugular in a spray of crimson.

Another raider lunged with a tentative swing, but Magumi was quicker, her maw clamping on his hand and ripping it away, then driving her teeth into his thigh, all in one fluid, deadly motion.

Two raiders squared their stance, drawing their bows, aiming at the fierce beast before them. Eurotasu's world narrowed to that moment, his heart pounding in his ears.

One raider's breath fogged in the night air, his rotten teeth bared in a grimace as he took aim at Magumi.

Eurotasu's paralysis shattered, anger and adrenaline propelling him forward. In two swift strides, he was upon the man, his dagger plunging into the raider's chest, silencing his malicious intent forever.

Without pausing, Eurotasu lunged toward the next assailant, his hands ready to strike.

Fate was quicker; an arrow launched from a bowstring found its mark in Magumi's shoulder.

She roared in pain and fury, closing the distance between her and the archer in a heartbeat.

Her jaws closed on the archer's face, tearing it apart in a gruesome retribution. His screams filled the night as he thrashed on the ground in agony.

The last raider, seized by fear, turned to flee, but Magumi was relentless, chasing him down with the wrath of the wild.

A wave of relief washed over Eurotasu as he watched the final raider fall. He hurried to Magumi's side, where she lay panting, her fur matted with blood. Gently, he examined her wound—it looked painful but not life-threatening. From his pouch, he drew a cloth, wrapping it carefully around her shoulder, his hands steady despite the chaos of his emotions.

"Magumi, you're incredible. You saved us all—the village owes you its life. I'm sorry I hesitated; sorry you were hurt because of me."

She gazed up at him and licked his face. "Eurotasu, there's no need for apologies. You were valiant. You stood and fought. You protected me. You're the best friend I ever had. I'm proud of you. That's what matters," her voice firm yet gentle.

They embraced, the distant cheers of victory reaching them. The raiders had been driven back; the village stood strong.

As they returned to the hamlet, the cost of victory became clear. Four brave souls had given their lives in defense.

The raiders, outmatched, had retreated into the night.

"We should pursue them," Eurotasu said, his voice a growl.

"No," Magumi replied. "We stay. We heal. We rebuild. Chasing an unknown enemy in the forest in the dead of night is a terrible scheme."

Eurotasu relented. He got down to the task of helping. His hands wouldn't stop shaking. His heart still pumped in his chest. After an hour, he went and slept on the grass near Hirona's hut.

As dawn's light crept over the horizon, Eurotasu lay reflecting on the night. Mixed emotions churned within him—pride for standing and fighting, sorrow for the lives lost, and a simmering anger that began to take hold. He vowed to grow stronger, to protect his village and those he loved. The next raid would not catch him unprepared, and his resolve hardened into a fierce determination. Eurotasu knew that the peace of this morning was just a respite, and the fire of his anger would not be easily quenched.

CHAPTER 28

281 B.C.E. Niitsu, Japan

The sighting of a venomous serpent triggered a blend of fear and anger as memories slithered back to encounters with treachery, venomous words, and hidden dangers. Magumi felt sadness down to her core, thinking about the things Eurotasu said the morning after his first battle.

Eurotasu paced back and forth, his voice rising with each step. "Why must the world suffer such senseless violence? It's irrational, beyond my comprehension. The survival instinct, the predator's hunt, the defender's stand—I understand these as life's cycle. But senseless cruelty, cold and calculated violence parading as reason, that's what truly baffles me."

"It's all so twisted. 'Logic' becomes the mask for illogical actions. We tout reason, yet twist it to excuse our darkest deeds. In conflict, each side claims righteousness, battling for land, wealth, power, beliefs, legacies. But violence for pleasure, for the twisted joy of pain—that darkness is incomprehensible, with no place in a civilized world," he continued, shaking his head in disbelief.

Magumi's eyes darkened with memory. "Your father would quote philosophers for hours by the fire. He spoke of a different violence—the silent kind born from inaction, wielded by the state to control or suppress. But the demons? Their desires are far darker," she murmured, turning to tend to the villagers.

As the tiny village of Ni reeled from the attack, Eurotasu seethed. The day after the attack, people were still in shock. There was a mix of mourning, relief at being alive, and exhaustion that only fighting for one's life can bring. Despite the recent turmoil, the village of Niitsu demonstrated remarkable resilience. The advanced techniques in metallurgy were evident as blacksmiths repaired tools and weapons. Women skillfully wove new textiles from hemp, ensuring the community remained clothed. Even the children contributed, gathering firewood and tending to the gardens. The collective effort embodied a spirit of cooperation and innovation, a legacy that would endure through the ages.

He had never been so angry in his life. Everything and everyone made it worse.

A young girl named Rin smiled and tried to offer him some fresh-squeezed berry juice through tiny hands as he sat in the grasses by the entrance to the village. He barked at her like an animal. He was infuriated that she smiled. What was there to smile about? He was irate that someone had tried to give something to him. "I'm not a baby; I don't need help," he said. He was annoyed and cross with anyone who came across his path. He was ashamed that he yelled at the unfortunate child as he watched her run off.

After a frenzied look around to make sure the villagers were okay for the moment, he gathered himself and set off for his hut on the top of Akiha Mountain, full of self-loathing and shame. Magumi met him halfway, reading his mood and deciding not to comment, as he spared her not so much as a glance. She fell in line behind him on his trek up the hill while he shouted and cursed. "Why hadn't the men here fought better? There should have been more people patrolling the woods. How dare I freeze in action? How long have I trained just for such a possibility? How many times had Father drilled home the message, 'to hesitate is to die'?"

Magumi remained silent, her presence a comforting shadow as he vented his frustration. They reached the hut, and Eurotasu collapsed onto the ground, exhaustion finally overtaking his anger. Magumi sat beside him, her eyes filled with understanding and patience.

"Eurotasu," she began softly, "violence is a part of life, as much as we might wish it weren't. But what sets us apart is how we respond to it. You fought bravely, and you protected your village. You did not fail."

He looked up at her, tears of frustration and guilt streaming down his face. "I froze, Magumi. I let you get hurt. I couldn't protect everyone."

"No one is perfect," she replied, her voice gentle yet firm. "Even your father has faced moments of hesitation. What matters is that you learned from it. You acted when it counted. You saved lives."

He took a deep breath, her words slowly sinking in. "I just… I want to be better. I want to protect everyone I care about."

"And you will," Magumi assured him. "But you must also accept that you cannot do it alone. We all have our roles to play, and together, we are stronger."

Eurotasu nodded, the weight of his guilt beginning to lift. "Thank you, Magumi. I'll try to remember that."

The days that followed were filled with hard work as the villagers repaired the damage from the raid. Eurotasu threw himself into the tasks, channeling his frustration into productivity. He helped rebuild homes, tended to the wounded, and reinforced the village's defenses.

As the village slowly returned to normal, Eurotasu continued his training with renewed determination. He practiced his sword forms, honed his archery skills, and meditated with Magumi. He also spent time with the villagers, building stronger bonds and earning their respect.

One evening, as they sat by a fire, Eurotasu spoke to Magumi about his parents. "I miss them," he said, his voice soft. "I wonder if they're proud of me."

Magumi smiled. "They are. I hear it in their letters when you read them aloud. They speak of you with pride and love. They know you are growing into a fine young man."

Eurotasu gazed into the flames, the warmth of the fire soothing his soul. "I just want to make them proud. I want to make you proud too, Magumi."

"You already do, Eurotasu," she replied, her voice filled with affection. "You have a good heart, and you are learning to use your strength wisely. That is all anyone can ask."

As the fire crackled and the stars twinkled above, Eurotasu felt a sense of peace. He knew the road ahead would be difficult, filled with challenges and dangers, but he was not alone. He had his parents' love, Magumi's guidance, and the support of his village. With these, he could face whatever came his way.

And so, Eurotasu vowed to continue his journey, to become the protector his village needed, and to honor the values his parents and Magumi had instilled in him.

CHAPTER 29
WINTERING IN THE MOUNTAINS

A sudden cold breeze reminded Magumi of the previous winter. As she settled into her meditation, the winter winds whispered through ancient trees, carrying echoes of frost-kissed tales. In the tranquility of her contemplative state, she found solace in the quiet majesty of the snow-covered landscape. Her thoughts drifted to the crisp air and the delicate beauty of snowflakes, each one a fleeting masterpiece in the grand tapestry of winter. Beneath the icy surface of her memories lay an undercurrent of anticipation, a yearning for the promise of the impending spring.

She envisioned the gradual thawing of the frozen earth, the emergence of delicate buds, and the gentle caress of warmer breezes. In the sacred realm of meditation, Magumi nurtured the hope that with the changing seasons, a renewed sense of life and vitality would bloom, transcending winter's cold grasp into spring's vibrant embrace. The village of Ni had recovered, and so had her foster son. She felt glad to see the joy of life back in his eyes.

Eurotasu sat on the fur-lined floor of his hut by the fire, back propped up against Magumi's body. Overnight, two feet of snow had fallen, leaving Ni and the surrounding areas at a standstill. With little to do, they chatted.

"These winters in Ni can be relentless, can't they? Stretching on for months," Eurotasu said.

"I've heard tales of harsher climates up north. We're fortunate, in a way," Magumi replied, shifting her weight for comfort.

"Yes, but it's the endless snow and overcast skies that truly test us. And the mountains become treacherous. Still, there's comfort in the harvest. Cabbages, leeks, radishes... They warm the soul."

"You seem to enjoy relaxing in the hot springs," she smiled.

"It breaks up the monotony. Winter has always been our time for growth. Training began early for me, chasing after Father and Mother in the forest. I miss them," he said, bringing a cup of hot tea to his lips.

"You were so eager, copying their exercises, learning to swim. I remember your father encouraging you to jump into the lake."

Eurotasu laughed. "Flailing arms and legs, but I did it. And you, Magumi, you taught me to float and not to fear the water."

"You've come far since then. Reading, writing, math... And you're training in weapons and tactics."

"I learned the hard way about fighting with honor. Father's punishment for picking a fight taught me more than any drill."

"Yes, your father hates bullies. Now look at you, a young man continuing your training with dedication. And I'm still here to guide you, Eurotasu. Soon this winter will be over, and I've got quite a bit of training planned for you."

"Thanks. Now, what should I cook for dinner?"

Magumi's ears perked up at the mention of food. "How about a stew? We have plenty of vegetables stored, and I think there's still some venison left from last week's hunt."

"Perfect," Eurotasu said, standing and stretching. "A hearty stew will do us good in this cold."

IN THE LAND OF NI

As Eurotasu began preparing the meal, he thought about the coming spring. He had grown so much in the past years, both in skill and wisdom. The hardships had forged him into a resilient and capable young man, but he knew there was still much to learn.

Magumi watched him with pride. Despite the challenges, Eurotasu showed remarkable strength and determination. She knew he was destined for great things, and she was grateful to be part of his journey.

As the stew simmered, filling the hut with a delicious aroma, Eurotasu sat back down beside Magumi. "Do you think Father and Mother will be home by spring?" he asked, his voice tinged with hope.

Magumi thought for a moment. "It's hard to say, but I believe they will. They have important work to do, but they also have a strong bond with you. They will come back as soon as they can."

Eurotasu nodded. "I hope so. I have so much to show them, so much to tell them."

"They will be proud of you, Eurotasu. Just as I am," she said, nuzzling him gently.

They ate their meal in comfortable silence, the warmth of the stew and the fire creating a cozy haven amid the winter chill.

Afterward, Eurotasu cleaned up and prepared for bed, the promise of new adventures and challenges in the coming spring filling his dreams.

Magumi curled up beside him.

CHAPTER 30

280 B.C.E. On the Road to Yahiko, Niigata

Spring in Wa arrived late, with life finally stirring as the snow receded. The thaw revealed a muddy mess, but resilient weeds, mosses, and budding trees added splashes of green.

The pines stood undaunted, their dark green a testament to their endurance. Spring here was fleeting, often joked to be as brief as a mosquito's life—winter one day, summer the next.

Eurotasu emerged from his tent into the misty hills, the musty scent of melting snow mingling with the fresh dawn. He had grown accustomed to this land, once an outcast, now embraced by his community.

A plan for revenge brewed, with Eurotasu at its heart. The villagers respected his combat knowledge, inherited from his parents. While some had more experience in brawls, Eurotasu's expertise lay in true battle. In two days, they would act, setting their strategy into motion.

Standing on the outskirts of Ni, Eurotasu gazed at the familiar houses and winding paths that had been his home for as long as he remembered. The air carried the faint scent of wood smoke, herbs, and the earthy aroma of thatched roofs. A bittersweet tug at his heart accompanied the realization that this departure might mark the end of an era.

Ni, nestled amidst the trees, had been a sanctuary of simplicity and routine. The laughter of children, the communal meals, the comforting rituals—they were over. Beholding the town, the blacksmith's house, and the storyteller's corner clung to Eurotasu's mind.

His eyes rested on Magumi. Eurotasu's hands tightened around the hilt of his father's sword, a symbolic link to the legacy he carried.

Turning away from the village, he started walking. Eurotasu's heart raced as his thoughts swirled. His hands trembled and a wistful smile flickered across his face. Deep within, a warm, fierce sensation burned.

With Magumi by his side and a contingent of a hundred men from Ni, Gosen, and Furutsu, Eurotasu ventured into the wilderness. He carried the echoes of Ni in his heart, unsure if the village would fade into memory or await his return as a changed man.

They hunted the same group that had attacked the villages of Ni and Furutsu. The enemy had eyed Gosen, but being a bigger village, had decided on two easier targets. Eurotasu's men learned this from hunting parties that had spotted these Northmen. Gosen's village elders had sent scouts to follow and monitor the Northmen's movements. *Where had those fuckers wintered?*

A woodsman reported, "I spotted roughly fifty men but took care not to be spotted myself. They are traveling towards Yahiko."

Eurotasu's men marched hard for two days. The road to Yahiko wound through fertile valleys where clusters of stilt houses rose above the floodplains. Along the way, Eurotasu's band passed communal granaries, their thatched roofs sheltering the precious harvests. Farmers, bent over their fields, tended to the crops with devotion.

Using shortcuts, they arrived near Yahiko a full day ahead of their foe. Sending runners with word, the people of Yahiko responded with thanks, provisions, and additional manpower. An extra hundred men had been gathered. They learned that towns and villages along the coastlines had been harassed by pirates in recent years, and many people came to Yahiko seeking shelter among its trees and shrine.

That evening in camp, the men discussed strategy. Eurotasu suggested, "Since we now outnumber the enemy four to one, I will split the men in half. The ambush will be located on a forest path to the village."

"What about hunting traps and archery positions?" chimed one of the hunters, drawing in the dirt to illustrate his point.

A built lumberjack from Gosen added, "My axemen can attack head-on, with others springing traps from the sides. Not a bad plan, I say."

"Considering most of us are not accustomed to battle," a small eye-patched man said.

"Yes, and we have the element of surprise and know the land," Eurotasu added. He stopped to pick up some stones to add to the hunter's dirt sketch.

"Still, something my father said gnaws at me. I remember hearing of two ambushes my father survived and one that my father had laid himself. That's three times the amount of experience we have."

"Two, don't forget the raid at Ni," someone from the back of the campfire shouted.

"In my recollection, there were two themes. One is that while surprised, the ambushed get back into the fight. This does not bode well for us," Eurotasu continued.

"Shit, we ain't scared of some painted-faced Northmen," another shouted.

"It's not about being scared. Our prey are fighting men—

pirates and mercenaries who know their craft. We must be smart. The second lesson I gleaned from my father was that head-on charges could be met with spears, swords, bows, and shields. Most of us have no armor. Weapons relish the chance to penetrate squishy flesh. No, if we are going to win, we need another edge."

"What do you propose?" huffed the axeman.

"I would have the axemen split as well. We've spent all day preparing. The scouts reported in at dusk, and the enemy would arrive sometime before dawn, seeking to attack before first light, much as they had done in Ni," Eurotasu finished. The final agreement on the plans was made over dinner.

Eurotasu turned in early. "I'm not yet old enough to drink rice wine with you men," he told them.

He wanted to talk with Magumi. "What do you think, what's your hunting assessment?"

"Eurotasu, the hunt is like a dance. It requires precision, grace, and an understanding of the rhythm of the wild. Your plan has these elements," she said, nudging him with her snout.

"Men are going to die tomorrow, on both sides. Have I planned enough? Thought it all through? Will we perish?"

Magumi was his everything. She provided an ear, and her voice soothed him, stoking his ego, reminding him, "You saw battle before Pausanias, the mighty Spartan."

He finally dozed off by her side.

Magumi woke him before dawn. Soon after, they went down to where his half of the men were forming up.

It took another ten silent minutes to see the first signs of the enemy. They came on, moving with serious intent. A strange sight indeed, most of these Northmen still wore hide clothing and wild face paint.

Their weapons were bronze, and no one looked like the next. Elaborate tattoos and jewelry covered some men, while others were bald and plain. Still, others had long hair down their backs, tied in weird braids.

Eurotasu counted fifty-four men.

Strangest of all was what was in the middle of their formation, four horses pulling a giant box covered in red sheets. *What's under those sheets?*

Eurotasu's men were well hidden on both sides of the forest path. The weeds and shrubs grew thick here. Another ten seconds, and the signal was given. A flute pierced the pre-dawn silence.

Huge hammering thuds soon followed towards the front and back of both sides of the enemy formation. Men looked up to see trees coming down towards them.

Before anyone reacted, the screaming started.

The trees had been cut almost to the point of falling over the previous day, and now a chop or two from an axe finished the job.

Somewhere between fifteen and twenty trees fell in quick order.

Most of the enemy were able to jump clear and avoid being crushed, but a couple were not so lucky. Still, others were left exposed between fallen trees, unable to form any type of fighting position and rally with their comrades.

The hissing sound of projectiles followed. The screams intensified. Eurotasu himself howled as he fired three quick arrows. He notched a fourth as the middle ground was being littered with shafts. Some found their marks, and more men went down.

However, some mercenaries started to return fire with their bows.

"Ring, ring," roared a tall mercenary. They regrouped and formed a circular defensive formation.

Eurotasu fired his fourth arrow and drew his sword. He screamed, "For Wa!" and charged down the hill. Men on both sides of the ambush took up the battle cry and raced down along with him.

About twenty of the best archers in his ragtag army stayed behind in reserve, taking shots.

At least twenty of the fifty-four enemy were dead or injured. Another thirty to go; the enemy would come to their senses when they realized they were outnumbered and surrender, Eurotasu thought. However, these mercenaries were hard men.

The enemy formed a turtle shell of shields, spears, swords, daggers, and arrows.

Larger and faster than Eurotasu, some of the villagers had already reached that wall, throwing themselves on it, hacking and slashing with axes, scythes, and too few blades. They fought angrily but without much effect. These men were not trained for war.

The sheer weight of their press pushed the defenders back. Small holes opened, a leg slashed here, an outstretched arm hacked off there.

About twenty paces from the front action, a strange and terrible thing happened. One of the mercenaries broke from his position and unlocked the lock that held the red sheets over the wheeled box.

Eurotasu found himself face down on the forest floor. Confused, he tried to rise, only to feel the weight of a giant paw on his back.

"Stay down, back, back," yelled Magumi.

Looking up, he wished he hadn't.

The lock and red sheet came off the box, and a large wooden door at the center exploded open.

First, a massive black clawed hand emerged, followed by a nightmarish face, accompanied by a roar that halted every man, friend, and foe alike.

Four Oni spilled out, roaring as they advanced. Their bodies were furry and bear-like in muscle; they walked upright, tails dangling. Their faces—all fangs, horns, and huge blood-red eyes that glowed.

Magumi began pulling Eurotasu back, her teeth locked onto his shirt. Most men were now screaming in terror.

The mercenaries recovered and started cutting down the

shocked villagers as the demons raced into the ranks, swinging their claws and biting with abandon.

Men were dying at an alarming rate, few bothering to fight back. *Are we all going to die here, shivering in terror?* Eurotasu remembered his earlier shame and terror from the night raid on his village, and his rage grew.

Back on his feet, he elbowed Magumi in the snout hard. It didn't do any damage, but it surprised her, and she let go of his shirt.

"Get off me! Stand, men! Fuck these demons!" he bellowed. Something in the power of his voice worked. Men started to swing back, and arrows once more flooded in from the tree lines.

Some were still too caught up in the terror. Blood soaked the forest grounds; the smell of piss, shit, and the demonic stench permeated the air.

Magumi also had her spirit back. She targeted a demon and launched herself like an arrow. Her fangs buried in the neck of the demon, who himself had a mouth full of human thigh meat.

It tried to turn, but Magumi, heavier, brought it down. However, it still battled back, thrashing wildly with its claws, slicing into the side of Magumi's head. Before it caused further damage, Eurotasu buried his father's sword deep in the demon's back.

Again and again, he ripped the weapon out and plunged it in. "Die, die," he wailed. A crunch from Magumi's jaws made his wish come true.

The demon went limp.

His anger had not. He bounded over Magumi and the corpse and slashed the face off a Northman. Dodging a swing from another with a perfect roll, he arrived back on his feet in balance.

The man leaned in too far, exposing his foot. Two quick blocks and a parry, and off came the foot of his adversary, who fell backward screaming as Eurotasu's blade caught him right between the eyes with a downward thrust.

Magumi was back up and at his side. Magumi and Eurotasu turned as one.

"They can die," he shouted again and again. Magumi took up his mantra. "They can die, the demons can die." Most men facing the foe were too busy to respond.

However, the chant arose from the trees, and the archers sent volley after volley at the monsters and their handlers. Some arrows struck true in the fiends' hides but didn't bring them down. The hides were too thick to penetrate very far.

Pain and distraction were crucial, as some villagers, upon finally seeing the monsters bleed, found their courage.

Hacking and slashing back, some villagers scored small hits. The Oni were fast, jumping between humans, felling them with clawed hands, snapping with powerful maws.

"Circle them," someone had the good sense to shout.

Magumi and Eurotasu rushed toward the nearest demon and joined the fray. Dodging, blocking, and reacting through instinct, the boy and wolf's countless training sessions fighting together were starting to pay off.

Eurotasu's fear, shame, and rage were shoved down. He focused entirely on the moment, pushing his arm out ahead of him as bait.

The monstrosity couldn't resist and lunged forward, only to be met by a ferocious bite to its midsection. It roared in pain before five or six men were on it, stabbing, thrusting, seeking revenge. The horror was dead, but the fighters were not satisfied. They turned and ran towards the next foe.

The last two remaining demons were outnumbered by twenty to one. Villagers stood their ground and fought.

Some didn't make it; the demons were stronger than ten men, and one swipe of their hands could send a person flying.

Eurotasu's attention lay elsewhere as he whistled to Magumi. They saw the few surviving mercenaries gathered by their box, trying desperately to fend off double their number. Without hesitation, he jumped on her back, and they were off towards their prey.

"Frog style," he yelled into Magumi's ear, bringing a huge grin to her face. Right before reaching the enemy, she pulled up and turned her body at the last second.

Eurotasu used the momentum to jump off her back, clearing over the heads of the adversaries, flipping like an acrobat and landing behind them. Mouths agape, he sent the dagger at his hip into the throat of the man closest to his left, with a beautiful throw. He thrust his sword into an eye of the man to his right. His blade passed the guard of the Northman's sword, which got into position a fraction too late.

Without a word, the mercenary dropped. The man to the left was still trying to talk, although it was all gurgled and bubbling nonsense.

Three other opponents were killed in short order by Eurotasu's comrades.

One more was brought down by Magumi's hind legs, which she used like a horse to kick the man hard into the dirt. With the immediate threat gone, Eurotasu turned in time to see the last demon brought low.

A heavy axe crunched into its skull, brain matter flying. Eurotasu had never seen something so glorious. It was over.

CHAPTER 31
HEROES' RETURN

280 B.C.E. Camping outside Yahiko

Eurotasu, Magumi, and their brave companions' return sent waves of excitement through Yahiko. Villagers buzzed with anticipation. Flags caught the wind's eager whisper, snapping a welcome in vibrant hues. Drums beat as they welcomed the heroes who vanquished the looming threat.

Children perched on tiptoes, gaped in awe, eyes wide as moons. Elders blessed the warriors with nods and full smiles. The air filled with the scent of incense. Amidst the celebration, Eurotasu, with Magumi at his side, pondered his mixed feelings. He was crying and laughing. "Why are my emotions so conflicting?" he asked, fingers pressed on his chest, as they stood in front of the gathered crowd.

"It's never easy to go to war," Magumi replied.

"No, I suppose not," he said, wiping his tears.

Eurotasu acknowledged the villagers' gratitude with nods and smiles, but the toll of war shadowed his gaze.

The chief clasped Eurotasu's arm. "Thank you, Eurotasu. We are alive because of you."

Yet, Eurotasu's mind wandered to the fallen and the stark realities of battle.

As night fell and the village feasted, Eurotasu found comfort in the people's fellowship. Sitting at the bonfires, its flicker reflected his inner turmoil. Magumi lay next to him, her silent support offered solace as he scratched her neck and grappled with the duality of his heroism and the war's lingering specters.

His thoughts turned to a distant childhood memory; a time unburdened by duty. The bonfire's warmth blurred past and present, invoking simpler days.

Eurotasu cherished his nightly discussions about war with his father, a tradition that began when he was just three. In their hut, candlelight would cast enchanting shadows while his father recounted battles, filling the boy with wonder.

A tiny fire sprite often flickered alongside them, its dance lending a whimsical air to their lessons. It cocked its head as if listening, though its comprehension remained a mystery.

Once, at seven, he missed a minor detail about an ancient battle, and his father's reaction was fierce.

"Battle of Sphacteria, what went wrong?" his father roared.

"Terrain, distribution of forces, and lack of guards at night."

"Yes, yes, but what else, boy? Think for yourself. Do not just give me the answers I want to hear."

"Perhaps assumption and arrogance," he replied.

"How so?" gruffed Pausanias.

"They thought themselves mighty Spartan warriors. That they could defeat anyone. They assumed that the Athenians would not attack, that they weren't willing to sacrifice men for something negotiable."

"Good, good," his father said, calming down ever so slightly, his tone relaxing.

Eurotasu knew it wasn't really so; the fire in his father's eyes said otherwise.

Pausanias's next statement was said with calm and destruction all mixed into one.

"Answer the following: when did the Spartans get their revenge and how?"

"At the battle of Mantinea, Agis acted quickly. Seeing his left flank losing, he stopped attacking the Athenians at the right and brought his men to fight the Mantineans and the Argos warriors. Caught them while they thought they had the advantage. Those Argos warriors caused the Skyrites and Brasid fighters to flee and thought victory was at hand."

"Why couldn't the Athenians attack their backside?"

"Because the Spartans' allies, the Thebans, and Spartan cavalry, held the right side. Also, two of the Athenian strategists were killed, which led to confusion among their ranks."

"Best answer you've given all night. Last question, screw it up and you must run an extra mile tomorrow morning. Who won the battle of Kadesh?" Pausanias asked with a genuine smile.

Egyptian wars had never been Eurotasu's forte. He relished too much in the stories of his father's homeland. He gulped, sensing a trap.

"Neither side won; the Egyptians under Pharaoh Ramses II won the field battle but failed to secure the city itself," Eurotasu answered with confidence.

"Who led the Hittites?" Pausanias asked.

"Muwatalli."

Pausanias smiled devilishly. "Wrong, it was Muwatalli II. Looks like you are running a little extra tomorrow, huh?"

"That's not fair; you said only one more question," argued Eurotasu.

"War is never fair, dummy. Now go to bed before I ask you ten more questions."

As Eurotasu started to respond, he saw his mother on the

opposite side of the hut. She had been busy mixing potions and scrolling through tomes, but now she gazed intently at her husband. Before a gasp left his mouth, his mother motioned with her hand.

He understood the gesture, turned, and went to his "room," which was little more than heavy cream-colored sheets pulled across one small section of the hut, offering him some privacy.

It gave his parents time to talk and be alone.

Although in such an enclosed space, Eurotasu heard their whispered voices.

"You do not need to be so hard on the boy. He does everything you ask and more," his mother said, to his shame.

She should not need to stick up for me; after all, I am seven years old, he told himself.

"If you wanted to see hard, you should have traveled to Sparta. He would be damn near battle-ready by now," quipped his father, adding, "He must be ready."

"Ready for what exactly?" his mother asked. She had run through this conversation before and was tired of it.

"For his destiny."

"Mind filling the rest of us in on what that is, or is it some grand secret to be taken to your grave?"

"You know of what I speak. You saw the boy's potential, his latent magical energy, his ability to pick up new information, languages, his athleticism. He is meant for something great," his father said.

"Then the fates have decided it so, and pushing him won't change the outcome."

"A Spartan has to be pushed to become a real man."

"He's not a Spartan, you fool; but you're right about one thing, maybe I should travel to Sparta."

"And why is that?"

"Well, I need to find a real man," she replied.

Pausanias had fought many battles, faced demons, deserts, jungles, and endless seas. However, dealing with a strong woman was his weak point, and he knew when he was defeated. "Perhaps I'll go help you find him. What hair color interests you these days? Maybe a blonde-haired stallion," he jested.

"Red hair, I love it," his mother said. They both laughed then, but Eurotasu didn't hear the next words they spoke as he drifted off to sleep.

The next morning, he woke up early and finished his extra mile run before his father had even gotten out of his bedroll. I will show them all, he thought as he plowed through his run like a bear.

Magumi came along for the run, which always made it more entertaining. She tried to act all haughty but occasionally would bound off to chase a bird or rabbit. She easily caught up, and when she did, her tail was wagging, and her tongue was hanging out like a puppy.

A loud pop from a log on the bonfire brought Eurotasu back to the present.

"C'mon Magumi, let's go to sleep."

Magumi lifted her head and gave Eurotasu a playful nudge. "Alright, but only if you promise to let me chase rabbits in my dreams."

Eurotasu chuckled and scratched behind her ears. "Deal. You deserve it after today."

They walked together to a nearby hut prepared by the people of Yahiko for the visiting warriors. The embers of the bonfire cast a warm glow on their faces. Once inside, Eurotasu wrapped himself in his fur-lined blanket while Magumi curled up next to him, her body radiating comforting warmth.

"Thank you for being by my side today," Eurotasu whispered, his voice filled with gratitude.

"Always," Magumi responded softly. "You are never alone, Eurotasu. Remember that."

As sleep began to claim him, Eurotasu felt a sense of peace. The day's battles and victories faded into the background, replaced by the soothing presence of his loyal companion. He reached out and patted Magumi one last time before closing his eyes.

"Goodnight, Magumi."

"Goodnight, Eurotasu."

With that, they both drifted into a deep, restful sleep, ready to face whatever challenges the new day would bring.

CHAPTER 32

The next day, Eurotasu began sword practice. The air in Yahiko village was heavy with the sweet scent of cherry blossoms as the sun dipped below the horizon. Engrossed in his techniques, the rhythmic clash and metallic ring echoed through the training grounds. He found a couple of men who knew the sword, and like him, they needed a return to normalcy.

Amidst the training, a figure emerged from the shadowy tree line, wearing a pin on his cloak that marked him as a messenger of the Order. The man approached Eurotasu with an air of urgency, his forehead glistening with sweat.

"Are you Eurotasu?" he asked, panting.

Eurotasu, still gripping his sword, nodded. "What news do you bring?"

Regaining his breath, the messenger said, "Your parents, Saoka and Pausanias, are in great peril. A village near Nagaoka is under siege. Demons and mercenaries have joined forces, threatening to overrun the village. Your parents, valiantly defending it, are in desperate need of aid."

Eurotasu's eyes widened as the gravity of the situation sank in. He sheathed his sword and stepped closer to the messenger. "Tell me everything."

With a solemn expression, the courier continued. "A fellow warrior witnessed the siege and managed to escape, reaching out to us for help. Saoka and Pausanias have fought hard, but the enemy forces are too numerous. The demons are wreaking havoc."

Eurotasu clenched his fists, his jaw set in determination. "What is the current state of the village? How many defenders remain?"

"The town teeters on the brink. The defenders are few and weary from the continuous onslaught. Your parents are leading the charge, but their strength is waning. Without reinforcements, it will fall within days."

A tremor ran through Eurotasu's frame, his breath hitched. The messenger handed him a map, detailing the location of the besieged hamlet.

"I understand the risks," Eurotasu said, his voice firm. "Prepare a message for the leaders of Yahiko and the men still here from the neighboring villages. We need warriors, supplies, anything that can aid in the defense. I leave in an hour. No one has to join me, but I would ask them to do so."

The messenger nodded and hastened to fulfill Eurotasu's request.

Eurotasu was more scared than he had ever been, but he reminded himself that Nagaoka was about a seven- or eight-hour journey from Yahiko. Would he arrive before all was lost?

Magumi appeared beside him, her presence a reassuring force. "You know they would not hesitate to save you, Eurotasu. We must act swiftly."

Eurotasu took a deep breath, steadying his resolve. "You're right. We've faced darkness before, and we will again. For them, for the village, for all that we hold dear."

As the hour passed, warriors and villagers gathered, armed and ready. Eurotasu addressed them, his voice echoing with conviction. "We fight not just for survival, but for the hope of a future free from this terror. Together, we can turn the tide. Let's bring our family back."

With Magumi by his side and the men of Yahiko behind him, Eurotasu led the march toward Nagaoka, the echoes of their determination reverberating through the mountains. This battle was not just for his parents but for the soul of Wa itself. As they journeyed, the hope for a brighter dawn fueled their every step, ready to face the darkness head-on.

About the Author

Greetings, I'm Chris Chaconas, an American author of historical fantasy who resides in Niigata, Japan. I grew up in the bustling city of Washington D.C., but I fell in love with the serene beauty of Japan 15 years ago while attending Temple University Japan and have lived there ever since. I own and operate Zippy's English, a cozy English school in the sleepy town of Niitsu, Japan.

I have a fervent interest in writing stories that explore the ancient past, especially the times before the dawn of civilization. My first novel, "IN THE LAND OF NI", is a historical fantasy adventure that blends my Greek ancestry and the name of the town I currently live in.

When I'm not writing, I indulge in cooking, traveling, and sports. I'm a proficient swimmer and an unskilled martial artist who has learned various Japanese disciplines. I share my life with my wonderful wife Yoko and our adorable Shiba Inu dog Hime. Writing a book has been a lifelong aspiration of mine, and I'm delighted to present it to you.

To learn more about C.G. Chaconas and discover more Next Chapter authors, visit our website at www.nextchapter.pub.

In The Land of Ni
ISBN: 978-4-82419-788-7

Published by
Next Chapter
2-5-6 SANNO
SANNO BRIDGE
143-0023 Ota-Ku, Tokyo
+818035793528

14th September 2024

Milton Keynes UK
Ingram Content Group UK Ltd.
UKHW041946091024
449514UK00006B/44

9 784824 197887